TINY DROPS

A NOVEL

DUSTI DAWN ROSE

Copyright © 2018 Dusti Dawn Rose

All rights reserved.

Editor: Erica Russikoff

Cover Designer: Kat Savage

Interior Designer: J.R. Rogue

ISBN: 9781720288299

No part of this book may be reproduced or transmitted in any form or by any means, electronic or mechanical, including photocopying, recording, or by any information storage and retreival system without the written permission of the author, except for the use of brief quotations in a book review.

This book is a work of fiction. Names, characters, places, and incidents either are products of the author's imagination or are used fictitiously. Any resemblance to actual persons, living or dead, events, or locales is entirely coincidental.

Brian,
When I started writing this, I thought it was for me. I realized somewhere around the middle, that it was for you. Thank you for choosing to walk beside me through this life. I love you.

PART 1

1995 - BRICE

1

WHAT'S HAPPENING TO ME?

I stir in my sleep, warmth waking my senses... I'm wet.

What the hell? How did this happen?

My covers slip from the bed as I toss my feet over. The floor sounds its protest at my sudden movement. Nighttime is for sleeping. I tiptoe to my dresser and grab a change of clothes. Opening the door, I slip out into the hall and rush to the bathroom. I can't say how many times I've already gone tonight. I haven't slept well in weeks.

My mind is racing as I sit back down on the toilet. It couldn't have been more than twenty minutes since I was here last, and it seems never-ending. I don't think I'll ever be able to rest again, and my body wants nothing more than that.

Glancing down at my panties, I try to stifle the sob as it escapes me; I can't hold it in anymore. I don't know what's happening to me, but it feels like dying, and part of me would welcome it. I've never before felt this bone-deep tired. I slip off my pants and toss everything into the hamper. I don't know what to do.

I'm fifteen years old; there's no excuse for bed-wetting.

I grab the undies that I brought in and slip them on. Pulling my mass of curls over my shoulder, I dip my head under the faucet and drink. I can't get enough. I've never been so thirsty before. It's no wonder I've wet myself. Every trip I make to the bathroom ends with my head under the faucet—drinking like I've been lost in the desert for weeks. What's wrong with me?

Sitting back down on the toilet, I go again. I won't go back to the faucet. I can't, not if I ever want to rest. But, as I try to swallow past the lump that's become a permanent fixture in my throat, I know that it's no use. The water may only offer a moment's relief, but it's all that I have, so I drink again.

When I look up at the reflection staring back at me, my whole body stiffens. She can't be me. I don't look like that. I reach my hands up and rub at the dark circles beneath my eyes. It's not traces of old mascara resting below my green irises—the dark shadows have moved in, taking a permanent place. How long have I looked like this? Felt like this? My skin's sickly, pale. I want to lie on the floor beneath the sink; I'm so tired. I lean closer to the image across from me. *"You can't live like this,"* she whispers, and I know she's right.

Goosebumps rise across my skin as I leave the bathroom, making my way down the hall. I have to wake her. She needs to know what's going on. We can't keep ignoring this; something's wrong. I lightly rap my knuckles across the wood before opening the door.

"Mama?" I whisper the words, stepping closer to the bed. "I'm sorry to wake you, but there's something wrong with me." A sob overtakes me as the blankets begin to stir. *There's something wrong with me.*

"Brice?" She reaches blindly for the bedside lamp, her voice laced with sleep. "What are you talking about? What's going on, baby girl?" Light replaces the darkness, and I take a step back.

"I...I....I wet the bed. I don't know what's wrong with me!"

"Shh... It's okay." She sits up, rubbing her eyes. "Maybe you have an infection. Whatever it is, we'll find out tomorrow. We'll get you to the clinic."

I knew I shouldn't have come; I knew she wouldn't hear me, not really.

"Go back to bed, try to get some rest. We'll get this sorted in the morning," she says.

I suck in a shaky breath. *I'm lost—all alone.*

It's not her fault. She works so much; she just doesn't have room for this in her life. I haven't really seen her more than in passing for weeks. She took a second job because Christmas is coming. When you're a single mom with two kids, that's what you do. I don't know how many times I've heard her say that or something like it.

Stumbling through my cluttered room, I reach the nightstand and flip on my reading lamp. Running my hand across the indent on the mattress, I feel no dampness on the sheets. My body sags with relief. I don't have the strength to change them. A stifled sob escapes me. Slipping under the covers, I ball the top sheet in my hand and cover my mouth with it—letting go, my body shakes silently as fear screams within, its voice blocking every other thought.

What's wrong with me?

2

WAKE-UP CALL...

"Brice, come on... Brice! Wake up! Mom said you weren't feeling well, and I should take you to the clinic before school. Come on!" Jesse yells, exasperated, right before he rips the covers off my bed.

I reach out blindly, trying to find something, anything to snuggle with. Coming up with nothing, I relent. Tossing my feet over, I slowly pull myself up, sitting on the edge of the bed. "You're such a jerk sometimes, you know that?"

Looking up, I pause as his amused smirk morphs, the corners of his mouth turning down—a valley of concern appearing between his eyes.

Everything about me feels slow: my movements, my thoughts. The only thing coming rapidly are my breaths.

"What? Why? Why...are...you...looking...at...me... like...that?" I ask, each word spoken between a big breath. My mouth feels thick and dry, like I can't get enough air. I try to stand, but I sink back down on the edge of the bed. I'm so weak.

Jesse drops the comforter and rushes to the closet. Why's

he acting like this? What's going on? Why do I feel like I can't catch my breath?

"What are you doing?" My words come out strained.

"It's okay, Little Bit," he says, coming over with my big boot slippers—the fuzzy ones I love that Mom claims are hideous. "We're going to get you to the hospital."

"Can't… Take me to the clinic. Mom can't afford the hospital, Jesse."

He's moving in slow motion now. *Did he hear me?* Pressure on my feet brings me back to the present, and I watch as he tugs the slippers on and then sits me up and pulls a hoodie over my head. When did I lie back down? Glancing down, I see that it's my soft green one with light gray, tiny doves all over it—my favorite. I smile, but it's an effort to raise the corners of my lips. Jesse's such an awesome person—even when he's being a jerk. Why can't he just let me sleep?

"If I do that, she'll just have two bills. I don't know what's going on with you, but we're not messing around with it." Scooping me into his arms, he walks to the front door.

My head drops onto his chest, comfort spreading through me. This is the way it's always been. Jesse's always here to take care of me. He's taking me to get help. I try to relax as he descends the stairs to our apartment two at a time.

I'll be all right.

"Whoa, is everything all right?" A gruff voice rings out across the parking lot. I look up at the sky, marveling at how brightly the sun is shining—despite the cold temperatures. Winter in the Yakima Valley is frigid, in spite of the desert climate. The rolling hills that line the valley have traded their dusty color for pristine white.

"My sister's not feeling well, Bernard," Jesse answers, without stopping. The car beeps as he unlocks it remotely.

Who's Bernard?

"Let me grab that door for you."

The face of our neighbor from across the hall appears in front of me. He must be Bernard. Why didn't I know that?

"Thank you," I manage to say on an exhale as I'm sat in the passenger seat, my tongue thick and strange in my mouth.

"I'll be keeping you in my thoughts, young lady," Bernard replies. Reaching up, he gives a slight tip of his funny little hat before he turns his attention to Jesse, who closes the door.

I struggle to listen to them, my mind slipping in and out of lucidity. Their words sound familiar, as if they're old friends. How does Jesse know him so well? Who is this man?

Jesse climbs in and gives a quick wave to Bernard before he buckles his belt and backs out of the parking space.

"How do you know the neighbor? I didn't realize the two of you were friends."

He glances over, eyebrow cocked in true Jesse fashion. "Wouldn't you like to know?"

"Yes, yes I would, which is why I just asked you, you jerk," I huff, my breaths starting to come rapidly again.

He glances back over, his brow wrinkling. "Just try to relax, Little Bit. We'll be at the hospital soon," he soothes, turning his eyes back to the road.

I turn toward the window and watch as the buildings pass, one by one. Sometimes it feels like there's no color in the wintertime—everything is either gray or white, and there's nothing else to see. Nature's life force is frozen—dead.

My eyes lull, closing slowly. I slump to the side, and *whack*, my head knocks into the window. "Ouch!" I sit up, rubbing the spot, and chance a glance at Jesse.

He's chewing the edge of his lip and drumming his hand on the steering wheel.

He clears his throat. "How long have you been feeling sick?"

My heart begins to race as I search for an answer to his question. "I don't know, a while. I'm just so tired. My whole body feels weighted, so heavy; every movement's like moving mountains." I lean back in the seat and close my eyes. "And I can't stop peeing—it's crazy. I'm probably peeing thirty or forty times a day."

"Jesus, Brice! Why didn't you tell me about this sooner?"

I flinch at the sound of his voice; it's desperate, afraid. "I don't know, I guess I just thought I would get better, and everyone is always so busy. I know you have finals this week; I didn't want to get in the way of that," I whisper. Turning back to the window, I see a little blue sign with a white H and an arrow pointing straight ahead. I guess there's color in winter after all.

3

TRAFFIC ON A FRIDAY

I'M SO GLAD I HAVE A BIG BROTHER. IF I HAD A SISTER, instead, I don't think she'd be able to carry me. It's a silly thought, but I can't help it as I hear the *whoosh* of the automatic doors opening. My eyes are closed; it's easier that way. I'm so afraid. I don't know what they're going to tell me here, but I know it won't be good. I know it's not normal to feel this way.

"Can we stop at the bathroom?"

"Sure."

He sets me on my feet in front of the ladies' room. "Thanks, Jesse," I whisper, gripping his arm while I try to get my balance. I take a step on shaky legs, and it's as if I'm trying to walk through quicksand. Pushing through it, I make my way into the restroom.

I take care of business, stopping at the sink to wash my hands. I glance up and freeze. My hair reminds me of Albert Einstein's—wild and curly, sticking out in every direction. I wish I had a scrunchie. Hopefully I won't see anyone I know here. I run my fingers through it, trying my best to tame it a bit. I stand for a moment and watch as it slowly loosens—

returning to its former shape. There's no fixing a mess like this.

Pushing the door open, I watch my brother for a moment. He's standing against the wall across from me, arms crossed, staring at the ground, his brow drawn together. His dark brown curls are almost as disheveled as mine. When he raises his head, I see a storm of emotion in his eyes—their usual clear, blue color replaced by a gray, turbulent sea. He tries his best to cover it, but he looks petrified.

"There she is," he says with a smile. "Let's get you checked in."

"Sounds like fun," I joke, swallowing to try to push down the lump in my throat. My whole body's shaking now, and I don't know if it's the fear or whatever is happening to me.

We put my name on the clipboard at the desk and take a seat in the front. There are only a handful of people in the waiting room—each of them lost in their own problems. None of them even take notice of the tiny girl with a head full of crazy curls. *Good.*

"Brice Garrison," I hear a lady call from the front of the room.

"That was fast," Jesse says, helping me to my feet.

"Don't get too excited," the lady sitting closest to us remarks. "They're just going to get you signed in, then you have to wait for the nurse, and then you have to wait for the doctor. Wait, wait, wait. This place is slower than traffic on a Friday." She shakes her head.

Jesse and I look at each other, not knowing how to respond. "Oh, okay. Thanks?" Jesse says. Wrapping his arm around my shoulder, he gently guides me toward the front.

"Slower than traffic on a Friday," I whisper, trying to stifle a sudden giggle.

"Shhh..." he whispers back, nudging me, a smirk playing at the corner of his mouth.

We take a seat in front of the window, and the lady behind the glass pushes a clipboard out through the small slot at the bottom. "You need to fill out these forms. What brought you to the ER today?" she asks, finally looking at us, her expression bored.

"My sister isn't well. She's really tired and has been going to the bathroom a lot, and her breathing is weird. Is there anything else, Brice?" Jesse asks, turning to me.

"Thirsty. I've been super thirsty. It's like I can't get enough water," I add, trying to think of anything else. How do you explain sheer exhaustion? "It feels sort of like I'm suspended in Jell-O or something. I can move, but every movement feels like there's some invisible force field pushing back against me." I feel the color rise in my cheeks when the lady behind the glass raises her gaze to me. I shrug, putting my hand over my mouth. Mom says I have an unusual way of explaining things.

"Wait here for just a moment. I'm going to go speak to the nurse," she says.

"Looks like today is our lucky day," I whisper between breaths. "Seems like we might get to skip the wait."

Jesse reaches over and squeezes my hand. His grip is so tight, it hurts. I wiggle my fingers, urging him to loosen his hold. He gives one final little squeeze before he sets my fingers free. *Thank goodness...*although I sort of miss the comfort of it.

As if he heard my thoughts, he reaches back over and grabs it again, only this time, his grip is light, controlled.

We sit like that for what feels like eternity. I squirm in my chair as the need to go to the bathroom again takes over. I'm just about to say something to Jesse when the lady returns, and an older man with kind eyes and a shock of white hair comes up behind her.

He glances down at the chart in his hand before he looks

up at me. He doesn't even look at Jesse when he starts to speak. "Brice? I'm Wayne. I understand you're not feeling well. We're going to get you better," he finishes with a kind smile before stepping away for a moment. When he returns, he's pushing an empty wheelchair.

"Why don't you take a seat, and I'll take you back to where the action is."

I nod and drop Jesse's hand so I can sit in the wheelchair.

"That's not really necessary, is it?" Jesse asks, standing to face the nurse.

"Just relax, big brother. We'll take great care of your little sis, and I can assure you, she's probably not feeling up to walking," he answers, as he begins to push me toward the back. "You're welcome to come along."

"Have you ever been to the hospital before, Brice?" he asks, his tone light, kind.

"I got stitches once, but that was just at the clinic over on Tieton Drive. The one across from Albertsons," I answer, shifting uncomfortably in the chair. "Can we stop at the bathroom before we go to the room?"

"Sure, you can collect a sample. They're going to want to look at your blood and urine—it helps us figure out what's going on. There are cups on the shelf and instructions on the wall for getting a clean catch."

"Okay," I answer, unsure of what to say. It's embarrassing to think about collecting my pee. "What do I do with it when I'm finished?" I question, my eyes on the floor as I struggle to stand.

"I'm going to give you this sticker. It has your name and all of your information on it. Just put it on your cup and leave it behind the door in front of the toilet when you're finished. If you need any help, pull the string beside the toilet, and I'll be right in to help you."

I glance up at him, relaxing when I see the inner glow in

his kind eyes. He does this all day long, every day. It's normal for him to collect bodily fluids from people, even if it's not normal for the people giving the sample. *It's normal for him.* He reaches out and gives me the sticker before he helps me to my feet.

I sway a bit as I get my balance. I'm glad we didn't have to wait—that there was no Friday traffic for us. We lucked out with 2:00 a.m. Tuesday morning traffic.

I find the cup and open the lid, setting it on the counter while I walk over to the toilet. I fill it and glance up at the little silver door in front of me. There is a sign on the front of it that says, *How to obtain a clean catch.* I quickly read through it. *Oops.* It says I'm supposed to start to pee in the toilet before I go in the cup, then finish in the toilet. Well, I got it half right. I finished in the toilet. I hope I didn't mess it up too bad. It's strange to learn there's a certain way that you're supposed to do something as simple as peeing in a cup.

I open the door, and both Wayne and Jesse rush toward me. When they each slide an arm under mine and help guide me down into the chair, I'm grateful. This weakness is unlike anything that I've ever felt before. I want to close my eyes and let it overtake me.

As soon as I'm settled, Wayne continues pushing the chair. This place is busy. There are people rushing every which way, each wearing their own set of vibrant colors and patterns. A bright contrast to the sterile gray walls. It's noisy, too. For some reason, I always thought that hospitals were sort of like libraries—everyone's meant to be quiet, use whispered sounds.

I jump in my seat when I hear a loud, angry voice. "You people can't keep me here!"

"That's nothing to worry about, kiddo. Sometimes people are brought in when they're not mentally well. He's harmless," Wayne says.

"Is it always this loud here?" Jesse asks, walking quickly beside Wayne.

"This is a tame day," Wayne answers, shaking his head. "You should see it on a multiple-code day. There's no escaping the noise. It goes home with you, and you hear it in your sleep." I shudder at the image his words paint and hope I won't be here long enough to witness it.

4

DK WHAT?

"Ouch!" I yell out, covering my mouth with my hand. I didn't mean to say anything; it just really hurt. This is the third time they've tried to start an IV, and it keeps going bad.

Wayne glances up. "Sorry, kid. I know it hurts. But the good news is, this one looks like it's going to hold."

I lean back and relax. "Thank God!"

I watch as he pulls blood back from the line and passes it to the other guy who's in the room. The room is really large, with a big, round light hanging down right above me. It feels weird—like I'm on display. Jesse is off to the side, pacing back and forth.

"Jesse, just sit. Relax. You're making me nervous," I tell him, even though that's really not fair. I'm sure this is tough for him. He's had an aversion to hospitals ever since our dad passed. Dad was in and out of hospitals for months before it happened. I was really young and don't remember a lot of it. But Jesse was twelve when Dad died.

"Is there a phone I can use? I need to call my mom," Jesse asks Wayne.

"Right there on the wall." Wayne nods toward the left.

I look that way and see a white phone hanging on the wall.

"Just dial 9 to get out," he adds as he puts a clear bandage sort of thing over my hand with the IV. I stretch my hand, glancing down at it; I've never had an IV before.

"Get a glucose, Eric," Wayne says to the other man in the room.

I feel a bit relieved hearing his name. I don't like not knowing a person's name. This is all so weird, and my head is foggy—like I can't get my thoughts straight.

Leaning back into the pillow, I rest my eyes.

"Morning, Edna," I hear Jesse say with a smile in his voice. He loves Edna. She's the owner of Mel's Diner, where my mom serves breakfast every day except Saturdays—that's Mom's one morning off. Edna gave her Saturdays because she's her favorite. That, and she's got a soft spot for Jesse and me. "I need to talk to my mom. Is she around?"

I open my eyes and see him leaning against the wall. His expression doesn't match the light, airy tone of his voice.

"Sure," he says. He looks over at me, his face relaxing when his eyes meet mine. He points at the phone before he holds it away, grabbing his ear lobe and pulling on it while shaking his head. Edna always yells when she's on the phone—it's hilarious in person, but has a way of making your inner ear vibrate when you're the one on the other end of the line.

"Hey, Mom," he says, before turning his body the other way.

"Brice? I'm Eric. I need to see one of your fingers, but before we do that, why don't you help me out by telling me your last name and date of birth?"

"Garrison, and my birthday is May 22, 1980." I hold my weak hand out to him. It's hard to hold up a finger, so I give them all to him. *He can choose.* I let my eyes drift back closed. I just want to sleep.

"Ouch!" I yell for the second time. Looking down, I see

him squeezing a drop of blood from my finger. "What'd you do that for?" I question, immediately throwing my other hand over my mouth. I can't believe I just said that. "Sorry, you just surprised me."

"No, *I'm sorry*. I thought you knew what this was," he responds. When I really look at him, I see the same kindness that I witnessed on Wayne's face. "I'm checking your blood glucose level. This little machine will tell us what it is in just thirty seconds."

We sit and wait, both staring at the little machine. When the time is finally up, Eric's eyebrows scrunch together.

"What's wrong?" I ask him, my heart racing.

"Looks like we'll have to wait for the lab results," he says with a tight smile, as he gets up and walks over to where Wayne is. I watch as they talk quietly to one another before they both leave the room.

"Hey," I feel a tug on my sock.

"Get off," I mumble, pulling my foot free as I roll onto my side. I'm so tired.

"What did they say?"

"Who?" I ask, rolling back over and pulling myself up onto the stretcher. No matter how many times I try to sit up on it, I keep sliding down.

"The nurses," Jesse huffs.

"I don't know. Eric—" I pause, wondering if he knows who I'm talking about, "—that's the other guy that was in here. Anyway, he tried to take a test. He poked my finger." I hold up my finger to show him the wound. It already feels like there's a tiny bruise there, and I keep bumping it. "But, the test didn't work, so they said we'd have to wait for the results from the lab. What'd Mom say? Is she coming?" I try to swallow past the lump in my throat.

"Of course, she's coming, Brice. You should have told her

how bad you were feeling," he finishes, a hint of irritation in his voice.

"I've barely seen her... I tried to tell her last night! You know, when I peed the bed. Did she tell you that this morning? Did she tell you that *I peed the bed*?" My voice is hoarse and I'm completely drained. I reach up to wipe a tear from my face. The attempt is futile; another one takes its place. "She told me to go back to bed, that we'd deal with it in the morning. Then I wake up to *you*. As usual. She didn't even come check on me."

"She never would have left this morning if she had known how serious it was."

"Well, she would have known how serious it was if she'd *listened*." The stream is continuous now, and I don't know how to get it to stop.

"You know that's not fair. You know how tired she is. How hard she works," Jesse says quietly, sitting on the edge of this monstrosity that I've been condemned to lie on. "She's coming. We'll figure this out together."

All I can do is shake my head. The tears have stolen my voice and locked it inside. I feel like if I try to speak, the scream that's down deep in my belly will rise up faster than the words and escape before I can stop it.

We sit quietly together. He picks up my foot and holds it in his lap. Both hands are wrapped firmly around it, as if he's afraid that someone is going to come and steal my foot away. "So, they didn't say anything before they left?" he questions again.

My mouth is so dry. I haven't had anything to drink, and I'm beyond thirsty. My tongue is fat and bloated. Not a part of me, but its own thing, the surface dry and cracked—like the ground beneath a puddle after the sun comes out and bakes the once-quenched earth.

"Will you get me some water," I whisper, my voice sounding as dry and cracked as my tongue feels.

He drops my foot and walks over to the sink. I watch in a haze as he searches for a cup. I begin slipping down the gurney again, but I don't have the energy to try to pull myself up. I wonder why they make the surface of these things so slick. I curl around myself and let my eyes close. I can't keep them open any longer.

"So, what're you saying?"

My mom's voice stirs me from my sleep. *How long has she been here?*

Opening my eyes, I'm shocked to see the amount of people in the room. I sit up quickly, pushing up with my heels, and let out a frustrated sigh as my body slowly slides back down. I feel a hand on my shoulder and am relieved when I look up into the kindest eyes I've ever seen. Harrison. I feel the flutter that happens every time our eyes connect. Then I remember my hair and that little flutter is replaced with sheer panic. *I can't believe he's seeing me like this.* I resist the urge to reach up and smooth it. Then he might know what I'm thinking, and I don't want him to *ever* know what I'm thinking. He can never find out how I feel about him; it'd be the most humiliating thing ever.

Wait a minute. Why is he here? I hope this doesn't mean that I'm dying or something. How long was I asleep for? My eyes scan the room quickly. My mom is off to the left talking to a woman I've never seen before. Is she the doctor?

"Do they know what's wrong with me yet?" I croak, the words dry and desperate.

Everyone in the room stops. It's as if I've hit the pause button with my question. My mom's eyes connect with mine and I see that hers are dark pools of sadness. Oh God, maybe I am dying. "Say something," I urge. Their silence is more frightening than anything they could possibly say.

The silver-haired woman in purple scrubs, who's speaking with my mother, recovers first. She makes her way over to me, her eyes full of quiet reassurance. "Hello, Brice. I'm Dr. Buck. I understand that you've been feeling unwell." She pauses for me to say something, but all I can do is shake my head in affirmation. "Your lab results indicate that you have a condition called type 1 diabetes. This means that your pancreas—a large gland that hangs out behind your stomach—isn't producing insulin anymore." *What?* The words float around the room, sounding like a foreign language. "Because your body quit making insulin, it caused a buildup of glucose, or sugar, in your blood. It's this buildup of sugar in your blood that's making you feel so weak."

"I don't eat much sugar." Why did I say that? Everyone in this room that's known me for more than a day knows how much I love chocolate. But still, I don't eat that much of it. "I thought only old people who eat poorly get diabetes. That's what my friend, Jayden's, mom said when there was a commercial on TV about it."

"That's a very common misconception. Type 1 diabetes is much different than type 2. People with type 2 diabetes still produce insulin, it's just that the insulin isn't as productive," she pauses to give me a reassuring smile. "With proper diet and exercise, this condition can be reversed, since their pancreas still produces insulin. Making these changes can result in better productivity of their insulin." Her mouth drifts down, and my heart begins to race. "Type 1 diabetes is an autoimmune disease. The antibodies in your system attacked the islet cells that produce the insulin and destroyed them. You will have this for the rest of your life."

I try to listen, but my mind is racing as fast as my heart. "Forever? I'm going to have this forever?"

She smiles again, and a wave of nausea hits me as she continues her speech. "The good news is, there are ways to treat it, and with some proper education, we can prepare you to treat it at home on your own. Right now, there is so much excess glucose in your bloodstream, you are suffering from a condition called diabetic ketoacidosis—what we call DKA. This means that several of the chemical components of your blood are out of range. This causes the anion gap to open. We need to get that back where it should be, and I suspect that once we do, you will be feeling remarkably better than you have in a long time."

"How do we treat it?" I ask, remembering the painful little poke to my finger. I run my thumb over the spot, wincing when I touch the little bruise.

I see her face fill with sympathy, and I hate it. Whatever I need to do, I'll do it, but I don't want people looking at me like that. I don't want anyone to feel sorry for me. If this thing is going to be mine, then I'm going to own it. I must have changed the look on my face, because the sympathy she wore just moments ago has been replaced with a small, knowing smile.

"You will need to do insulin injections twice a day and check your glucose before and after meals. We're going to keep you here for several days. We'll have someone teach you how to properly draw up your insulin dosage and do the injections. You will also meet with someone who will teach you about your new diet."

She looks like a mom or a grandma. Not someone who should be delivering this life-altering news. I'm glad people can't hear our thoughts because mine are screaming right now.

"But for now, our main focus is going to be getting that gap closed and getting you feeling better. There will be plenty of time to learn in the next few days," she says, effectively ending the conversation. She walks back over to my mother, leaving me to process everything she's just told me.

I don't know what to think about any of this. How is it possible to be completely full of questions, and yet, not be able to pluck one of them free? I have things I want to ask but no idea where to begin. Maybe once the DK whatever goes away, I'll be able to think clearly enough to come up with a coherent sentence.

5

NOTHING AND EVERYTHING HAS CHANGED

I LIE BACK, LETTING MYSELF SINK INTO MY BED. I THINK OUT of everything, *it's* what I missed the most this last week. It feels so good to have a moment to myself. At the hospital, it never really felt like I was alone. Because even when there wasn't someone in the room with me, I could hear them right down the hall—talking and laughing. Telling each other stories about everything from patients to boys.

I reach up, grab a corner of my comforter, and pull it to my nose, slowly inhaling the scent of pure sunshine. I don't know what it is that my mom does differently, but when she does my laundry, it always smells amazing. Sitting up, I take in the rest of my room. The old blue swivel chair that sits in the corner and always has at least ten sweaters tossed across it is completely clear of everything…except a new throw pillow that's shaped like a flower and a big, fluffy, purple blanket draped across the back. It's also new.

I haven't had help cleaning my room since I was seven, and that had been Jesse. He got so frustrated with me because I wouldn't stop playing while he was trying to help me clean. I remember it like it was yesterday. He threw down my She-Ra doll and screamed, *"Figure it out for yourself,"* slamming the door on his way out. I walked straight up to that doll and picked her up. She was exactly who I needed to rescue Barbie from the evil teddy bear who was running away with her. I figured it out in my own way. My room may not have gotten clean, but my imagination was always well fed.

I sort of feel like she invaded my space, coming in here and cleaning everything when I wasn't home. But my bed smells so lovely, I guess it evens out. Plus, I know this is how she shows her love. And the new things look really nice—like the perfect spot for reading. I love to read—anything and everything. The weirder the better. I don't want to read something predictable; I like things that surprise me. I've been really into Christopher Pike lately. His writing is really out there. There's nothing I love better than going into Waldenbooks at the mall and picking out a new book.

Just the thought of it gets me feeling excited. Maybe if I have enough leftover babysitting money, I can talk Jesse into taking me down there this afternoon. If Mom will let me leave. Freedom is a thing of the past. I crave the feeling I get running my hand over the perfectly aligned spines, each one a promise of a new adventure—an escape from my strange new reality.

I don't mind the shots, not really. Most of the time, they don't even hurt. I glance down at my hands in my lap. I pull my right hand up in front of me and look at the tiny bruises on each of my fingers. That was the worst of it: being woken up in the middle of the night—when I actually *could* sleep—and blindly passing my finger out from the covers, while squeezing my eyes closed. I think the anticipation of it was always the worst. I knew it was coming, but I never knew exactly when. Some of the nurses were nice and quick about it, that was better. But one of the nurses hovered, and she always had a look of trepidation on her face; it made me want to apologize. I kept having to bite my tongue so I didn't say, "I'm sorry you have to poke me. I can see it's hard for you."

Sometimes, if I just squeeze my finger, it will start to bleed again. They said my fingers will get used to it, they won't always bruise. I'm ready for that to happen because right now it hurts to even brush my hair. Diabetes. It still doesn't seem real. I know I can do it—the treatment doesn't scare me. What scares me is the look I keep getting from people. The look that says, *she's fragile, we have to be careful with her.* I'm afraid I'll never be independent again, never be trusted to be alone.

The creek of the door opening startles me from my thoughts. *Harrison.* He's never been in my room before. What is he doing here?

"Hey," I say weakly, standing from the edge of my bed. "What's up?"

"Since your mom had to go to work, and Jesse had a study session, they wanted me to come hang out with you."

The internal groan is so loud. I'm glad it's in the depths of my imagination and I didn't let it slip. It's humiliating enough to need a babysitter. I don't need to be making absurd noises on top of things. My only visible reaction is the slight hitch of my left eyebrow—it's always been the more active of the two.

"What? Is an afternoon with me so bad?" he questions, a teasing smile on his face. "Come on, Rice. Get your shoes, and let's blow this Popsicle stand."

I feel a little tingly every time he calls me that, which is silly, I know, but I love that he gave me a name no one else uses.

"What does that even mean?" I deadpan.

"We need to get out of here, you know—go walk around—experience life…"

I stare at him for a moment, enjoying this banter and the small smirk still playing at the corner of his mouth. My heart rate quickens as I take in the sight of his mouth. That perfect mouth. Ugh. *Get a grip, Brice.* I move my gaze up to his eyes —the color of warm, dark honey—with lashes so long, they almost sweep the lenses of his glasses. I'm glad his eyes aren't full of the pity and guilt that my mom and brother's have been swimming in for the past week. My cheeks warm as I realize that I've been standing, staring into his eyes for way too long.

"Right, shoes," I say dumbly, quickly stepping around him and out my bedroom door.

I slip on my snow boots once I reach the front entry. The weather has been really bad, with record snowfall already, and winter has just begun. I don't mind it. It seems fitting for the way I've been feeling.

When I turn, Harrison is standing there, holding my coat. "Do you need to check your sugar before we go?"

And this is why I need a babysitter. As soon as he opened my bedroom door, I completely forgot about all things diabetes. Although, I could argue that, had he not come at all, I wouldn't have been distracted by him and forgotten. See, I still don't need a sitter.

"Yeah, I probably should." I hang my jacket back on the hook and walk the short distance to the kitchen. From now on, my life is going to be measured in tiny drops. Tiny drops of my blood given to see how I'll measure up—how I've done. If I'm maintaining like I'm supposed to. What will the answer be?

I go to the drawer Mom set up for my needles and supplies. It's such a weird thought, that I will need something as permanent as my own drawer for this stuff. I can never go without it —at least, that was the running theme at the hospital. They each talked to me about it, in different, not so subtle ways. There was the talk about loss of kidney function if you aren't good with your dosing. Amputations. Loss of eyesight—which freaked me out the most. If I couldn't see, I couldn't read, and I don't think I could survive without books. I thought about Braille, but with the way my fingertips are feeling, that doesn't seem plausible. I never knew that when you get a disease, they talk to you about all of the horrid things that could and *will* happen to you if you don't take care of it. Of course, I'm going to take care of myself. I want to live. I want to do everything I need to do to keep it in control.

I set the monitor on the counter and snap open its hard outer case. We were sent home with it from the hospital. After they released me today, we stopped by the pharmacy and got everything I need. I don't know how my mom is going to afford to do it all the time. Just the strips to check my blood sugar cost nearly seventy-five dollars. I'm not even sure if one hundred strips is enough for a month. They want me to check it first thing in the morning, before and after each meal, and before I go to bed each night. If it's out of range at all, they want it to be checked in the middle of the night, too. That's at least eight strips a day. The doctor did say that once I get the hang of things, if I have good control, I can just check before meals and bedtime. That'd be nice.

"Does it hurt?" Harrison asks, his eyebrows pinched as he stares over my shoulder. He's so close, I can feel the tiny hairs at the back of my neck stand from the proximity—a foreign anticipation of touch.

"Not really," I lie.

"I'm proud of you, Rice. You're taking this really well. I don't know if I would have," he whispers, each word tickling my skin.

My heart begins to race as I let my imagination play out a scene where I turn and wrap my arms around him.

"You're like a sister to me, and if you need anything at all —ever—you just say the word." His words are strong, confident.

I glance down at my chest, fully expecting to see the handle of the knife that must surely be protruding from the center of it. I can almost feel the blood dripping down from the wound his words left there. I swallow my humiliation and do my best to recover. "Thanks, Harrison. I'm glad to have *two* big brothers. One could never be enough," I say playfully, bumping into him.

My monitor beeps, displaying my reading on the screen—109.

"So, is that good?" he asks.

"I think it's right where it should be."

"Great, let's get out of here."

I follow him back to the door and grab my coat. "So, what're we going to do?"

"It wouldn't be any fun if I told you," he replies, making quick work of the steps leading to the building's front entry. There isn't much to it. One wall is lined with locking mailboxes, and in the opposite corner, there's an old, sad-looking chair. I couldn't imagine sitting in it, and often wonder why it's even there. There's a long rip across the seat, causing the stuffing to spill up and out of the wound. Its wooden legs look uneven and wobbly, and the fabric that isn't torn is a dull, dirty pink—the color my mom would call *dusty rose*.

Exiting the lobby, I wrap my arms around my middle as a strong shiver courses through me. It's so cold. On our way to Harrison's pickup, we run into the man I saw on the way to the hospital. I don't remember what his name is. That whole day is pretty hazy.

"Hey, hey, Mr. Shelton, do you need a hand with your groceries?" Harrison asks him.

He stops in front of us, a playful smile on his face. "Now, how many times have I told you to call me Bernard or Bernie? I retired, remember? I left that name at the school." Walking to the door, he sets the bags down to open it.

As soon as they're out of his hands, Harrison swoops over, gathering them up.

"I'm just going to take these up. I'll be right down,"

Harrison says. Setting down the two from his left hand, he reaches into his pocket for the keys to his truck. "Go ahead and start it, warm it up." He throws me the keys.

I make a lame grab for them, but my attempt falls short. Truth is, I tend to lean the other way when things are flying at me. I'm not sure why, but it's a bit embarrassing. I scoop them up off the ground and run across the parking lot. The cold has completely seeped into me now, and I can't stop shivering.

Once I get into the truck and turn it on, I slip across the bench seat to the passenger side. Harrison knows my mysterious neighbor, too. I wonder why I've never talked with him before. I look around the inside of the truck. It's the first time I've been in it—Harrison and I don't hang out. As frustrated as I am at the fact that my family thinks I need to be watched, but didn't think they should discuss it with me, I'm totally psyched to get to hang out with him. It's clean in here, and there's a faint smell of coconut. The little orange tree that's hanging from his radio knob is likely responsible for the smell.

I glance back to the front of the apartments just as he opens the door. *Harrison.* He's been a fixture at our house since he and Jesse both sat on the bench for nearly the entire season they played football when they were twelve. It was the same year my dad died, and I think his friendship really helped Jesse. He lost something that year—we all did—but he gained something, too.

It's a well-known fact that Harrison's mother loves all things *Star Wars*. Her favorite actor? Harrison Ford. I've only met her once, but the whole time I stood in their living room, waiting for the boys to grab whatever it was we stopped to get, she went on and on about her favorite hunky heartthrob. It was hilarious. Most people call him Harry. Except my idiot brother, who has always called him Ford. And me. I like the way Harrison sounds. It's a great name, and calling him Harry cheapens it, makes it less than what it is. Some things don't need to be changed.

"Sorry about that. I couldn't let him carry that all up on his own," Harrison says, climbing into the truck.

"Of course, I should have thought to offer," I reply.

"You haven't met him yet, have you? On the way upstairs, he was asking about you. Said he hadn't had the pleasure to meet you yet. He retired before you got to the high school. It's a bummer; I know you would have loved him."

"Oh, he's a teacher? I was wondering how you guys knew him. What'd he teach?"

"He taught English. Introduced me to a lot of the greats in literature. He really inspired me because he could stand in front of this group of kids who didn't want to be there—kids that were too busy paying attention to each other to pay attention to him—and all he had to do was begin speaking," Harrison begins, a fire in his eyes I've never witnessed before. His voice so full of admiration. "He was captivating. So passionate about everything he was speaking of. That kind of self-assurance demands attention, and it didn't take long for him to transform the whole class. He made English cool," he finished, bobbing his head to the music playing in the background.

The world is a vampire, sent to drain.

"What is this?" I nod toward the radio. "I've never heard it before, but I kinda like it."

"Smashing Pumpkins' 'Bullet with Butterfly Wings.'"

"What?" *What did he just say?* "Is that the group? Smashing Pumpkins? Weird..." I hope that didn't sound offensive; my luck they're probably his favorite group.

"It's a weird name, but that's their style. Out of the ordinary. That's why I dig it, you know?" He smiles, and I reach over to turn it up.

Despite all my rage, I am still just a rat in a cage.

My body moves slightly with the music as I think about the lyrics. I feel that way now—a rat in a cage, absolutely no freedom. But I don't mind—at least not today—in this moment, here with Harrison. I reach over and absently draw a heart with my finger in the window steam, before rubbing my palm across it. *I hope he didn't see that.*

My mouth pulls up when he turns into the parking garage behind the mall. I sort of thought we might end up here. Jesse told me more than once that Harrison loves the bookstore as much as I do.

"I was thinking you might like something new to read. My treat," he says as he puts the truck in park.

"Are you serious?!"

"Totally serious. You're the only person I know who loves to read as much as I do. I thought this might take your mind off things. Besides, I needed to pick something up, anyway."

"That's so kind of you," I say, my heart melting into a gooey puddle of unreciprocated feelings. Oh well, at least he doesn't know how I feel. I think I'd die if he ever found out.

Waldenbooks has always been my favorite out of the two bookstores in the mall. It has more of the books I like to read, and there's a whole shelf of Christopher Pike books. I pull three from the shelf that I haven't read. This is my ritual—I read the back of each, then place them behind my back and awkwardly try to shuffle them around. Then I move two to one hand, and the third to the other. Whichever one is by itself is the one I choose. I have a hard time deciding things, and this sort of takes the pressure off—leaves it to fate.

I finish with my weird little routine and glance down at the book in my left hand. *Remember Me.* I hope it's good.

"Did you find something?" Harrison asks, breaking my

thoughts, startling me. I'd been alone in this section just moments before.

"I did. Are you sure you don't mind getting it for me? I actually think I have enough at home. I'll get you back when we get there."

"Don't be ridiculous, what is it? Four dollars? I think I can handle it, Rice," he replies, the easy smile on his face making my knees wobble.

6

CHRISTMAS VACATION

ALONE. IT'S THE FIRST TIME I'VE BEEN COMPLETELY ALONE IN almost a month. It feels really good. I enjoy solitude, complete silence. I've always found it sort of rejuvenating, and I've craved it for the last several weeks. It's time to fill myself up with the kind of quiet that is needed to deal with all this noise.

Going back to school was a nightmare. Everyone wanted to talk to me. Normally, the only people I talk to regularly are my teachers and my best friend, Jayden. I mean, I'm casually friendly with a few other people. And if I get paired up with someone for a project, then of course I'm cordial, but I learn better when I'm not distracted by everything else. And unlike most of the inhabitants at my school, I actually like to learn.

There's an endless amount of knowledge, and I wish I could learn it all. I used to wish that I was one of those savants. I mean, if you're going to get stuck with a disability, wouldn't extreme intelligence be the way to go? But nope, fate didn't smile on me. Instead, it left me with this lame disease. Guilt trickles in as soon as I have the thought. I don't want to feel bad about it because I'm going to have it forever, and I don't want to feel like *that* forever, so I better not feel like *that* at all.

I'm sure this wouldn't make sense to anyone else, which is why I keep these thoughts to myself.

Every time I'm with my mom and brother, all they want to do is talk about it. How am I feeling? When did I check my sugar last? What was my sugar? Did I have a snack? I should have a snack. Snacks are important. It feels so bizarre. So unlike my normal life, just a month ago. Back when my meals were my business. Of course, they made sure I ate, but no one really cared *what*. We don't eat meals together often. Everyone has a busy schedule. My mom works mornings at Mel's, and she's been working in the evenings at Shopko, stocking shelves for Christmas. Jesse is here sometimes, but he's been spending a lot of time with his new girlfriend, Tori.

My mom just left for work, and Jesse didn't come home last night, so I'm blessed with time to myself. I walk into the living room, knowing exactly what I need to do today. It's time to make Christmas come to life in here.

We have a tree, with pretty, little twinkling lights, and we all hung the decorations on it together, but besides that, nothing's been done. My mom normally sets up her village that lights up and tells its own Christmas story—it's always been one of my favorite parts of Christmas. But this year, she hasn't had time for anything, and she's been so stressed out. Maybe if I do this, it'll make her feel better.

It's only 7:30 in the morning. I should have loads of time before anyone gets home. Satisfied with my plan for the day, I pull my hair back using the scrunchie on my wrist and head for the hall closet. The closet is as deep as our bedrooms and about half as wide. I always thought it would make a good office, but then where would we put all this stuff? There're so many boxes in here; it's going to take some work to find the right ones. Good thing I had a big breakfast before Mom left.

I've gained nearly ten pounds since I was diagnosed. I had been losing weight for months, but I didn't realize when they admitted me to the hospital I only weighed sixty-five pounds. I looked like a skeleton, and I hadn't even noticed. There were so many signs I should have seen. I don't know why I let it get as bad as I did before I asked for help. But, now I'm eating a ton and feeling *so* much better. I'll be back up to a healthy weight in no time.

My mom's been waking me up at 6:00 a.m. every morning and feeding me eggs, toast, and whichever breakfast meat she decides to make. There is always fresh fruit on the side. When she's short on time, she makes me apple cinnamon oatmeal. Not everything about this disease sucks. It does have its perks. Spending time with my mom is definitely one of them. I try not to complain because she works so hard, but sometimes I really miss her.

Standing just inside the closet, I know why we haven't done any more decorating. I'm going to have to move at least ten boxes to get to the red totes in the back. They hold everything I need to turn this place into a winter wonderland. If I get this done in time, I think I'll make some snowflakes to string from the ceiling, too.

Everything is so haphazardly placed in here. I'm afraid that I'll accidentally grab the *wrong* box and it will all come tumbling down, leaving me pinned until someone hears me scream. Lucky for me, the first box I grab isn't the cursed *wrong* box, and everything stays in place. It ends up being a pretty quick and easy task once I've started.

I love Christmas. Every year when we get out the decorations, it's almost like seeing a loved one that's been away for a long time. All the past Christmas memories come out to play when I hold an iconic piece of our family history in my hands. These boxes are plum full of history and memories.

I stack the last box standing between me and the treasures I seek out in the hall. Now I just have to take the four big totes out to the living room, and I'll be ready to reload the closet.

What was I thinking? I huff, blowing a stray curl from my face, and stretch my shaky arms. I may have been a little hasty taking on such a big project, although it does feel good having a little independence.

The first two totes are super light, but I know the one on the bottom holds the village and probably weighs more than me at this point. I laugh quietly, even though I'm well aware it's not funny. I'm suddenly struck with an emotion so deep it catches my breath, and I feel a tear slide down my cheek. As I reach up to wipe it away, I see the slight tremor in my hand. That's weird. I shake my fingers loose, trying to quell the tremor.

Picking up the third box, I'm determined to finish the task at hand. I'm not even going to attempt to move the last one. I'll just have to unload it from its current position. When I get to the living room and set down the box I'm carrying, I feel a wave of dizziness and sit on the sofa. I'll be so glad when I don't feel so weak anymore. I'm tired of feeling like this. Moving a few boxes around shouldn't have worn me out so fast.

I take a deep breath before I stand. I still feel a little dizzy, and my heart is a steady gallop, but I'm sure it's just because it's been awhile since I was so active. I want to power through this so I can get it done before anyone gets home. I'm excited to surprise them.

When I get to the closet, I pop the lid on the tote and smile down at the tiny world it holds inside. I'm surprised to feel moisture on my cheeks again. Why am I so emotional? Maybe I'm going to start my period soon. I brush the tears away, reach inside, and pull out the bakery and the school. I can only hold two at a time. The walk back and forth is quick, and before I know it, I've moved enough of them to lighten the box. I pick it up, surprised at how badly my arms are shaking. I slowly make my way out to the living room. Placing the box on the floor, I lie down beside it.

It's what my body is telling me to do, but my mind's fighting it. Why do I feel like this? As soon as I question it, I see the answer like a neon sign flashing in front of me. My blood sugar's low. I sit up, feeling the panic kick in. I need to check it.

Racing to the kitchen, I pull open the drawer. I try to open the case, but everything feels foreign, like I've never done this before. I close my eyes and take a deep breath. "Pull it together!" I scream, my voice causing another form of panic to set in. My words sound so distant, even though I know they came from me.

I finally manage to turn the little machine on and put the strip inside. I poke my finger and place the drop of blood on… too soon. I use my shaky hands to pull the strip out and put another in. My blood is so runny, it's covered the end of my finger, and once the machine is ready, it's all I can do to soak the little dot with blood. It doesn't want to go where it's needed. It just wants to coat the end of my finger and run down my hand. The tears are continuous now, and I feel so helpless. When the agonizing thirty seconds are up, my panic doubles. Forty-two is the number flashing at me.

Ok, I need to get a grip, panic won't help. I sit, staring for a moment, trying to remember where my mom said she put the glucose tablets she bought. I. Can't. Remember. I don't have time to go searching, I know that. I can feel it in my floaty thoughts—my mind keeps traveling without me, and my body keeps telling me to sit.

I fight the urge and make my way to the fridge. Where's the juice? There's no juice! Why isn't there any juice? Okay, it's *okay*. I remember something about milk having sugar in it. I'll start with some milk. I go to the cupboard and grab a cup.

My hands are shaking so badly now, the cup tips and rolls to the floor when I try to set it on the counter.

"Come on!" I yell. Why is everything fighting against me? I reach down for it, feeling a wave of dizziness. I can do this. I channel all of my will, and with two hands, set the glass down on the counter. When I pull the gallon of milk out of the fridge, I know I'm in trouble. I can't lift it above the glass. There's no way. My hands are shaking so badly now, I don't even think I have the energy to hoist it onto the counter.

I slump to the floor, my back pressed firmly against the cabinet drawers, their handles digging into me. I twist the cap off the gallon, and with two trembling hands, pull it up to my lips. The whole jug is shaking so badly, I'm afraid I'll swish it up my nose and drown myself. As I pour, I feel it run down my chin and all over the front of me. But I guzzle it like it's life or death, and in a sense, I guess it is. The action of doing something to combat this feeling gives me a resolve to escape this hell.

Slowly, I stand and make my way to the snack cupboard. I pull out a box of graham crackers. Opening the box, I take out a package, and then stop to grab my glass before I sit back on the floor. Holding the glass between my legs, I use both arms to steady the jug. Most of the milk I pour goes in. I open the cracker package, my hands still trembling, and dip the first one into my glass. I sit like this—mindlessly eating until the last cracker is gone. I push the gallon of milk to the side and lay my whole body down.

"Brice?! Brice, honey, come on, baby! Wake up!"

I pat my mom's hand away, wanting to continue resting in this dream space. "I don't want to get up yet. Just let me sleep," I mumble, as I roll over, the cutting pain of my hip digging into the floor grabbing my attention. "What am I doing on the floor?" I ask, suddenly very awake.

"Come on, baby, get up. We need to check your sugar."

"No, I just—" I pause as I remember everything that happened. I feel the dry stiffness of my milk-covered clothes and shudder when I realize that the weird yellow glow is the light from the inside of the refrigerator. I wonder how long I've been sleeping? "You're right, let's check," I finish, standing.

She leads me to the table where the monitor is still sitting. She gently guides me into the chair, quickly pulling out the used strip and setting it aside. Her hands are shaking as she resets the machine and grabs my hand. The little snapping noise the poker makes when you push the button always freaks me out worse when I'm not the one holding it.

387.

"Wow, that's really high. What happened?"

I turn my face toward her and take in a deep breath. I don't even know how to begin to explain what just happened. It was the scariest thing that's ever happened to me. I don't ever want to feel that way again. I rub my hands across my face, trying to find the words.

"It got low," I whisper.

"How low? Are you here by yourself? Where's your brother? Is he still not home? Were you moving all the stuff from the closet by yourself?" Her face evens out as she tries to mask how she's feeling, but I know she's scared. I am too.

"I was trying to surprise you. I wanted to make it feel like Christmas in here. I was just busy, and I wasn't paying attention. I won't let it happen again," I say, suddenly feeling guilty for ignoring the symptoms, and worse for not being smart enough to recognize them. Now I've just caused her more worry.

We sit at the table, having a silent staring contest. She's

beautiful. I always think that when she's holding still right in front of me. She's generally a flurry of movement—I suppose you can't have two children, two jobs, and a clean home without constant motion. Her expression turns playful, a mischievous light flicking on in her emerald eyes.

"You need to dose two units of your R insulin, and then you need to come with me into the bathroom so I can show you something."

I'm not sure where she's going with this, but I'm curious to find out. I walk over to the fridge, pop open the butter compartment, and pull out my insulin…but only the bottle she said to. Normally, I do them both together, but this is the one that works quickly. The other—the NPH—releases more slowly. It makes sense that she would want me to take a couple units of the fast-acting. I grab a needle from the drawer and pull the cap off the bottom. Then I turn until I can see the numbers, pull the plunger back to the 2, pull off the orange cap, and stick the needle into the vial. Pushing the air inside, I turn the vial upside down and draw out two units of the insulin, lift the hem of my shirt, and gently stick it into the skin of my stomach. Sounds brutal, huh? The crazy thing is, this part doesn't hurt at all; most of the time, I can't even feel it. I'm grateful for that.

When I put the insulin back in the fridge, my mom comes up beside me, wrapping her arms around me. "Are you ready, baby girl?"

I nod. "Let's do this thing."

She slides her hand down to mine, and together we walk to the bathroom. "I'm not sure that you're ready for this. Are you ready for this?"

"Mom! I already said I'm ready, geez!"

"All right, I just had to be sure. This is going to be life changing," she finishes, a slight smile on her face, trying to hide the sadness that lies right under the surface. She opens the door, flips on the light, and pulls me into the bathroom.

Glancing in the mirror, I stop cold. I have crusty milk all over my face, my hair is matted straight up on one side, and on the other, it's plastered to my face, the milk working like glue to hold it there. And there's a long streak of blood across my nose. I look completely ridiculous. Absolutely *wretched*. I shudder at the thought of anyone other than the two of us seeing me like this.

"Oh my God," I say in disbelief.

"I know, right? I was surprised, too, but then I realized what this was, and had to share it with you. This is the face of a warrior. You even have the tribal paint to go with it. Today you fought a battle, and you came out the other side. Do you know how strong you are? You astonish me every day. You amaze me. Don't you ever put the blame of this on yourself. Do you hear me? I'm so sorry this happened to you today. I'm so sorry no one was here for you. I won't let that happen again. But baby, I'm so proud of you," she finishes, wrapping her arms around me.

I let myself relax into her. Nothing in the entire world feels better than a mom hug. I feel so safe, wrapped in a cocoon of love and strength. I fight the urge to let the tears go; I've done enough crying for one day.

"Now, maybe you should take a shower while I clean up the kitchen." Her laugh is shaky, the fear she's trying to mask slipping out.

She kisses me on the cheek, and I watch her walk out the door behind me. As it closes, I lean into the mirror and watch my breath fog it, taking comfort in it. *I'm still here.*

7

SNOWFLAKES AND NEIGHBORS

"What would you like for Christmas?"

The question surprises me, pulls me from my quiet thoughts. I hadn't really thought about the gift-giving and receiving part of Christmas. I've seen the kind of money Mom's been spending on all of my supplies. She says it's only temporary—she's applied for insurance for me that will cover everything. But right now, I can't imagine she has anything to spare. I put down the scissors I'm holding and take a moment to think.

"I could use some new socks, and maybe a journal," I answer, giving her a soft smile.

"You want socks? For Christmas?" She shakes her head, barely containing her laughter. "Hey Jesse, come here a sec, would ya?" she shouts toward the living room where Jesse and Harrison are busy hanging all the snowflakes we're making. When she turns back to me, her eyes are full of glee. "Just wait, this is hilarious. You two are something else." She shakes her head again, causing a curl to spring free from the confines of her top knot.

My brother walks in and grabs a handful of M&M's out of

the red dish in the center of the table. My mom made it a point to strategically place candy throughout the house after my first run-in with low blood sugar. She looks up at him, raising her left eyebrow. *That must be where I get it from.* Jesse casts his eyes down, and, smiling sheepishly, holds his hand back over the bowl, dropping several of the M&M's back into it. "Sorry, they're just so good," he says on a laugh.

Mom shakes her head. "What did you say you wanted for Christmas?" she asks him, turning her attention back to the folded paper she is cutting small shapes from.

It's my brother's turn to exercise his brow, and once again it's the left one. *Interesting.* It must be a family trait, or maybe it's just because we're around each other so often, we mimic behavior.

"I just told you this morning. I need socks." He gives her a puzzled look before turning to me. "No more wine for Mom. I think she's had enough."

"Oh, shut up! I know what you said; I wanted your sister to hear it." She laughs, swatting at him.

Harrison walks in, leaning his arm on Jesse's shoulder, a full head taller than my brother. He reaches into the center of the table, grabbing a handful of candy. "It's a winter wonderland in there. I think we can halt the snowflake production," he says, popping the candy in his mouth.

I turn my gaze away, hoping I wasn't staring for too long. When I glance back up, he gives me a kind smile, and I feel my cheeks heat.

"Are you ready to check it out?"

"I can't wait!" Pushing my chair back, I stand up.

Mom gets up, clapping her hands with glee, pure joy alive and free on her face. I feel the strain on my cheeks and know that it lives on my face, too. I take her hand, and together, we follow the boys into the living room.

"Whoa." I reach out, touching a snowflake, the movement

making it dance in the twinkling lights. They catch its glitter, casting magical shimmering light across the room. It's mesmerizing. The work they've done has truly transformed the room into a winter wonderland. Snowflakes hang from varying lengths around the room, with lights strung in between. It's beautiful. I feel a swell of emotion for this gift and the boys who gave it to me.

"Wow, this is amazing! You two have outdone yourselves. Where did all of the lights come from?" Mom asks, spinning around in the center of the room, her arms out and face turned up. I imagine her tongue popping out, expecting to catch a snowflake from the sky.

"We each picked up a few boxes. I guess when I said we need to get some lights, Ford thought I meant *he* needed to get some lights." Jesse playfully punches Harrison in the shoulder. "We couldn't let them go to waste," he says, swooping in, picking Mom off her feet. "Love you, Mama. Glad I could make you smile."

Harrison glances at me, rolling his eyes at their shenanigans. "What do you think? Is this Christmas enough for you?"

"More than enough; it's truly magical." I smile, the stress of the last month forgotten, my heart fully in the joy of the moment. "Thank you." I turn my eyes to the ceiling. When I glance back at him, the eruption of butterflies in my belly is like a little hurricane. He almost looks shy. It almost looks like… My thoughts—interrupted by the doorbell. Who could that be?

"We invited Bernard over for game night. He doesn't really have anyone, and he's a great guy. Just straight across the hall, if you ever need anything," Jesse says while Mom answers the door.

Ah ha! I'm being set up with a new babysitter. I glance down at my boots and take a deep breath. I know they're doing this because they care about me, and they worry, but it still sorts of sucks.

"He just cares about you. When he heard about the other day, it really freaked him out. Me too," Harrison whispers my thoughts back to me.

The *me too* at the end makes my toes tingle. I like the thought of him caring about me. Does he think about me the way I think about him? I glance over at him, and he gives me an easy smile, the deep dimple in his cheek making me want to reach over and touch it—measure its depth with my finger.

Bernard steps into the apartment, and I study him closely. This is the first time I've seen him not bundled for the weather. He must be close to seventy, but his smile is youthful, making him appear younger. I've always thought that age was something you carried in your eyes. But the relaxed way he holds his face, and the ease of his smile, totally contradict the wisdom in his eyes. His short hair is full of salt and pepper, although I'm sure it was dark before it changed. His skin is the color of light cocoa, and he has a smattering of freckles that dust his cheeks and nose. In his hands, he holds a pie. It. Looks. Delicious… Figures, my first temptation dessert would have to be pie. Pie is my absolute favorite.

I'm a little mad that he would bring pie. Of course, it's the neighborly thing to do, but I'm sure they told him about everything. Why couldn't it have been cake? I wouldn't have even thought twice about cake.

"It's great to see you, Mr. Shelton." Harrison steps forward. "Let me take that for you," he says, taking the pie.

For some reason that's even worse. Now, both of the things I want, but can't have, are together. I feel myself start to salivate, but I don't know if it's because of the boy or the pie.

"Thank you, Harry. This is a real treat. Two of my favorite students." He looks back and forth between Harrison and Jesse, shaking his head slightly. "I sure lucked out with this apartment." He smiles, his eyes full of merriment. "Glad I finally sold that big house. It was too much for an old man to take care of." The smile slips for a moment. What's his story?

"That apartment's been empty for ages. It's nice to have someone in there, finally," Mom says, giving him a side hug.

She's a hugger. I once saw her hug a stranger at the grocery store. She didn't walk up to him and randomly hug him. Nope. He was standing behind us in line, and, of course, started telling her his life story. This is just something that happens to Mom, too. People tell her the most bizarre, personal things. It's like a superpower or something. So, while we stood there waiting on the slow cashier, the man proceeded to tell us all about how he'd just lost his son to leukemia. I don't blame her for hugging him. I probably would have too, if I hadn't been so frozen in place by the story. It was so sad, it nearly stopped time for me.

"We're so happy you're here." Her eyes turn to me. "Have you met Brice?"

"I haven't had the pleasure," he answers, his smile so genuine, I almost forgive the pie. *Almost.*

"It's nice to meet you, sir," I say, offering my hand.

He takes it between both of his, smiling at me kindly. "It's a pleasure to meet you, young lady," he finishes, giving my hand a final squeeze before he releases it.

I cross my arms as a small smile takes over my face. Maybe I can forgive the pie. I've always had a soft spot for the elderly, and he's adorable. I want to know more about him. I've never been one to hold a grudge, and it's not like I'm the only person here. I'm sure they'll all enjoy the *pie*.

"Is Jayden coming?" Mom asks.

"She's babysitting this evening. Mr. Tillman's supposed to drop her here after," I tell her. Sometimes I wonder why Jayden's my best friend—we couldn't be bigger opposites. But I love her to pieces; everyone does.

"I don't believe you," I say, because it's true. Jayden can tell some whoppers. She plumps her stories, always adding just enough color to make it more fascinating. But, sometimes she takes it over the top.

"It's true." She points her fork at me while she chews the roast beef she just tucked into her mouth. Roast beef has always been my favorite dinner. I love everything about it.

"How many of you believe this story?" I ask around the table. My gaze sits a moment too long with Harrison, his amused smile making me falter, but when he sends a playful wink my way, I find courage and continue around the table. "Anyone?"

"I think it's possible. It could have happened," Jesse says, a mischievous glint dancing in his eye. I know he's just saying it to challenge me. "What is it you find so hard to believe?"

"For starters, the whole mouth-to-mouth bit. We all know there's no way Mr. Tillman is going to put his mouth on a dog's. Period. *No way*," I say, pointing my fork at Jayden. "That's where you lost me. You took it over the top this time, Jay." I laugh. Her porcelain-white skin colors, and she laughs, too.

"Okay, but he did hit a dog. And we did get out to see. And the dog *did* run off," she says, midchew. "So, the story is mostly true. Mostly," she finishes, with a dramatic sigh, rolling her big, blue eyes at me.

"I think I may have retired a few years too early. You two would have been fun to have in class," Bernard interjects. The creases around his mouth deepen before a big belly laugh breaks free.

His laugh is contagious, everyone in the room on the brink. As we all give in to the titter, I realize that this is the first time since my diagnosis that everyone has let go of the fear and sadness. We're enjoying ourselves. I think the worst part of all of this is the hollow ache in my gut that says I've made them unhappy. I've caused this sadness to fall over them, and now they're living in constant worry. The rational part of me knows it's ridiculous. I know I didn't cause this—at least that's what the doctors say—but there's this little part of me that feels like maybe I did.

"Whew, I haven't laughed like that in ages." Bernard takes a big breath, shaking his head. "Brice, where you at tonight? Do you think you can have some pie?" he asks, taking me off guard.

"No, no, thank you. I can't have pie." I smile politely, picking at the hole in my jeans.

"Why not? This is a special pie, no sugar. Just apples, cinnamon, and a couple of teaspoons of apple juice concentrate, and of course, a little butter. You gotta have butter. I was 103 when I left my apartment, so I'm having pie." He winks, rubbing his hands together in front of his face.

I'm stunned. Is he diabetic? He's not overweight. "You're diabetic? But you're so thin. I thought type 2s were bigger?" I realize, as the words escape me, how insulting they sound. "I'm sorry, I just haven't met anyone else."

He leans back in his chair and steeples his fingers. The expression on his face is still amused, but I can tell things have shifted. He's gone from guest to teacher, and I'm about to be schooled.

"Do you think that only young people have type 1? Is that why you assume I'm type 2?"

His question surprises me, and I nod, even though I realize as I do, this is a ridiculous notion to have.

"But, you know there's no cure for type 1 diabetes, correct?" He pauses, waiting for me to supply the answer. I give another silent nod. "Then it stands to reason that there could be people of all ages with the disease then, correct?" he finishes, his tone sincere and uncondescending, the corner of his mouth turned up slightly as he waits for me to speak.

"I don't know why I didn't think about that. They call it juvenile diabetes. I guess it didn't dawn on me. Of course, there would be adults that have it. How old were you when you were diagnosed?"

"I was twenty-seven. They misdiagnosed me at first with type 2. The doctors sometimes think the same way you did—type 1 is only for juveniles, when that simply isn't true."

I'm amazed at the level of quiet around the table. I'm not sure it's ever been this noiseless in here. Normally, everyone has something to say—an opinion on everything. Especially Jesse and Jayden—neither one of them know how to stay still for more than a moment.

"You've lived with it for a long time." *Again* with the insulting comments. I should really take a hint from the rest of them and just be silent.

"Yes ma'am, and I'm not dead yet," he responds, chuckling quietly.

"Let me get some plates for this gorgeous pie," Mom says, standing to head to the kitchen. "Brice, I don't see why you can't have a small piece."

I chance letting my eyes meet Bernard's and relax as I do. He doesn't look angry at all. If anything, he looks a little amused, his eyes full of understanding. "Don't beat yourself up for not knowing everything there is to know about this disease. Hell, I've had it for over forty years, and I'm still learning." He winks, rubbing his hands together as Mom sets a piece of pie in front of him.

8

READY OR NOT...

"Where are you going?" Jayden asks.

I look at her chin. How can she hang her head upside down like that without getting a headache from it? Her blonde hair hangs straight to the floor, its corn-silk straightness looking the same upside down as it does right-side up. Perfectly in place, just standing on end.

"It's in the basement of the library," I tell her for the third time. Maybe the words don't stick because her brain's upside down. "Wanna help me pick something to wear?"

She rolls over and hops up so fast, you would have thought I just told her Brad Pitt walked through the door. He's this super hunky new actor that she's been hung up on ever since we saw the movie *Legends of the Fall*. I totally get it.

"Will you actually wear what I choose?" she asks, her eyes conveying her skepticism. She's right to not trust me. I've never gone along with one of her choices before.

I look her over carefully before I answer. "That depends... Will I be dressing for a meeting in the basement of the library, or am I going to look like I'm getting ready for the prom?"

She bites her lip as she studies me. "Okay, okay. I'll try to tone it down, but there's never a reason to be drab. You could use a little color in your life. This is a new experience; these people don't know boring you. This could be an opportunity for you to be exciting." She wiggles her eyebrows at me, turns, and begins rifling through my closet. "And who knows? Maybe there'll be a cute boy there."

I feel dread building in the pit of my stomach as I walk backward toward the bed. The back of my legs hit, and I sink down on the mattress, watching her continue the search. At least she's not foraging through her closet—who knows what I would end up in, then. I study the outfit she's wearing today. "Are those bell-bottoms?"

"Yes! Don't you love them? They don't call them bell-bottoms though; they're flare-legged. Aren't they great?!" she squeals, propping her foot out, moving it back and forth, the loose fabric floating all around.

I shake my head. "Only you could get away with something like that, Jay." She makes everything look adorable. *Everything*—even the hideous silver bowling shoes she has on. When did they start making silver shoes? "New shoes?"

"Yes!" she squeals, jumping up and down. "They're great, right?"

"They're something else." I smile, hoping she doesn't see what I really think.

She smiles her bright, beautiful smile at me and turns back to the closet. I lie back on the bed, willing the dread to go away. I don't know why I'm so nervous about this. It's not like I don't know Bernard now. We've been keeping each other company on the days when there's no one here. He's actually a really cool guy, and I can see why the boys like him so much. I hate meeting new people, though, and I think I may actually have to talk to people there, too.

"So, whatcha think?" Jayden asks, holding a forest green

sweater and a pair of faded blue jeans up to herself, as if the outfit were for her.

"That's it? That's your choice? Seems a bit…understated," I say, getting up. I didn't even know I had a sweater like that in my closet, but I love the color; green's always been my favorite.

I run my hand over the sweater's soft texture. I get to the sleeve and notice a tag hanging at the cuff. I look up at her; she grins sheepishly. "Okay, so I may have picked this up for you at the mall yesterday. But, you have to admit the color is gorgeous, and it's going to make your eyes look amazing."

"I don't deserve you," I say and mean it.

She waves her hand, brushing off the comment. "Try it on, I can't wait to see it."

I pull the soft fabric on over the tank top I'm already wearing and step in front of the long mirror on the back of the door. It's gorgeous. I think I'll live in this sweater from now on. Turning, I throw my arms around Jayden as she squeals in delight.

"I knew you'd love it. I just wanted to make you happy, Bri. You've had a really crummy month. You deserve something to smile about." She pulls back from the hug to look me over. "I made you something, too." Reaching into her pocket, she pulls out a green beaded bracelet. Holding it out to me, I see she has a matching one on her wrist. "This way, we'll always be together. Now, will you let me do your hair?"

"Ugh, that's even worse than you picking out my clothes," I groan, rolling my eyes at her.

"You are such a child sometimes." She laughs, shoving me toward the stool in front of my vanity.

She runs her fingers through my tangles as I watch from the mirror, the look on her face comical.

"How do you even manage to work with this mess?" she

jokes. I cringe as I feel the cold water from the spray bottle shower my head. I close my eyes, fingering the beads on my wrist. Emotion swells within me as I toss her words around in my mind.

Gentle tugs carry me away as she twists and pulls, working her magic. All movement stops and I open my eyes. The front of my hair has a small French braid, effectively holding it out of my face. It's perfect.

"Jay, you know I don't want to meet any boys, right?" Our eyes connect in the mirror. She lets out a disheartened sigh, her gaze falling down to the floor.

She looks back up, her smile firmly back in place, but different somehow. "I know, Bri, but sometimes fate has a different idea. Who knows, maybe this is one of those times." She shrugs, a hopeful gleam in her eye. She thinks my crush on Harrison is hopeless and I'm wasting my heart on an impossibility.

"Thanks. For the sweater, the bracelet, and for just being you. You're the best."

I can't hold back my laughter when my eyes meet hers in the mirror.

She gives a little wink as she fluffs my curls again. "I am, aren't I?" A devious smile lights her face, and I know that I'm in trouble. "You know what you need?" she asks, sitting down on the edge of my bed and slipping her feet out of her shoes. "These will look fabulous with your outfit. Just a touch of funk."

9

WEDNESDAY EVENING MEETINGS

"Are you sure you're okay to drive?" I ask Bernard as he slides in behind the driver's seat. The look he gives me says I'm out of line. "I'm sorry, I'm just nervous."

"What are you nervous about? My driving?" he asks, shaking his head. "Girl, I've been driving at least twice as long as you've been alive. Actually, I take that back, probably more than three times as long."

"It's not that, it's this whole thing. Meeting new people is hard for me. My favorite people are all book characters."

"I understand that, but the problem with *those* people is they can only say what they're destined to say. I personally like a live conversation sometimes. I like it when people surprise me, and if I don't ever talk to anyone, how are they going to surprise me?"

I study him as he drives. He's wearing the same little hat he was the first time I saw him—the day my life changed forever. Will I always think of it like that, *before and after?* My life has a definitive line down the middle now.

"It gets easier."

I swear this man is a mind reader. He's always doing that—reading my thoughts, answering my unspoken questions.

"What does?" I question, even though I know what he's talking about. I need to hear him say it. I spin the beads at my wrist, marveling at the different textures beneath my fingertips.

"This...all of it. Pretty soon, the shots and finger pokes won't be any more troubling than tying your shoes. Just another part of the day. At least I hope that's the case for you." He glances over, making sure he has my attention. "The way I see it, when you get this disease, you have two choices, and it's up to you which one you choose. You have the right to choose either, but there's only one right choice. You can fight each and every day. Fight to live a happy, healthy life. Or you can ignore it—rebel against it—and die a slow, agonizing death. It's not much of a choice, really, but there are some who will choose the wrong path."

I look away from his piercing gaze, wiping sweaty palms on my jeans.

"Not you though. I can see it already. You're stronger than that."

I'm quiet as the severity of his words sink in. I think about all the horrible complications the doctors have been stressing to me since day one. Kidney failure, blindness, amputations, the list goes on and on... I'm not even sure what all of it is. The one thing I knew right from the start was, I didn't want any of it to happen to me. *Who would?*

I look down at my sore, bruised fingertips, slowly running the pad of my thumb over them. I can understand wanting to ignore it, too, though. It may not be my choice, but I understand it.

"That gets better too," he says, holding his hand out so I can examine his fingers.

Unlike mine, I see no bruises at all. Instead, the very end of his first three fingers have a hard callus on each side. Looking closely, I see countless little dots—poke marks.

"The calluses make it nearly painless. I really don't even feel it anymore—" he pauses, putting his hand back on the wheel. "I do suggest that you stick with just a few fingers... makes it a little more bearable while they're still tender."

The pain in my fingers is a constant reminder of everything. Every time I try to pick something up—hold a pencil, fork, or hairbrush. It's not excruciating, but it's painful, and it's been one of the hardest things for me to get used to.

"Thanks for the tip." I smile, glad for the shared knowledge.

"I hated the finger pricks the most, too," he says softly, seemingly lost in the past. "But don't you ever forget what those tiny drops add up to." His words become stronger, challenging me to listen, begging to be understood. "Those tiny drops of blood are a small sacrifice for the years that you'll get because of them. You can and *will* have a full, healthy life if you do what it takes."

"I will," I whisper, suffocating on my emotions.

I turn my attention back to the window, surprised to see that we're already pulling up to the building. The front of it is lined with massive windows—allowing the readers inside to have natural light by which to travel through their stories. I take a deep breath, willing myself to relax. This will be all right...good, even.

I've always felt a calm when walking into a library that I've never felt anywhere else. This one is no exception. I love the sacred silence, the smell of the old books, and the faint giggles of children—breaking the quiet with their unbridled joy. And the inevitable *shh* that always follows their laughter. I remember being one of those children, and I'm thankful my mother loves reading as much as I do.

"Shall we?" Bernard says, breaking the magical hold the

library has over me. He extends his arm out for me, and we walk toward the door that leads to the basement. "You're in for a treat. J.C. is quite a guy. You'll make a lot of friends here," he assures me. I know he's smiling, even though I can't see his face—I hear it in his voice.

I've never been in the basement before. I imagined a dark, dank space, so what I find surprises me. We walk through a large, arched doorway, and I'm met with a warmth that begs you to come closer, to be wrapped up in it. The source of the heat is a large fireplace. The flames dancing within are small and the coals are burning brightly. The room is so cozy, I want to find a comfy chair and curl up with a book. That would be heavenly.

"It's quite magnificent, isn't it?" Bernard asks, breaking me from my thoughts.

"It is. Can anyone come down here? It looks like the perfect place to read."

Bernard smiles. "It's open to the public, except when they have meetings." Stepping closer to the fireplace, he holds his hands out to the flames. "Trouble is, they have meetings almost daily. There's a schedule upstairs."

"Hey, hey, there he is." A man walks into the room, straight toward us. Bernard lets out a soft chuckle. He's wearing a baseball cap backwards. It gives him a youthful appearance that makes placing his age impossible. He has a few days' worth of scruff on his face, but it doesn't hide the deep dimples in his cheeks when he smiles at us. I like him already. He puts his hand out to Bernard, and when they shake, he pulls him in for an embrace.

"And who do we have here?" he questions, doing his own survey of me.

"Brice. I'm Brice," I say, stepping forward with my hand out. I'm surprised when he pulls me in for a hug like he did with Bernard, moments before.

"J.C. It's a pleasure to meet you, Brice. How do you know this old man?"

"He's my neighbor—and friend."

"So, are you here to support him? Or are you a member of the exclusive club?"

"Excuse me?" I ask, confused.

"Are you a type 1?" He laughs. "I've always felt like it's a secret club… Other people couldn't join, even if they wanted to."

"Oh." I let out a laugh of my own. "Then, yes, I'm a member of the club."

Because we arrived first, Bernard and I have the pleasure of sitting by the fire. I run my hand over the rough texture of the chair. How can something so abrasive be so comfortable to sit in? We helped J.C. arrange several chairs from the room in a semicircle around the fireplace. The only thing to do now is wait for everyone to show up. I wish I knew how many people are coming. Taking a deep breath, I count the beads circling my wrist. Twenty-two—my lucky number. Did she do that on purpose?

I glance at Bernard, surprised to find his eyes closed.

"Are you okay?" I whisper, worrying about his health. In the week that we've been hanging out, this is the first time I've even thought about his health. The realization leaves a bitter taste in my mouth. This man has done nothing but show concern and friendship for me. I hadn't even thought to ask him how his health was.

Just as I stand to go to him, he opens an eye and smiles at me. "Don't mind me. Sometimes being an old man means that random cat naps happen, especially when I'm in a place that feels as comforting as this."

I sink back into my chair, relieved. "How's your health?" I ask, before I let the moment slip away from me.

He sits up from his relaxed position and leans side to side, stretching his back. "I've nothing to complain about. Complaints never make anything better; they just compound it, give it strength, make it bigger." He smiles. "Concentrate on the good. It makes life better."

"So, you're not going to answer me, then?"

"I'm alive, that's answer enough." He laughs, causing me to shake my head.

Glancing over at the doorway, I see the first person has arrived.

"Lori, what a pleasure!" Bernard jumps up from the chair with youthful joy, taking her hand in both of his, grasping it tightly.

She's probably Jesse's age, or a bit younger. The dark rings under her eyes speak of sleepless nights. *What's her story?*

"We missed you last week," she tells him, pulling her hand back. "Everything all right?" Her eyes do a quick search of the room and settle on me. A slow smile spreads across her face, causing her eyes to light up.

"Just busy. Even in retirement, life is always moving. Sometimes the current doesn't go the way you want it to, but this time I was lucky. I got a new friend," he tells her, turning his attention to me.

I've been sitting on the edge of my seat, not sure if I should stand or not. But, now that he's looking at me, I spring to my feet, self-conscious.

"Lori, this is Brice," he says, looking back and forth between the two of us. "Brice." He nods toward me. "Lori." Back toward her. "Brice, here, is my new neighbor. And friend."

"It's nice to meet you." I smile, unsure of myself. This is what I hate about being social—I always feel like I need to fill space but never know what to say. I glance down at my black Docs, the sight of them reminding me of Jay, and I smile again. I can't let her win all the time...have to draw a line somewhere.

"It's great to see a new face. I'm not the newbie anymore." She takes a moment to scrutinize my face, her expression soft. She leans toward me and asks quietly, "Are you diabetic?"

"She was diagnosed last month," Bernard says, answering for me. "She's been a warrior about it."

I don't really know what to think when people say stuff like this. I hardly feel like a warrior or brave. That's another thing I hear all the time now, *'You're so brave. I couldn't do it.'* I think that one bugs me the most. Of course, they could—if they had to.

"Glad to hear it," Lori says. Turning her attention to J.C., she continues, "Is Kristy coming? Did you hear how the surgery went?"

"I haven't heard anything." He leans back in his chair, lacing his fingers behind his head. "I always figure no news is good news in a situation like this," he finishes, his expression calm, words easy.

"I hope so." Lori sinks into the chair beside him and lets her purse drop to the ground.

"How many people normally come?" I ask, sitting back down.

"It depends—" she pauses, as if to mentally count the people she's met in this room, "—but the most we've ever had since I started was eight. It's a pretty small group. Most of the time, there are four or five of us."

"Sorry I'm late guys," a woman says, coming into the room.

She's beautiful. You can tell she lives a happy life; it shows in her dark, almond eyes. She quickly makes her way to the chair beside Lori and takes a seat.

Lori leans over and asks, "How'd it go?"

"It went okay. Dad's still in ICU, but everything looks good, and Mom is doing great. She's so strong. Two days after major surgery, and she's already up moving around." She pauses her story when her eyes meet mine, and she tilts her head to the side before continuing. "We have someone new? I'm Kristy."

"Brice. It's nice to meet you."

I hope this is it. All of these introductions are making me uncomfortable. They all seem so easy and relaxed with one another. I'm an outsider. I hope I don't have to tell my life story.

As if the thought was plucked from the air, J.C. says, "Why don't you tell us about yourself, Brice? What brought you to the meeting tonight?"

I swallow past the lump in my throat, trying to decide what to say. "Well, Bernard brought me." *Wh,y exactly, did I agree to come?* "I guess I just wanted to meet other people who understand all the things I've been dealing with. I can't voice my feelings with anyone else," I finish, wiping my sweaty palms on my jeans. I wish I hadn't sat so close to the fire.

"Well said." He smiles again, and I notice for the first time that he has a syringe tucked behind his ear. The sight of it makes me laugh, and I place my hand over my mouth to muffle the noise.

They all look at me expectantly. I straighten in my chair. "Your syringe." I nod toward him. "It caught me off guard. Sorry."

He winks. "I like to catch people off guard, that's why it's there." He reaches up and pulls it down. "Plus, I always like to be prepared."

"I was about your age when I was diagnosed," he says, taking over. Thank goodness. I'd much rather hear their stories than have to tell my own.

"I used to do this just to mess with the kids at school, and truthfully, I enjoyed the attention. I don't do it anymore, but I thought it might help break the ice for you tonight." He glances down at the needle in his hand before he continues. "Growing up with diabetes is weird." His eyes meeting mine. "It changes the way you think, who you are. The strangest thought is knowing that you could die...like *now*. That definitely changes the way you think. The way you feel." His smile is light and easy, despite the weight of his words. "I think we all understand that here."

"For me, sometimes the hardest part is the overwhelming support and care," Kristy says, her face serious and full of emotion. "It's like all the extra care and support just makes me feel guilty. Because I know they feel it all so much too." She stares at her hands, folded in her lap. Her shoulders rise as she takes a deep breath, struggling with the emotions. "I guess I just love them so much, that I wish they didn't have to struggle with all of this, too. Sometimes it gets to me." When she glances back up, her eyes are bright pools of unshed tears.

"Yeah, I totally get that," I say, thinking about my own family and what I've put them through since the beginning of all of this...and it's only been a month. My blood sugar gets low so often now, and each time is so different, it feels unpredictable, like at any moment it could happen and turn a regular day into its own strange battle. They all react quickly, set to pounce on this disease and tell it who's boss. Sometimes, it's pretty easy for me to take care of on my own, but there are times when it really gets me. Those ones are the worst. The times when I'm simultaneously happy they're there to help me through, and guilty, because they have to be. So yeah, I totally get what she's saying."

I hold her gaze for a moment, struggling for words. "I hate feeling helpless." I pause... Is that even what I mean? "No, that's not right, it's not helpless. I'm not sure exactly how to describe it."

"There's no one here that hasn't felt what you're feeling at one time or another. Finding out that you'll have to deal with this for the rest of your life is a lot to take in," Lori says, her voice encouraging. "Just say whatever you're thinking. We'll all understand, and it's good to get it out."

"It's like I'm fragile now. My mom used to go on and on about how responsible I was, that she had nothing but trust for me. Now, it's like she doesn't trust me anymore." I stop and take a drink of the tea J.C. brought me. "That's not entirely true either, though. In my mind, I know *that's* not true; it's this disease she doesn't trust. But it's like this disease is me now, and I'm *it*—there is no dividing line…so it feels like she doesn't trust me." A strangled laugh escapes me echoing oddly through the room. "Just ask Bernard, he's been my main babysitter since we met last week." I reach up, swiping the stray tear from my cheek. I hope they didn't see it.

"Babysitter? Is that how you think of me?" Bernard shakes his head. "And here I thought we were friends." He reaches over, taking my hand.

The hour passes quickly, and when we leave the room, I'm a little lighter than I was before we came in. And tomorrow, Lori is going to come get me. She wants me to go to some radio competition bingo game with her. If she wins, she'll get a new Toyota Tercel. She seems like a nice girl; I enjoyed talking with her and since I don't have anything else to do, I thought it would be great to get to know her better.

10

BINGO!

"Well," I say into the phone as I glance at Harrison. He tilts his head to the side, eyeing me with curiosity. "Maybe we can still go. Hold on just a sec."

I put the phone down on the counter and turn to him. "Lori's car won't start. Would you maybe want to take us?"

"Sure, I don't have anything going on today. Sounds like fun." He smiles, causing dimples to grace his cheeks.

"Thank you!" I squeal, throwing my arms around him.

He pats me awkwardly on the back. I come to my senses and let him go.

"Sorry, I just really wanted to hang out with her. I'm intrigued. I mean, sure, I have Bernard to talk to about the diabetes stuff, but I would like to get another teenage girl's perspective on everything."

"You may want to pick the phone back up then, before she thinks you hung up on her." He laughs, shaking his head.

"Oh, right." I grab the phone from the counter. "Lori, my friend said he can take us. Will that work?" I take the notebook from beside the phone, jotting down the directions as she gives them to me. "Sounds good. See you soon."

"Thank you, thank you! A million thank-yous," I say, dancing out of the kitchen to put my boots on. "Are you sure you don't have any plans?" I holler from the front room.

Every time he has a day off lately, he spends it with me. The teenage girl in me hopes it's because he's secretly in love with me. But, the objective thinker knows it's because he's worried about me spending time alone. Maybe it's a little of both.

"This is it." I point to the building marked with a big letter D on it.

Harrison pulls into a free space in front of the building. I release my seat belt and open the door, putting my feet out just as Lori appears at the bottom of the stairs. The dark circles under her eyes look more pronounced than they did yesterday. I wave my hand and she smiles, giving a quick wave back.

I slide to the center of the truck, making room for her to climb in, a jolt rolling through me when the exposed skin on my wrist grazes Harrison's hand. Does he feel it too—the electricity that dances between us every time our skin meets?

"Thank you both for coming to get me," Lori says as she closes the door. "I know I don't have very good odds of winning, but there are only ten players, so it's worth a shot. Plus, now that my car isn't working, I need it more than ever."

"How'd you get a seat to play?" Harrison asks, pulling out onto the main road.

"I'd been trying to get a seat for weeks. Calling every time I heard the tune on the radio. I finally managed to get through as the tenth caller the last time."

"Lucky break," he replies. Glancing her way, he smiles, his dimple coming out to play.

My stomach rolls and I bite my lip. Was this a bad idea?

We pull into the Valley Mall parking lot, and I see where they have the stage set up at the far end, next to the outdoor restrooms and concession stands. Red, white, and blue balloons are flying from each corner of the stage. Chairs are set up in front of it for the audience.

When we get out of the truck, Lori sways a bit and grabs the door for support.

"Is your sugar okay?" I ask, unsure if I should or not. I don't know if it's proper diabetic etiquette. I hope I didn't offend her.

"It's fine. I've just had a kidney infection. I think I'm over it now, though."

"That sounds serious. Are you sure you're all right to do this?" Harrison asks, coming around to our side of the truck.

Lori's silent for a moment. "I'm sorry, what were we talking about?" she asks.

"Your health," I supply, growing more concerned. "Are you sure you're okay?"

"Of course, I'll be fine." She waves off my worry, and the smile that lights up her face makes me feel like maybe I was overreacting.

"I'm surprised that they're holding this outside in the middle of winter," Harrison remarks.

"I know. I'm cold already." I rub my hands together, blowing into my palms.

"Why don't you guys get some seats? It looks like they have big heaters set up over there, and I'll see you as soon as it's finished," Lori tells us, turning to head to the stage.

"We'll be rooting for you," I call to her as she fades into the growing crowd.

"Do you think she's really all right?" Harrison asks as we take the two seats closest to a heater.

"I hope so." I put my hands out to feel the warmth from the red glow. "I noticed the dark circles under her eyes yesterday, but today they look even worse." I jump as the speaker that's positioned to the right of us lets out a loud squeal.

"Sorry about that, folks, I just wanted to take a moment to introduce myself and our ten players before the game begins. I'm Shawn Michael, and I'll be hosting this event. One of these lucky participants is going to drive out of here in this brand-new beauty—" he pauses, sweeping his arm out theatrically toward the shiny, red Toyota that's sitting directly beside the stage. "Contestants, when I point your way, do me a favor and call out your name."

"I'm Anna Finkelstein, and I'm so excited to be here!" a lady in a fuzzy pair of earmuffs and a bright pink coat says. Her cheeks are rosy, and her eyes are full of merriment, and I hope as I witness her joy that if Lori doesn't win, Anna does.

I close my eyes, tuning out the noise as Shawn Michael continues his playful banter with the contestants and crowd. I let myself feel the moment. I've been overcome with the need to do this a lot lately. The need to close my eyes and feel—*feel* the way the air moves around me with a spark of energy on its tail. The sensation of the warm sun on my back, despite the cold air that's biting my cheeks. Something about this disease has made me want to be grounded yet fully immersed in every moment. Each day is more precious as I learn to navigate as this new me.

Electricity sparks to life when Harrison reaches over. Taking my hand, he gives a quick squeeze before letting it go. My eyes fly open, shocked by the contact from him. What did he think—seeing me sitting this way, with my eyes closed, face turned to the sky?

I dare a glance in his direction, and he leans over, whispering in my ear, "You're beautiful."

My face flames as a horde of locusts are released inside of me, their movement causing such a stir of emotion, hope, and excitement, I can barely contain myself. I don't want to look at him…*can't* look at him. The only thing I can do is take his words, write them on a piece of paper in my mind, and slip them into the box that holds my favorite memories.

I snap out of my haze when a chair falls over on the stage. I look up and see Lori standing, panic in her eyes.

"Miss, if you leave now you'll be disqualified," Shawn Michael says as she hops down from the stage and runs toward the bathrooms.

I stand up and sit back down. I don't know what to do. "Do you think I should see if she needs anything?" I ask, a slight quiver lacing my words.

"Let's head over there." Harrison stands, and begins walking toward the bathrooms. I spring to my feet, closing the distance behind him. "If she doesn't come out in a few minutes, you should go in and check on her."

We stand against the cold stone of the bathroom that has immersed us in shadow, and I can feel my teeth beginning to chatter. I'm not sure if it's from the cold or the fear of the situation. We've been waiting an eternity. Or minutes, I'm not sure which. Lori pushes open the door, and I release a pent-up breath, relief flooding me. It's short lived as her eyes fill with dread again, and she retreats back into the bathroom.

"You go."

"I'm going," we say simultaneously.

My hands tremble as I place my palm on the door.

"I'm right out here if you need me," Harrison encourages.

I give a quick nod and step into the bathroom.

When my eyes adjust to the new light, I see all of the stall doors are open except the one at the very end. Violent retching fills the space, and I step tentatively toward it. "Lori, let me in. I want to try to help."

"Why are they doing this?" she questions through the door.

It throws me off. I'm not sure how to answer.

"What do you mean?"

"The experiments? Why are they doing this to me?" she cries, her voice full of anguish. "I just want the experiments to stop." Her hair pools out beneath the door as she lies on the floor.

My heart begins to race. The fear in her words consumes me. I push back through the bathroom door, my eyes connecting with Harrison's. "She needs help. Have someone call an ambulance." I don't wait for a response. Turning, I rush back inside.

I can see her cheek resting on the cool blue tile floor. "Lori," I whisper, getting down on my knees. If I can't get her to open the door, I'm going to have to try to squeeze under. "Lori!" I shout. My loud voice pierces the eerie silence, echoing back toward me. Chills erupt across my skin. I hope someone comes quickly. I don't know how to get a hold of her family.

A long sigh escapes me as she begins to stir on the other side of the door. "Lori, can you hear me?"

"You should go," she whispers, "before they get you."

"I-want-to...I do, but...I want to take you with me. I want to stop the experiments. But in order to do that...I need you to open the door." I hold my breath, eyes squeezed tight, and wish with all of my might for her to open the door.

A scream bubbles out of me when the door bursts open, and I'm suddenly sitting on the floor amongst a crowd of legs and wheels. I scamper to get up, and feel relieved when my eyes lock on Harrison's. The concern I see there is surely mirrored in my own.

"Come on." He holds his hand out to me and I grab it like the lifeline it is. "Let's get out of the way."

We stand in silence outside the bathroom. My heart's racing, and I can't get the shaking to stop. I don't know what was happening to her. But I know that it was because of diabetes. I don't even realize I'm crying until I feel a drop land on my hand.

"Hey, shh…" Harrison wraps his arms around me, enveloping me in warmth. "It's all right, it's going to be okay," he whispers, as we watch the stretcher being pushed from the bathroom.

11

GIRL TALK

"He told me I was beautiful," I sigh, eyes closed as Jayden brushes my hair.

"Who?" Her hand pauses mid-stroke.

"Harrison."

"Harry told you you're beautiful?" she asks, the note of disbelief making me feel dejected.

I open my eyes and stare at her in the mirror. A million different things travel through her mind as we speak without words. Finally, the silence is broken as she begins to brush again.

"Well, he's right. You are beautiful—inside and out."

"He's going to take me up to the hospital to see Lori. She can finally have visitors." I change the subject—talking about myself makes me uneasy. It's been three days since Lori was taken to the hospital. I'm still not sure what happened. Bernard said she'd been in DKA and her kidneys had nearly shut down. Truth is, I don't really know what any of that means or why it happens.

"That's why I'm doing your hair." Jay pauses, taking the small section of hair that she's pulled together on the side of my head and twisting it tightly. She slides a bobby pin back inside, effectively hiding it in the twist. She quickly does this five more times, making little twist-rolls across the front of my hair. The back is wild, the curls free.

"I wondered. I was wracking my brain trying to remember if you'd ever asked me to do it before. I couldn't come up with one time when it was your idea—not mine."

"It's getting too long in the front." I wiggle my eyebrows, trying unsuccessfully to loosen my hair. It's so tight. "You're my best defense against curl chaos."

When my hair is down and in its natural state, the curls fall into my face. No matter how many times I brush them to the side or tuck them behind my ear, they spring free and half blind me. The best I can do is a slide barrette on the side, but I feel like it makes me look like a little girl. The last thing I want is Harrison seeing me as a little girl. I put up with the torture for the sake of beauty.

"What time is he coming?" she asks, glancing in the direction of her house. Even though there isn't a window to look out, I know she's wondering if there's anyone home. Her mom's a drunk and gone more than she's there. When she does come home, most of the time she's not alone. I'm not sure what's worse. We rarely talk about it. Jayden's funny that way—as sugar sweet as she appears on the outside, you'd never imagine her life is in a constant state of disarray.

"Soon."

I see the slight slump of her shoulders and scramble to fix it.

"Do you want to come? Harrison said he wasn't going into Lori's room with me—something about giving her privacy. I'm sure he'd like the company while he waits."

Her blue eyes lighten in the mirror as she glances up into it. "Are you sure you don't mind? I mean, I do have a few presents I need to wrap, so I don't have to come if you'd rather I didn't," she says softly, waiting with bated breath.

"Of course, I don't mind. Just gives me an excuse to sit beside Harrison in his truck." I giggle, knowing all talk of Harrison secretly drives her crazy. She would never tell me it does, but I'm perceptive—I see it in her body language every time we talk about him. I think she thinks I'm going to end up hurt, no matter what the outcome is, and maybe she's right, but isn't that what love is all about?

"Should you check your sugar before we go?"

I let out a long sigh. I have moments when I don't have to think about diabetes, but they never last long and are grabbed away without warning—*all the time.*

"Yeah." I get up from the stool and make my way toward the kitchen, pausing when I hear voices in the living room.

Jayden's hand rests on my shoulder as she comes up behind me. "What are we doing?" she whispers.

Finger to my lips, I turn so she can see. I want to be able to hear this—the tone in their voices unlike any I've ever heard from them before. Something must be wrong.

I creep toward the end of the hall, hoping the shadows are enough to keep me hidden. Jayden's breath is warm on my cheek as she squishes close to listen.

Harrison's back is toward us, his body blocking most of Jesse. Jesse's hands are balled in tight fists at his side, and the part of his face I *can* see looks red, angry.

"You can say what you want, Ford, but I can tell you have a thing for my sister." Jesse steps closer, causing Harrison to take a quick step back. "She's got enough shit going on right now; she doesn't need you messing with her."

Harrison lets out a harsh laugh, and I hold my breath, my heart pounding so loudly in my ears, I'm afraid I won't be able to hear his response.

"Fuck you."

I step back further into the hallway, those words the last thing I expected to hear.

"I've known her nearly half my life; what I'm doing is being her friend. She needs someone to be here for her. To be strong for her. Seems to me, you and your mom are both hiding from her, taking on extra shifts... She practically lives alone."

The ringing in my ears doesn't hide the truth in his words. They're hiding, avoiding me, all of this. I know they need to work, but they need to be here too. Jayden's arm comes around my shoulder, and she squeezes me tightly.

"When you're not at school, you're with Tori or working. When was the last time you had a conversation with her that lasted more than five minutes?" Harrison's tone softens, his words imploring. "It doesn't matter how I feel about her. I know she's just a kid."

I stand statue-still, his words so faint I'm not sure I heard them right. When he turns and his eyes lock on mine, heat floods my face. Jayden squeezes my hand, stilling. She had been jumping up and down beside me. My heart's racing and her jarring stop is suddenly too much—it's all *too much*.

"Are you okay?" she whispers.

"I need to check my sugar," I say, averting my eyes from everyone, everything, as I rush through the living room into the kitchen.

I pull the drawer open, quickly, my hands shaking. I snap open the case on the monitor, the movements starting to feel second nature after the last month. I'm sure in another few, I'll be able to do it with my eyes closed. I push the button, turning it on, pop open the strips, and pull one out, waiting for the little arrow to tell me to insert the strip. The tremor in my hands is so intense, I can't get the strip into the little slot at the bottom of the machine. I laugh at the irony of this happening seconds after my previous thought. Jayden grabs the strip from my hand, putting it in for me.

"Just breathe for a minute. I've got this for you," she says, wiggling her eyebrows as she grabs the poker. Pulling back the end to cock the needle, she holds out her hand for mine. "I've been watching." She beckons for my hand as I hold back. "Come on."

I reluctantly give it to her. I would have rather done it myself. She pushes the end of the poker up against my finger, pressing the button on its side to release the needle. I flinch as it pierces my skin, never sure if it's the pain that causes me to jump, or the sound.

I pull my hand from hers and place a drop of blood onto the tiny dot at the center of the strip. The boys come into the room behind me. The tension they bring with them makes the air feel heavy and dark.

The screen flashes, 45.

"Whoa, that's low," Jayden says. "Go, sit, I'll get you something."

The concern I see in her eyes is too much for me. A wall of emotion bubbles up from inside, and I'm helpless to stop it as the tears spill over. I'm having a hard time connecting thoughts. I know we were going somewhere, but I can't remember where.

"We're going to be late," I say, my eyes connecting with Harrison's as he crouches in front of me. He's not scared. He's always so calm.

"There's plenty of time. First, we need to take care of you." He rubs his thumb across my cheek, wiping away a tear. He takes the glass of orange juice Jayden is holding and hands it to me. I put it to my lips and take big gulps, finishing the glass quickly. I imagine the orange juice rushing in to save the day, and I let out a laugh. Harrison doesn't ask why, just smiles, squeezing the top of my arm before he stands back up.

"Where were we going? I can't remember." My cheeks flush.

Jayden sets a plate of crackers with peanut butter smeared on top beside me. She has the biggest fake grin, her bright blue eyes brimming with tears. "We're going up to the hospital to see your friend, but not until you have a snack." Her voice shakes.

Jesse steps from his spot beside the wall. "Maybe you should just stay home."

The idea makes me angry. I won't change my plans because of this, even if I couldn't remember what they were moments before. "Why? Why should I just *stay home*? Because this just happened? News flash, Jesse, this has been happening *every single day* for the past few weeks." I pull a deep breath, trying to reign in my anger. It's not his fault. "I'm not going to stop living my life because diabetes is happening to me. I won't. I'll feel fine as soon as I finish my snack," I finish, picking up a cracker. That last part's a lie. I won't feel fine—I'll feel worn out, tired—but I'll push on anyway. I won't stop living my life. I refuse to.

"What do you mean it's been happening every day for weeks? Jesus, Brice, did you tell Mom?" Jesse says.

The anger in his voice surprises me, makes me drop my cracker. It lands peanut butter side down on my pants. Of course.

"Lay off, Jesse," Harrison growls, the cuffs of his flannel not quite hiding his clenched fists.

"Fuck you, Ford. I don't know why you think my little sister's life is any of your business, but you're wrong," Jesse answers, his tone colder than I've ever heard before. It's hard to believe he's talking to his best friend. I hate this more than anything. I don't want them fighting, *especially* over me.

"Relax, Jess, of course I told Mom. I have an appointment next week. It's the soonest they could get me in because of

Christmas. Which is in two days if you've forgotten, so I suggest you two kiss and make up." I giggle, trying to make light of the situation. He meets my gaze, shaking his head.

I finish my crackers in silence. The room is still, devoid of sound except the crackers crunching as I place them, one by one, into my mouth. By the time I finish the plate, my thoughts are clearing, thank goodness. I don't like losing control of my mind. That's the scariest thing of all.

"I'm sorry, Little Bit." He lets out a sigh, anxiously popping his knuckles. "I'm just worried about you—constantly. It's driving me crazy, but I shouldn't take it out on you." Jesse pulls me up from my chair, hugging me tightly.

I want to accept his apology, but not without a reminder first. "Don't you think you're apologizing to the wrong person?" I pull back so I can gauge his response. "Don't get me wrong, you were an ass to me, too, but Harrison is the one you should be apologizing to."

He takes my face in his hands, looking at me for a long moment. "I love you, sis." He leans down, placing a kiss on my forehead. Then he turns, leaving the room without another word.

12

DKA MADNESS

Part of me wants to fill the silence, but mostly I'm glad no one's speaking. Enough has been said today already. Maybe what we need is total silence for the rest of the day. I don't know how to do that, though. My thoughts could never be quiet. Sometimes they're so loud, I forget I'm the only one who can hear them. I'm the worst at giving half-sentences and expecting the person I'm speaking with to know the other half of the conversation.

As we pull into the hospital parking lot, a sigh escapes me. That was the longest ten minutes ever.

"Are you all right?"

I jump, his voice shattering my thoughts. He drops his hand from the steering wheel and gives my knee a little squeeze.

"Don't worry about Jesse. He'll get over it."

"I hope so."

"Me, too," Jayden says, her voice sounding far away.

I'm sure she's been swimming in thoughts of her own during the drive. I know without a doubt I'm going to hear all about it as soon as we're alone.

"Do you know what room she's in?" Harrison puts the truck in park, pulling the key from the ignition.

I'm not sure about this. What if she doesn't want company?

"316. Bernard said they moved her from the critical care unit this morning."

I wish Bernard had come with us. Going into her room by myself is scary. I'm hardly more than a stranger to her. I'm not sure why it felt like such a good idea before, but now I want nothing more than to turn around and run back to the truck. I find the beads on my wrist. Spinning them, I take a deep breath. *Calm down.*

"That's good. She must be doing better." Jayden smiles. Looping her arm through mine, we head toward the entrance. I'm glad she's here, propelling me forward.

"Same floor you were on," Harrison remarks as he steps inside. "That's good. There was a nice waiting area up there."

"Are you sure you don't want to come in with me?" I ask, my fingers crossed inside my coat sleeve.

"She probably doesn't even remember me, Rice. I'm not going in there."

Relax, I tell myself, stepping onto the elevator. It's weird being back at the hospital again. I hadn't been here in years, and now I've been twice in just as many months. I hope this isn't a trend. Hospitals make me itch—there's too much feeling floating in the air. I watch Harrison as the elevator begins to ascend. His hair could use a cut, the dark locks curling at the edges. His eyes meet mine. I smile, but it feels like plastic on my face—fake.

"Lori," I say, awkwardly, my face to the crack in the door. I'm not sure if I should go in or not. Maybe she's not even in there; maybe they've sent her home.

"Yes?"

"It's Brice. I wanted to come see how you're doing." I look at the floor, holding my breath. I don't know why I'm so nervous.

"Come in."

That was easy. I push open the door and see Lori lying in the bed closest to it. The second bed is unoccupied. She looks so much younger than when I first met her—the dark circles are gone. She looks refreshed. "Wow, you look great."

She laughs. "I guess almost dying will do that for you." Her tone is laced with irony.

"Is it all right that I came? I wasn't sure."

"I'm glad you did. I wanted to explain what was happening. I'm sure it must have been really scary for you." She's all seriousness now, the humor in her voice from moments before gone.

There's a folding chair beside the sink. I grab it, setting it out beside the bed. "I was really worried, but I'm glad you're okay now. You are okay, right?"

"I'm getting better. My kidneys were shutting down, but my numbers are improving, looking better every day."

"What happened?"

Lori looks at her lap, and for a moment I think she isn't going to answer. After a year and a minute have gone by, her eyes return to mine. "It's a long story. Are you sure you have the time?"

"I'd like to know, if you want to tell me." I hold my breath as I wait for her reply, silently pleading with her to tell me. The whole experience really freaked me out. I need to understand it. *Please tell me.*

"I'm new here. Did you know that?" she asks but doesn't

wait for a response. "This is the first time I've ever been out on my own. About a month ago, I accidentally knocked my bottle of R insulin off my desk—it shattered. I didn't know what to do, or how to get more, and I didn't want to worry my mom with it, so I just took my long acting." She pauses, her eyes on some image from the distant past. "I had run out of strips, too, but I felt totally fine. I had been exercising so much, I thought I was maintaining fine without it. I didn't think there was anything wrong." She looks up at me, her eyes begging me to understand, and I do. I've only been diabetic for a couple of months, but I can already tell there is a fierce need to feel independent about dealing with it.

"What did it do to you? Was your sugar too high? Is that what caused you to hallucinate?" What's wrong with me? Why do I keep asking so many rude questions? I glance back at Lori and return her soft smile. *I'm sorry,* I mouth, and she laughs, releasing me from my awkwardness.

"I was in DKA, diabetic ketoacidosis. When your body can't process the glucose, it causes all sorts of problems with everything. It has a domino effect; one thing gets out of whack, causing a multitude of other things to follow." She pauses, letting me process what she's saying. Her next question sort of throws me. I'm not sure how it ties in. "Have you seen the movie *Outbreak*?"

"Jesse took me to see it this summer. He's my brother."

"I saw it this summer, too, with my boyfriend. I think that's why I was hallucinating about experiments. I'm sorry if I freaked you out, and if I haven't said it already, thank you. You saved me, Brice." She reaches over and grabs my hand for a moment. "Do me another favor—promise you'll never go without. I've learned a lot in the last few days, but that was the most important lesson of all. Even if you think you're fine, going without insulin is a sure way to wind up in trouble."

"Seems like the more I know, the more questions I have."

"Right? Too bad they don't give out a handbook with this disease: *One Hundred Things Every Diabetic Should Know.*" Lori smiles, and I realize how good it feels to sit with someone who understands completely.

13

DOCTOR KNOWS BEST

"Brice? Come on, we have to leave now or we'll be late!"

Mom's been yelling at me for several minutes, but it isn't helping me find my boot. I'm never late, mainly because I just don't care that much about how I look. I've searched everywhere. I'm starting to think there's some sort of boot conspiracy going on here.

"Mom! Did you take my boot?" I huff, stomping into the living room, one foot safely enclosed in my lucky boot—my favorite boots—the other's bare, exposed to all the dangers of the world, but it only takes one to make this bad day worse.

"Ouch." I hop up and down, squeezing my poor toes. I mis-stepped, trying to avoid the boxes lying all over the living room—waiting for Christmas decorations to be tucked back in them.

Mom laughs as I melt in a heap on the floor.

"Don't laugh at me! It hurts!" I fold into a crisscross position and cradle my foot in my hand. Ever so slowly, I begin to wiggle my toes. Pulling my sock off, I cringe at the sight of my blue toe. "It's blue! I think I broke it. Can we just stay home?

Can you call in sick to the doctor?" Giggles erupt from me, despite my pain.

"Oh, honey…" she pauses, still trying to contain her laughter as she sits on the floor in front of me. "Here," she beckons, "let me see it."

I groan as I set my foot in her lap. Throwing myself backwards, my head smacks the edge of the coffee table. "Ahhh…I hate this day!" I scream, rubbing the spot on the back of my head.

Mom's hands still, and all traces of the humor she sat down with are gone. "Baby, you've got to stop beating yourself up. We'll get this all figured out. You'll see."

All I can do is nod. It doesn't seem like anything will ever be figured out again. Nothing is ever stable. I try to follow the diet—I do the medicine when I'm supposed to, I drink lots of water, I exercise. Okay…maybe the exercise thing is a stretch. I walk—if that qualifies. I'm trying. I do all of these things, but the numbers are always wrong. I can't imagine what it'd be like to have one day where it wasn't bouncing all over the place. It makes me crazy, sad, tired, angry—most of all, I feel defeated and I *hate* it. "Are we going to be late?"

She glances at her watch, "Nope, not if we ditch the boot and just grab your slippers."

You'd think chairs in a waiting area would be comfortable. Especially if you're going to be waiting for a long period of time. But no. I roll from one butt bone to the other, giving each a reprieve from the pressure for a few moments. I can't take it any longer—I stand, twisting from side to side, my muscles needing to move. I drop at the waist and shake my body out. Two hours is too long to be sitting in a chair—waiting.

"We'll get lunch as soon as we get out of here," Mom

whispers. Glancing at her watch, her eyebrows furrowing, she lets out a deep sigh and drops her hands back to her lap. Her chuckle surprises me. The woman closest to us glances over the cover of her magazine, her eyebrow reaching higher, until I imagine it running into her hairline. Wow, I guess laughter is frowned upon here.

She came in right after us, and I keep wondering who will get to go first. I lean closer to my mom, keeping my eye on eyebrow lady the whole time. "What's so funny?" I whisper.

"The fact that I was in such a rush to get here." She stretches her arms up above her head. This must be torturous for her. She doesn't sit still—ever. Mom could be defined as life in motion.

"I was talking with your brother this morning…"

I groan as her words hit me. Eyebrow woman sets her magazine in her lap. She adjusts her position, getting comfortable for the show.

"I know how much you care for Harry—we all do. But what I need you to understand is at this stage of your life, he's a man and you're still a child. For the sake of both of your futures, I need you to promise me you won't pursue these feelings you're having." She reaches over, giving my hand a little squeeze.

Of course she would bring this up here. I shrug her off, positioning myself away from her. The door opens and a woman in bright red scrubs with little pink hearts all over them walks out, holding a chart. I wish with all my might that my name is printed at the top.

"Marsha," she says, smiling kindly at eyebrow woman, who looks at me triumphantly. Today, victory is hers. I have to fight to keep my tongue in my mouth as she gets up to leave.

Mom reaches into her purse, pulling out a little baggy with peanut butter cracker sandwiches inside, and I feel as if I've reverted somehow. I remember years ago, she used to carry little baggies of Cheerios to keep me happy when we were out and about. Now we're back to packing snacks.

"I think you should have a few of these."

I take the baggie from her and pull out a cracker. Someone clears their throat loudly as I stuff it in my mouth. I glance up to see the woman behind the front desk giving me a hard stare. Once my attention is hers, she nods to the sign hanging to the right of her desk. I pause midchew, barely making out the words from here—*No food or beverages in the waiting area.* Of course. I stop chewing, my mouth still full. "Sorry." Bits of cracker go flying with my spoken apology and I'm mortified. I throw my hand over my mouth. Slumping down in the chair, I quickly chew and swallow. This is ridiculous. I just want out of this place.

As I'm planning my escape, the red-scrubbed woman makes an appearance again. When my name leaves her mouth, I jump up, glancing back at Mom. She quickly follows.

"Are you with him?" She smiles at me expectantly.

What?

"Excuse me?"

"Are you here with Brice?" she asks, looking around me. Oh, I should be used to this by now.

"I *am* Brice," I tell her, fighting the urge to roll my eyes. I smile instead. *People.*

"Just eat a couple." My mom tries to push the crackers into my hand for what has to be the tenth time since we came back to the exam room. That sounds so sterile, but it's what's written on the tiny sign mounted beside the door—*Exam Room 13.* I knew it was a bad sign from the start. If you have more than thirteen exam rooms, patients are tucked away all over the place. I'm certain our lunch will be more like a dinner, so I reluctantly snatch the bag of crackers from her hand and pull one out.

After the second one, my mood improves a bit. There's a quick tap at the door and the feeling diminishes—gets pushed out by unease—as the doctor walks in. I pass the bag of crackers back to my mom, hoping that he doesn't see. My hopes are unwarranted, however, because he's failed to look up from the chart.

"Brice," he says, his hands still on the papers in front of him.

"Yes," I reply, unsure if I'm supposed to respond or not.

"I'm Dr. Edwards. I'll be reviewing your case today." His eyes are still cast down.

"Did you bring your blood sugar diary?" he asks, finally taking the time to look at me.

I have to stop myself from saying *hi* because we've already done introductions. You don't truly meet someone until you look them in the eye. His are icy blue. I bet women think he's attractive. I glance at my mom to see if she's noticed him yet. *She noticed.* She's running her fingers through her hair, and when she sees me watching her, she swats at my elbow.

I pull open my bag with my supplies and take out the tiny booklet. The stack of pages—held together by two staples in the middle—resembles a check register. My hand shakes as I pass it to him. I'm generally pretty good at tests…sort of goes with the territory of being someone who likes to learn. I imagine this is what it feels like to hand over a test you know you've failed. The numbers recorded in the book fluctuate like mad—despite all of my efforts to control it. I'll get it figured out—have a day where things are good. Then diabetes up and changes the game. I can't seem to win.

I watch his back straighten as he reviews the log. His expression turns to stone as he mutters, "If you keep on like this, you'll be dead before you're twenty-five."

Mom springs from her chair, knocking it to the ground as she moves. Her body is between his and mine, trying to shield me from his words. But it's too late. They've already pierced through my heart, ripping the very fabric of my soul. Tears well—silent drops rolling steadily down my cheeks as I sit, helpless to stop them.

"How dare you!" Her words are venom rolling from her tongue. She snatches my chart and diary from his hand, stuffing them inside the bag that's lying at my feet, and turns to grabs my hand.

"Where are you going? You can't take that."

"It's coming with *us*. You'll never touch anything that has to do with my daughter again," she says, inches from his face. "Ignorant."

"Excuse me?"

"You heard exactly what I said, don't play dumb. As far as I'm concerned, if you don't know kindness, then you know *nothing* at all."

I've never felt more defeated in my life, and now I've the equivalent of a grand piano hanging above my head by a piece of fishing wire, ready to drop at any moment. I glance at my mom who is shaking out her arms beside me as we stand, waiting for the elevator.

"We'll find you a new doctor." She pauses for a moment, lips pursed as her eyes search my face frantically. "I had to leave before I punched that fucker." She turns back to the elevator, and I smile. She keeps calling me a warrior—but I know who the real hero is.

14

SOGGY SLIPPERS

I STAND, SHIVERING AS THE SNOW THAT HAS TURNED TO SLEET pelts me in the face. I'm waiting for my mom to open the door. No key fob for this one. It doesn't even have automatic locks. She has to reach over to my side and pull up the little silver nob. I can feel the water seeping into my slippers, and the cold is making my toe throb even more. I knew I hated this day—I should have never left the house.

She gets the lock open, and I slide in. "You must be freezing. Are you freezing?" she asks, grabbing my hands and shoving them toward the air vent…which is still blowing cold air.

I shrug her off and place my hands under my legs. I can't stop the shivering. I'm not sure if it's a direct result of the cold or the doctor's words. The warmth of my tears on my face tells me that it's likely both. *Why would he say that?* "Why would he say that?"

"Oh, honey." She looks at me—really looks at me—and I notice for the first time that I'm not the only one who's crying. I see her trying to gather strength and the right words, but maybe there aren't any. I feel worse for her than I do me.

Moments ago, I wouldn't have thought that possible, but what do you say to your kid when someone has just told them they're going to die? Soon. Like within the next ten years. I know we never know when we're going to die, but ten years feels really short. I thought I had more time.

"Because he's an idiot. Because he spent all of those years with his head in a textbook, forgetting to take a moment to learn the most important lesson of all. He forgot to learn how to be human…or maybe he never was in the first place. I meant what I said in there. Learning to treat others with kindness—it's what really matters." She rubs her hand across my cheek. "I know things have been crazy, and we haven't been able to get a good hold on this, but we will. We can. I won't let what he said be true. I won't. It's *not*."

I nod, glancing quickly at my lap. I have to look away. A huge swell of emotion threatens to burst out in giant sobs at any moment. But I won't let it. I can't. She's been so strong for me. I don't want her to see me break.

I take several big breaths, trying to will the emotion back down. I see it as a thing and try to visualize it getting smaller until I can fold it up tightly and tuck it away somewhere. He's cracked my surface—I can feel it. If I give in now and let it out, I'll be totally shattered. I don't know if there's enough glue in the world to put me back together again.

"How's your toe?"

I love her more in this moment than I ever have before. She's brilliant—my mother. I'm sure she can see the crack and has offered up a bit of glue in the form of a changed subject.

"It hurts terribly," I say through chattering teeth. The cold has seeped inside of me, running like ice water through my veins.

"We're skipping lunch, obviously." She glances out the window at the darkening sky. "I think I have everything I need in the fridge for some chicken noodle soup. I even have a bag of those egg noodles you like in the cupboard. We'll get you inside, and while you take a bath to warm up, I'll fix us a feast." She reaches over and grabs my leg. The squeeze she gives it is almost too tight, but I feel the love there. I'm grateful for it.

"Thanks, Mom." My voice sounds *so* weak. I hate it. The hot tears continue to stream down my face—their warmth a constant reminder of their presence. I feel like I'll never be warm again. If I *ever* find my boot, I'm *never* letting it go. Who knows? Maybe this whole day would have turned out differently if I had started it properly—with my boots on.

We start the drive in silence, but it doesn't last. I knew it wouldn't. When feelings get so big they're thick in the air all around you, you have to talk about them. You just do. It's unhealthy if you don't.

"It's okay to feel sad. It's all right to let yourself break down." She pauses, coming to a stop at a red light. As soon as the car starts moving again, so do her words, as if her foot isn't just giving power to the car but fueling her speech as well. "If it were me, I think I'd let myself totally break down and sob. I'd probably put a time on it, though. I like things to feel orderly…even break downs." She laughs, but it ends on a strangled sob. My eyes flick to the time, 3:47. My throat swells and I manage to suck a deep breath before my sobs join hers—the dam has broken free. Fresh tears follow the trail of what feels like thousands before them. I'm able to take a deep breath as the tension leaves me, but the tears continue to flow.

I turn to look at Mom. She's staring at me, not the road, and I realize we're sitting in the parking lot at home. So lost in my despair, I didn't even notice we'd stopped.

She lets out a funny noise, causing her lips to huff out, flutter. She rolls her eyes at me as her lips dance and the laugh that escapes me is almost painful—like it could rip out another sob on its journey. But it doesn't. I take another deep breath. This one isn't so shaky; this one feels strong again.

"Thanks, Mom. I think I needed that." I glance at the clock and laugh for the second time. 3:52. I gave myself five minutes to break down. I hadn't expected to put myself back together in that time, too.

"Make sure you check your sugar before you start your bath." Mom closes the door behind us. The storm is getting worse. I'm glad we're inside now. I wish we never had to go out again.

I sit on the floor, pulling my feet out of my ruined slippers. Mom's staring at me, one arm wrapped around her middle, the other pulling at her lip.

"I'm sorry. Wearing your slippers out on a cold, wet day was a terrible idea."

I hate that she's tormenting herself over this. "It's no biggie, Mom. I think my toe would feel even worse right now if it had been crammed in a shoe all day." I offer her a smile that I hope she's willing to accept.

I glance around the living room, noticing all the boxes and decorations are gone. Christmas has mysteriously disappeared. "Somebody's been busy today."

I spot a bit of fishing line still hanging from the corner, its snowflake nowhere to be found—the last remaining evidence of what has been. I have a sudden pang of longing for what once was, but I'm grateful we don't have to worry about cleaning it up tonight like we'd planned.

I push myself up from the floor and carry my bag over to the sofa. Sitting down, I pull out the monitor, open the case, and push the button. I pop the top off the vial that holds the strips and retrieve one. When the monitor says to, I insert the strip, pick a finger, push the gun into the side, and press the button that releases the needle. I jump—but just *barely*. Squeezing my finger, I apply the blood to the small dot in the center of the strip and hold my breath. *I hope it's a good number, I hope it's a good number*—my silent mantra continues as the machine counts down the seconds.

"379." My shoulders slump, and I bite my lip to hold back the tears. I was 105 this morning. The only thing I've had to eat since breakfast was the two peanut butter cracker sandwiches at the doctor's office. I've never been this high before when it wasn't a direct result of being low. I've been nauteous since we left the doctors office, but I thought it was his words causing it. Not my sugar.

"Whoa, that's high."

Her words make me jump, transporting me back to the here and now.

"I don't know what happened," I answer, dejected. "Why is this so hard?" I don't expect an answer. I know there isn't one. Not really.

She sits beside me, wrapping her arms around my shoulders, giving me exactly what I need.

We sit in silence—her holding me tightly, me letting her—until we hear voices coming up the hallway.

"You've got to get over this, Jesse. I told you I wouldn't do anything, and I meant it. But I'm not going to stop being her friend, and I sure as *hell* won't stop trying to make things easier for her."

I can feel Mom stiffen around me as Harrison's words make their way to us.

"Why don't you go start your bath. I'll get dinner started." She practically pushes me up off the couch.

My eyes lock on Harrison's as he and Jesse both emerge from the hallway. He gives me a soft smile, and some of the terrible from the day falls away—that's how powerful his smiles are. They can make a disaster like today seem insignificant.

My mouth tugs up to return the gesture before I remember the sleet. *My hair.* I start to panic, wishing I had moved more quickly. I shouldn't be here—standing before him like this. I reach a tentative hand up, trying to gather my mess of curls. Curls and water are a toxic mix.

Jesse steps forward, grabbing me in a bear hug. "Hey, sis. What'd the doc have to say?"

His question hits me like a punch to the gut. I don't know how to answer.

"Honey—" Mom drapes her arm across my shoulders, "—go start your bath," she says, effectively shooing me from the room. She even gave a little shove.

I don't know whether to be thankful or irritated, so I settle on something in between. Maybe it's melancholy. Doesn't that sound so much prettier than depressed or dejected?

I start the water in the tub, wondering what its sound is drowning out. I hate knowing that they're out there talking about it. About me. Somehow, I became a problem everyone needs to figure out. I try to clear my mind—strip it of thoughts as effectively as I strip my body of clothes.

The warm water is a shock to my throbbing toe. I bite my tongue to hold back the scream that wants to come as the pain intensifies. I relax into the tub and pull my foot up out of it, resting it on the side. It's bearable like this. I lay my head in the bottom, and let the sound of the water filling—rising over my ears—drown out everything else. I push out everything that happened at the doctor's office. If I hold onto it, it will be my ruin.

15

BERNARD THE MAGNIFICENT

"So, then what happened?" Bernard asks.

He's sitting across from me at Mel's. The sweater vest he's wearing is the exact same shade of navy blue as the hat that's sitting next to him on the bench seat. Mom is working a rare evening shift, and he decided it would be a treat if we surprised her. I think he enjoys our family. Feels like he's a part of it. I can't imagine living alone. It just seems so…lonely.

"I don't know. Mom practically shoved me out of the room to take a bath." My eyes dart around the diner, searching for her. She's waiting on the people at the table closest to the door. "They keep arguing about me—I hate it." I feel like I can tell Bernard anything. So I do. He knows all about how in love with Harrison I am. He thinks it's meant to be. He keeps telling me that all of the best things in life take time and patience. *Rome wasn't built in a day.* What does that even mean? I don't see the comparison.

"It's just because they love you." He pauses for a moment, but I know he isn't finished. He enjoys the pause. I've come to believe it's part of the lesson. "But—" his finger goes up, as if making a point of its own, "—they love each other, too. I've seen those boys together since they started high school. I don't think I've ever seen two friends closer. They're like brothers—*are* brothers. This is the first time they've disagreed on anything. They'll figure it out. But it's gonna take time. Rome wasn't built in a day." He winks, picking up his teacup, and everything is right in the world. Even if I still don't get it, it comforts me to hear him say it. Because even if it wasn't built in a day, it's still standing now, thousands of years later. It may have taken them a while, but they did it right.

He leans to set his cup back on the table, and I notice his hand is trembling.

"Are you okay?" I ask.

He makes this all look easy, each day he just…is. I've seen him get low, eat something, and carry on as if nothing happened. He doesn't stop for it. I hope I get there. It's only been a few months, but I'm tired of this disease controlling me.

He clasps his hands together on the table in front of him, but the tremble doesn't stop. He breathes, and I see a flash of something I've never seen from him before—sadness. I'm compelled to get up and go to his side. I pick up his adorable little hat, placing it on my head as I slide into the booth beside him. His mouth turns up a smidge, but the sadness remains.

"What is it? What has you so sad?" I lay my hand on his arm, unsure if I should hug him.

"This day is always hard, but this is the first time in a long time I didn't have to spend it alone." He reaches into the pocket of his trousers, pulls out his wallet, flips it open, and plucks a picture out of the sleeve, passing it to me.

"She's beautiful," I say because it's true. She looks like him, but not. She has the same caramel coloring, the same freckles gracing her cheeks, but her eyes are a startling blue. A red ribbon is tied in her hair, and her smile is bright, happy.

He looks me in the eye for a moment before he responds. It feels like he's trying to make a decision.

"She was." His voice is a soft whisper. "Evelyn, my wife, used to say she was the prettiest girl to walk the earth in all of its days." His voice strengthens as he continues. "She was right. Leila was the prettiest girl, and smart, and funny—like her mother." His smile is in the past, remembering some long-forgotten day. "Today makes thirty years since she's been gone, and I still feel the ache as if it were yesterday. The day it happened always makes it real hard—because instead of remembering all the good things about her like I do most of the time, the morning just plays over in my head, over and over and I wish, I wish, I wish." He stops, overcome with emotion.

I slide closer, draping my arm across his back, and lay my head on his shoulder. "If it helps, you can give it to me. Whatever it is, you can tell me and I'll help you carry it. That way, maybe it can feel a little less heavy." I give his arm a little squeeze, hoping this is the right thing. Hoping I haven't just made it worse by asking him to talk about it.

This time, his long pause isn't about weighing the information that's going to be given; he needs it to collect himself. I sit back up, giving him space, and pick the picture back up. The thought of this girl being in his life one day and then simply not, makes my heart hurt. The ache is physical, as if someone walked up and hit me there. I play over what he said and wonder about his wife.

"Where's your wife?"

I glance up just in time to see Mom coming our way. Our eyes connect and I shake my head subtly, hoping she changes course.

"I shouldn't have said, '*my wife.*' She hasn't been that in years." His words startle me. He'd been quiet just long enough for me to be lulled by it.

"She left about a year after. She blamed me. She never said, but I could feel it. Maybe she didn't blame me for that morning, but still she blamed me for Leila's fate."

My mom stopped when she saw my subtle indication, but she's now frozen, standing in the middle of the diner with her order pad in hand, a towel draped over her shoulder. I dip my face and pull it back up quickly, trying to give her a mental shove. My gesture's effective; she turns to wipe the empty table closest to her.

"That's terrible." I know I should say more than that, but I can't imagine losing everyone I loved in the course of a year. "I'm sorry, I shouldn't have said that…it just sucks, and I'm so sorry for you."

"It did suck, but I think we both needed it. She moved on, remarried, and had a few more kids. I'm glad she was able to do that. I never wanted to. I had my little piece of heaven, and it lasted nearly fifteen years. That's more than a lot of people get. When we met?" His eyes hold mine for a moment before they slip to the past again. "Evelyn and I—it was magic, the type of love that filled the atmosphere. And from that love came beautiful Leila. She was twelve when she passed. Twelve years old."

"That's so young." I'm appalled at the things that keep slipping out of my mouth.

He reaches up and squeezes my hand. "Yes, much too young. She was diagnosed when she was eight. Evelyn and I, we discussed it when she got pregnant. Of course, we should have thought about it before, but you don't think about those kinds of things when you're thinking about babies. At least, I didn't. To me, it didn't matter. Even if she did end up with it, we'd just deal with it the same way we dealt with mine. Ha—" the laugh he lets out is so harsh, I momentarily imagine it as a sharp blade slicing through the very fabric of existence, "—what I failed to realize until it was too late, is that this disease looks so different from one person to the next. It affects each of us differently. There's no neat little box it'll fit into."

His voice breaks, and he looks away for a moment to

gather his thoughts. A light tap on my hand tells me I'm squeezing too tightly. I pull my arm back and lay my head on his shoulder.

"Leila—she just never felt it—ever. They call it Hypo and Hyper unaware. We didn't have too much trouble from the highs—Evelyn and I watched for symptoms constantly. But the lows... They would sneak up on her, and she would just go white and drop. The first few times it happened—I can't even explain that kind of fear. But we got comfortable with it. It got her in the night. By the time morning came, it was too late."

Tears are streaming across my nose, dripping onto his shoulder. I feel him take a big, shaky breath and I sit up, trying to control my emotions.

"I'm sorry," I say, wiping at the tears on my face. I blow my lips out, making them flutter. He gives me a soft smile.

"You don't need to apologize for your emotions." He pats my leg. "Our emotions are a part of the vast universe inside each of us. Sure, we can learn to contain them—hold them inside with no visible cracks—but we can no more control them than the weatherman can control the weather. I say let it out...before the storm inside grows so big that it consumes you. Besides, I laid some heavy stuff on your shoulders, and you were already carrying a big enough load of your own."

"Is everything all right?"

Mom slides onto the bench across from us. For a moment, I had completely forgotten we were in a public place. I glance around, making sure no one is watching.

"Yeah, I was just talking to Bernard about the doctor and my day from hell," I say, quickly, hoping she buys it. I don't want to tell her about Leila. I couldn't.

"Brice, you watch your mouth," she says, in true mom fashion. "Although it was a pretty terrible day."

"Julie, why don't I give you the number for my doctor. He has a small family practice, which I think is a lot better than those big corporations that switch doctors from one visit to the next—you never know who you're going to see." He shakes his head as he casually drops his hand on top of Leila's picture, scoops it up, and places it back in his wallet. Then he pulls out a business card and passes it to my mother. It's all so slickly done. I sit, amazed. I had completely forgotten about the photo.

"He'll treat you right," he finishes, winking at me.

"Dr. Banting," Mom reads out loud.

"Irony at its finest." Bernard smiles, putting his wallet back in his pocket.

"What do you mean?" my mom and I both say at the same time.

"He'll fill you in; he never misses a chance for a quick history lesson." He chuckles, all traces of the sadness—I now know he carries—missing from his voice.

My mom slides out of the booth and pulls her notepad from her apron pocket and the pen from behind her ear. "So, what are we having?"

16

THE WEIGHT OF IT ALL

"What kind of surgery did Kristy's parents have?"

It's Wednesday, and we're driving to the library for another support group. I haven't seen Bernard since he told me about Leila, and it sort of feels like this *thing* between us. I'm not sure if I should talk about it or not. I tap my boot, waiting for his reply. I'm so thankful to be wearing them again. I've been condemned to sandals for the last week, waiting for my toe to heal.

He smiles, turning his eyes back to the road. "Ask her about it tonight. It's a really great story. It certainly gave my morale a boost when I heard it. Love is a wonderful thing."

What does love have to do with surgery? Maybe one of them gave the other one something. Like an organ donation. I'm full of questions, but I don't voice any of them because he's already told me to ask her when we get there. Maybe it was for the liver. I've heard it has regenerative properties. You can donate a small part and it can regrow. Now I have even more questions than I started with. Sometimes I wish I could just turn my brain off.

"I wanted to talk to you about the other night." His words are the switch, effectively turning off my obscure thoughts.

I shift from the window and study him. Tonight, he's wearing a dark brown wool hat. How many does he have? At least four that I've seen, but I get the feeling that's just the start. I'm stalling—letting my mind wander to hats, of all things. I pull myself up nice and tall in the seat.

"Sure." *Sure?*

He glances at me again. This time, he looks a little uncertain. "There are some things I should explain about Leila's condition. Testing wasn't like it is today. Back then, it took over five minutes—start to finish—before you got an answer, and it was just a range. We didn't have monitors then." He clears his throat. "Medicine has come a long way in the last thirty years. And the research they're doing? It's amazing. I think they're right on the brink of something big—something life altering for people with this disease. Anyway, what I mean by all of this is—I don't want you to think what happened to her is going to happen to you." His voice catches at the end. My heart trips over it, spilling over.

He's worried about me—how this could affect me. I hadn't even thought about myself once since he told me his story. Only how hard it must be for him. The fact that he's so worried about me makes me love him that much more. "Don't worry about me. I've gotten low a few times in the night already. I wake up like a jackhammer's going in my chest. There's no way I could sleep through that." I smile, shrugging my shoulders. I try to look at ease, but the thought of the nighttime lows makes my heart race. I turn away, taking a big, calming breath. It's not the middle of the night. I'm not there.

"It's nice when our body sends us signals that we're in trouble." He turns the whale of a car into the parking lot. "Not everyone is so lucky."

"Everything about your car reminds me of the ocean," I

say, changing the subject because I have to—I don't know what to say to his last statement. I can't go there right now.

"Oh, yeah? How's that?" he asks as he slides the car into park.

"There are so many things, it's hard to know where to start." I pick at the rip in my jeans as I try to figure out what it is about it that *really* reminds me of the ocean. It's sort of nothing and everything, but I can't possibly tell him that—that's the sort of stuff only Mom understands. "Well, of course you've got the color—blue—it's easy to see why that makes me think of the ocean. But it's not just that. Here, inside, we have the sand." I wave my hand over the dashboard. "But that's just what you see. I think what truly does it, is the way it feels like we're floating—a boat on the ocean."

The look on his face is priceless—a mix of humor and confusion.

"Doesn't it feel that way to you? You have to feel it. Seriously, we could be gliding across water in this thing."

"You shut up and get out of my car," he says, barely containing his smirk as he throws open his door. "Floating across the damn ocean," he mutters striding toward the library. "Sounds to me like you're calling my car a boat. Girl, what that car has is *class*. That's a classy car back there." He continues walking in silence, and now I can't really tell if I upset him or if he's just playing with me. I think it's the latter, but I can't be sure.

The basement is full of noise as we reach the last stair. We aren't the first to arrive this time. J.C. is talking with a young guy who's standing with his legs planted wide, arms held tight across his chest.

"They didn't have a right to take my license. No one got

hurt but me. I never go low. It was the ice cream…too much insulin for the ice cream." He shakes his head.

I hadn't thought about driving since I'm not old enough yet. I couldn't imagine going low while driving a car. How scary.

Kristy and Lori are talking quietly to one another over by the fire, another woman with them. I drift closer to Bernard, unsure of myself with the new people here—I hadn't expected it. I'm relieved when he heads toward the free chairs beside Lori. They're a bit further from the fire than we were last time, but I still feel its warmth.

I unzip my jacket and lay the dark green monstrosity across the top of my chair. I sit, causing it to slide down, momentarily covering my head before it drops to my lap. I blow out a huge puff of air. The hair that's obscuring my view dances for a moment, but it's not enough to get it out of my face. I push it back with my hand, but the thick, dark curl bounces free. My coat has stripped me of control; I'll be fighting this sucker all night. I swipe at my wrist, feeling nothing—no scrunchie. How could I leave the house without a scrunchie?

I hug Big Green, the quilted fabric comforting in my lap. When I glance at Bernard, he's shaking his head.

"What?" I whisper.

"You. And those glorious curls of yours. Why can't you just let them be free?"

"They're free. At this point, I couldn't change that if I wanted to." I slump further into the chair and rub the silken lining of my jacket. The softness helps to soothe my nerves, and my face begins to cool. I glance around the room, happy to see that most everyone seems to have missed my show.

"You have gorgeous hair," the woman that wasn't here last week says. "I'm Gloria, by the way." She points inward, a soft smile taking hold of her bright, kind face.

"Nice to meet you, Gloria. I'm Brice," I reply, taking her in.

Her hair is silver and styled in a short pixie cut that accentuates her long, slender neck. The smile, that was but a whisper moments ago, blooms to its full magnitude, changing her from simple to stunning. It's funny how a smile can do that—completely transform a person with just the tweak of some muscles.

"Looks like we're all here. How's everyone tonight?" J.C. asks, walking to the chair directly across from the fire. "Kristy, how are Mom and Dad doing?"

"They're both well. Mom recovered very quickly. Dad's off the vent now, and he's healing with no sign of rejection. We're hoping for a fast and complete recovery. If his body accepts this—" she stops and takes a big breath, her eyes brimming with unshed tears.

"What kind of surgery did they have?" I ask the room. I'm pretty sure I'm the only one here who doesn't know.

I'm surprised when Kristy answers, the emotion she was overcome with subsiding. "Sorry, I must have confused you with all of this. My mom gave my dad a kidney. Both of his were failing as a long-term complication of this God-awful disease. But, she's given him life." When she finishes, the slump in her shoulders is gone. She's now sitting tall, pride gleaming in her eyes.

"Wow" is all I can think to say. Now everything Bernard said makes sense. I hope one day I'll know that kind of love.

The conversation around the room continues, but I drift away on a sea of inner thoughts. I don't know if I would want someone I love to give me a body part. What if something happened to them because of it? It must have been a difficult decision for Kristy's dad.

"When are you leaving?" Gloria asks Lori.

I must have missed something.

"Friday. I would have gone home with my mom when she left, but I wanted the chance to say goodbye to everyone here. Even though I've only been in the group for a few months, I've really enjoyed getting to know other people who understand."

"Why are you leaving?" I blurt out, even though it wasn't my conversation. Mom says I have a bad habit of doing that.

Lori looks at me, her eyes full of sadness. "I'm not ready to be so far from home."

"Can I have your address? I'd like to stay in touch." I'm sad she's leaving. I liked the idea of having someone closer to my age to talk to about all of this. Bernard is amazing, and I love having him right next door, but I doubt he would have advice on hormone changes affecting blood sugar.

"Sure, that sounds nice." Lori reaches into her purse and pulls out a little worn notebook and pen. She jots something down, rips out the piece of paper, and passes it to me. This act calms me considerably. I don't mind goodbyes, as long as they aren't the forever kind.

"How are you feeling?"

"Better every day. I'm still worn out and tender around my kidneys. I'm not sure how long it will be before it all goes away," she answers, clasping her hands together in her lap.

"I was so sorry to hear you were sick," Gloria says, putting her hand on Lori's upper arm.

"Thank you, Gloria. I made a mistake—one I'll never let happen again," Lori replies, casually brushing Gloria's hand from her arm.

"Does anyone have anything they want to share with the group tonight? Something you're struggling with, or something you feel like you've conquered?" J.C. asks, bringing the attention back to the front.

Part of me wants to talk to all of them about what the doctor said—that I'll be dead by twenty-five. But I can't, because even though we all have this one thing in common, it's not enough for me to want to share something that shattered me so completely. I've only talked with Mom and Bernard about it. I couldn't even say it out loud to Jayden, and she's been my best friend forever.

I look around the room at each of the people here. I tune out the noise of what's being said and just watch them. They each have a story to tell. This illness hasn't been nice to anyone, and the people in this room are no exception. The only difference is the people here have someone to share it with. I know it gives each of them comfort, but I realize, as I watch, that I'm not *ready* to share—this is all too much for me. If I was willing to open myself up to them, share my struggles, then I could keep coming. But I'm not. I can't keep taking on the sadness this disease has brought to others. Not if I can't give some of mine, too. I'll suffocate under the weight of it.

I feel prickly heat under my arms, my heart racing. I wipe my sweaty palms on my jeans, glancing over at Bernard. He sits to attention, his back flush to the chair.

"What's the matter?" He leans over. "Are you low?"

"I need to go." As soon as I say it, I know it's true. I can't breathe in here. *I need out.*

I stand quickly, hugging Big Green to my chest. "I'm sorry, we have to go."

I rush to the stairs without making eye contact with any of them. I throw open the big library doors, a huge rush of cold air meeting me. It calms my overheated skin. Taking in a big breath, I relax against the rough brick on the side of the building and close my eyes. The sun warms my skin. Winter sun is my favorite kind—a promise of warmer days.

Bernard is standing quietly beside me when I open my eyes. I love him for not walking out in front and blocking my moment with the sun.

"I don't think I'm ready for this yet. It's too much." The words come out broken. I hope he understands.

He puts his arm around my shoulder, gently leading me to the car. "People come and go from the group all the time. It's not for everyone. Even though our time as friends has been short, I've learned many things about you. I'm observant. We have that in common." He drops his arm to unlock my car door, opening it for me. I slip inside and take in a calming breath. His car smells clean. I don't know if that's exactly a smell, but I can't pinpoint anything else. It's just *clean*.

He climbs in, buckles his seat belt, and starts the ignition before he continues. "I think you're the type of person that feelings stick to. You're lucky for that in a way. You feel life in a way that many others don't, but there are two sides to every coin. You may be blessed with feeling life more deeply—more beautifully, in a sense—but life can be tragic. It can be easy to feel as if the emotions are drowning you."

We drive in silence until we are almost to the apartments before he begins to speak again. This might be his longest dramatic pause yet. "I know all of this because I'm one of those people, too. I'm just in a different place in life now than you are. One day, a group like this might be exactly what you need in life. It's perfectly okay if that time isn't right now."

"Thank you for being such a great friend." It's true. His words soothe me, each and every time. "I'm going to have to tell Jayden that she's been replaced." I giggle as he glances over at me with his eyebrows scrunched, mouth in an o.

"Don't you dare go hurting that girl's feelings," he scolds me, and the world seems right side up again.

17

TATTERED SOULS

"Let's go over there," Jayden says, nudging me with her foot. Her back is against the inside of the couch arm, feet toward me. I'm sitting cross-legged, facing her. She's staying the night.

"What? Why?" I don't want to take her to Bernard's. He's mine—I don't want to share. Jayden is pure light…it's easy for her to over-shine everything.

"The way you talk about him. I can tell he means a lot to you…" She holds out her hand to examine the nails she just filed, her mouth tipping up just a bit. "And you mean a lot to me, so I want to get to know him. Are you embarrassed of me? Why don't you want me to hang out with you guys?" She slumps back against the couch, her forehead wrinkling as she tugs at her bottom lip.

"Jay…" I unfurl from my crisscross position and smack her shoulder. "Look at me."

She's glancing down at her lap. She's losing herself to insecurities and self-doubt. I can't imagine being Jayden and being anything but completely self-assured. The girl is gorgeous. I know *that's* not the only way one measures self-worth. I'm sure having the one person who is supposed to love her the most in the world always choosing the party over *her* has taken its toll. Once she finally glances up at me, I do the one thing I know will make her feel better. I give her the truth.

"I'm worried once he gets to know you, he'll like you more." Now that I've said it out loud, it sounds ridiculous. "You're just too cute. It's maddening."

Her laugh mixes with mine, lightening the air around us.

"Come on, let's go. I'm sure he'll love the company." I bounce to my feet and hold my hand out to her, pulling her up from the couch.

"Should you check your sugar?"

"Jay, you don't have to remind me. I'm not a child, all right?" I regret the words as they leave my mouth. It's hard—constantly having people hovering over me. Always reminding me, as if I could ever forget. I know what I need to do and when I need to do it. My mom, my brother, my best friend—they all have this way around me now. They treat me as if I'm fragile, delicate, and breakable. I hate it. I'm just me…I don't want to be anything else. Bernard and Harrison are the only two people left on the face of the earth who look at me and just see *me*.

She sighs dramatically, steps in front of me, and puts her hands on my shoulders. We are almost identical in size, but our similarities stop there. "I just really care about you. You're like a sister to me. I can't lose you, Brice." She bites her lip as her Mediterranean-blue eyes become liquid pools. I cave, wrapping my arms around her.

"You're right, I'll check it. I'll bring my insulin over to Bernard's, too. He likes to feed me dinner. But I don't need you to tell me that. I fully understand the responsibility, okay?" I smile, hoping she'll understand what I'm trying to say.

"Okay, I'll try," she says.

I leave a quick note, letting whomever comes home first

know where we are…although it should be a given. I love Bernard's place, and if no one's around, that's where I usually am. It's perfect.

185.

"Isn't that a little high?"

This is another thing I hate—feeling like I'm being judged by my number. She probably wouldn't see it that way at all, but that's what it feels like to me.

"It's a bit. I'll just do an extra unit of insulin with my dinner and lay off the carbs. It'll be fine." I'm not sure who I'm trying to convince—her or myself.

I grab my insulin and a needle, and put them in my bag along with my meter—just in case. I pretty much have to take it all with me all the time. I wouldn't want to need it and not have it, even though it's just across the hall.

"Let's do this," Jayden says, grabbing my hand and pulling me toward the door.

I slide my feet into my new slippers (Mom got me a pair of hard-bottomed ones after my old pair got ruined) and grab my fuzzy, green hoodie off the coatrack. Slipping into it, I lean against the door as I wait for Jay to put her boots on. She's never been one to hurry. It's almost as if she walks through each step in her mind before she repeats the process here—in the real world. As if she unzips the boot mentally before her hand ever touches the zipper. At least that's what I assume happens because there is always a three-second delay in between everything Jayden does.

Her second boot is zipped, and she has her coat in hand, so I open the door. There's nothing like a little action to speed things up. She'll take it off as soon as we step inside, anyway. I'm saving her a step.

I ring Bernard's doorbell, glancing at Jay. Her cheeks are flushed, and I can tell she's a bit bent about my sudden departure. "Sorry. You were taking forever," I say, sheepishly.

"I didn't know we were in a hurry." She huffs.

"It must be my lucky day," he says, pulling me in for a quick hug. He's a hugger. I don't mind because I am, too. "Are you girls hungry?"

"We haven't had supper yet," I answer, my stomach a hollow ache that follows a long-ago meal. I didn't have a snack after school, and it's almost six. I'm not sure why my sugar's high. I never know—it rarely makes sense.

"I've had chili cooking all day, and I was just getting ready to slip the cornbread in the oven. I was hoping you would join me. Now it's even more of a treat because you've brought your friend." He smiles at Jayden, reaching his hand out to her.

"That sounds delightful," Jayden replies, leaning in for a side hug. She's not much of a hugger, but she makes do. "I hope we didn't impose. Brice always talks so highly of you; I told her it wasn't fair to keep you all to herself. I think it's time she shares." She winks at me.

Bernard opens the door wide, and we step into his magical place. The bookcases are eclectic, and in many different sizes, scattered around the room. In one corner, he has two the same height which stand side by side with another one resting, staggered, across the two. The front room is a book lover's dream. The first day I came here, I did nothing but circle the room, taking in all of the titles, while compiling a list in my mind of ones I wanted to borrow…if he'd let me. He simply sat on his sofa with a pleased smile, letting me soak it all in.

I know it's going to have the same effect on Jayden because the one thing she enjoys almost as much as making up stories, is reading them.

"You're a book lover, then," Bernard says with an amused smile.

She drops her coat inside the door. Without a word, she steps up to the case closest to her, reaches out her hand, and slowly slides her finger down the title on each spine.

It's not just the books. There's a feeling in the room. Like it's a secret place where words go to rearrange themselves and become new stories—forever tumbling and shifting to reveal an ever-changing tale. And yet, the heart always remains the same. I don't know why I didn't think of this before, but now I understand what transpires here when I'm not around. "You write, don't you?"

He shakes his head, quietly chuckling. "You surprise me more and more each day." He walks closer to me.

Jayden is lost within herself, reveling in the stories surrounding us. This place is a tiny slice of heaven for those of us with tattered souls.

"So, what gave me away?" he whispers, a childlike sparkle dancing in his eyes.

"Wait! You *do* write?" I want to sit and soak in every word he's ever penned to paper—every hastily scratched bit; every long, drawn-out story; and every forgotten sentence. *I want all of it.* This is an opportunity to know him completely. I can't wait. "Can I read it?"

"Most of the time it's just my thoughts. The tired ramblings of a lonely, old man." He laughs, but I see the truth in the sadness that washes in like a wave at the end of his chuckle. "There's nothing of any value for a young girl like you in there. I did try my hand at a couple of stories, though. I sent them out, but never heard back. I suppose it was worth it just to tell the story—even if nobody reads it."

"I want to read it," I say, louder than intended. "I really, really do."

I'm holding my breath waiting for his response. I don't know why I'm so certain he'll say no, but I'm crossing everything that's crossable in hopes I can change his mind with will alone.

"Maybe in a few years, when you've been dealing with this

longer. I don't want to hit you with all of that right now. I'll dig through some things, see if I can find anything light in there."

I let out my breath, imagining my hope leaving with it. I feel deflated, both literally and metaphorically. I really want to read his stuff. "Whenever you're ready to let me, I'll be happy to read it," I say, hoping he can't hear the disappointment in my voice.

He holds my eye for a long moment before a knock at the door startles us both…and Jayden, too, from the sound of the scream she lets out.

"Are you expecting anyone else?" I ask, my hand clutching my beating heart.

"Nope. I can't imagine who it could be." Bernard walks slowly toward the door. He reaches it, and, leaning in, puts his eye up to the little hole in the center. He pulls the door open with a relieved laugh. I'm surprised to see Harrison and Jesse standing on the other side.

"What are you doing here?" I ask, as Jesse comes inside.

Things have been weird with Jesse, and weird-times-ten when Harrison's around, too. I hate it. I'm not sure what happened or how it shifted, but the dynamic of our relationship changed—not just mine and Harrison's—but mine and Jesse's as well.

Jesse and I have always been close—closer than close. Every time I've ever been asked what I wanted to be when I grew up, I've had a flash of my big brother. *Every single time.* He's easy. Easy to love and easy to laugh with. He always knows exactly what to do or say, and kindness is ingrained deeply within him. It's not a way to be; it just simply is who he is. I can't stand to see him being so nasty to his best friend. It's not him.

Bernard places his hands on my shoulders. "I think what your sister means is *welcome*. This is a pleasant surprise." He lets go, patting me gently before he removes his hand completely.

Harrison is lost in the magic of the room. "Your library is fantastic!" he says, spinning around, taking in all of the books. He steps to the shelf closest to him and pulls out a book. *The Adventures of Huckleberry Finn*. Carefully, he opens the first pages before he closes it and looks over to Bernard, who's still standing behind me. I let myself believe he's looking at *me* that intently. Warmth blossoms in my stomach.

"This is a first edition. Are these all first editions?" His words are an ice bath to the warmth growing inside me. *He's excited about the books.*

Bernard shakes his head. "Heavens, no. That shelf has some pretty special books, but then what book isn't a special book." It's a statement, not a question. He walks up to Harrison and takes the book from him, running his hand across the cover, as if remembering an old friend.

"Do you miss it, Mr. Shelton?" Jesse asks.

"The teaching?"

Jesse nods.

"It wasn't my passion for children that made me want to teach. It was my passion for literature that fueled me. Always. And I believe that's what made teaching so great. I wanted to tell people about these great stories—these heartbreaking, life-changing stories. And once I got into the classroom, I found I had a gift for it. It's easy to inspire others when you, yourself, are inspired."

A Cheshire grin takes over his face. "*This*," he says, bouncing the book in his hand—testing its weight. "This is what I live for. The people inside these books keep me company at night and in the morning while I drink my coffee. And now I am lucky enough to have all of you in my life. I don't feel like I'm missing anything. Except things I stopped wishing for a long time ago."

The room is silent. I know I'm the only one in here who knows about Leila, and the weight of his final sentence steals my breath. Harrison's eyes find mine, and my heart begins to beat just a bit faster. I look away, hoping Jesse doesn't see us and freak out.

The room is flooded with heat, so I peel off my hoodie. I can't stand being in it a minute longer. There are too many people in this room. "Can I get some water?"

"Of course," Bernard replies. Taking my elbow, he leads me into the kitchen.

His first stop when we enter the kitchen is the window above the sink. He flips the latch and pushes the pane upward. Holding it with one hand, he places a small piece of wood upright in the space between, letting the window drop down on it. He guides me to the spot directly in front of it. The cool air hits my skin, and I feel like I can breathe again.

Bernard sets a glass of water beside me, never saying a word.

I pick it up. It's moist in my hand from the condensation on the glass. There are ice cubes floating inside, and I smile down at them, thankful to have such a thoughtful friend. "I don't know what's wrong with me." The words surprise me. I didn't realize I felt that way.

"How do you mean?" he asks, closing the window when he notices the goosebumps rise across my arms.

I set down the glass and run my icy fingers across my arms in a futile attempt to stave the sudden cold.

"I don't know, it's like I can't be around people anymore. I feel like I can't breathe, especially when it's Jesse and Harrison."

"Ah…"

"What is that? *Ah*?"

"It sounds to me like you need to have a conversation. Whether that means with everyone all at once, or individually, is up to you. But you need to talk to them about how you're feeling." He crosses his arms and leans against the counter opposite me. "You leave it to me. I'll bring it around. You'll just have to be brave and speak up when the ball's in your court."

"How are your classes? Are you enjoying your education?"

Bernard's table is round and normally sits four comfortably. We brought a barstool in from the kitchen, and Harrison graciously accepted it for the night. It sits slightly higher than all the other chairs, so he's sitting with a bit of a hunch to his shoulders—as if to try to shrink in size, or maybe it's the weight of the room bringing him down.

"I don't know. I can barely see up from down right now. I never knew how hard it would be to work nights and try to go to school, but it's brutal."

Jesse's answer shocks me—he never once said anything to me about it.

"Maybe it's time to think about letting go of the job and just focus on the education," Bernard answers. It sounds so simple—an easy choice. But I know it's not like that—not for Jesse, not for us.

"Ha!" Jesse's laugh is harsh, bitter. "I've been working to help my mom crawl out from under the medical debt that's plagued her since my dad died. It's not shitty enough she lost her husband—she's spent years paying for it." His Adam's apple bobs up and down before he begins again. "It's the least I can do for her. She does so much for us."

"I understand family obligation. If you need help with any of your school work, come on over, any time. My door's always open to you."

"Thanks, that's very kind of you. I might just have to take you up on it."

I try to relax. Knowing Bernard is going to try to shake the tree, so to speak, has me seriously flustered. I let out a pent-up breath. Jesse looks at me, and ever so slowly, his left eyebrow rises. This is it. This is the start of it. My brows pull together, and I attempt a smile, but I know I can't pull it off. Not really.

"What's up with you, Brice? I barely see you anymore. Not like this guy—" he points his spoon at Harrison, "—*he* seems to see you every day."

"Not every day, but yeah. I've been lucky enough to get to spend some time with him." I'm so surprised at how sure and strong my voice is. It's okay for Harrison and me to be friends, and I won't let my idiot brother ruin it.

"What is it exactly that bothers you so much about us being friends?" Harrison asks, sitting straight despite his tall stool. "I don't get it, I really don't. Where's all of this hostility coming from? I thought I was your best friend. What's wrong with you?"

"I see the way you look at her. Don't you get it? She's my *sister*, and she's still a *child*." His voice is a low rumble.

"She's not a child, Jess." Jayden astonishes me—joining in.

This whole conversation feels surreal, as if I'm merely watching a movie and none of this is real. I'm glad she's here; I won't have to fill her in on this train wreck later.

"I don't really know what my feelings are for Brice. Am I attracted to her? Of course! Look at her, she's beautiful."

He may be talking to Jesse, but the only one he sees right now is me.

"Do I think I could love her? Yes. I think maybe I have since I saw her at that first football game all those years ago—sitting in the grass with dolls spread all around her, talking as if they were each their own person." His eyes break away from mine, his focus returning to Jesse—whose face is red and shaking.

I reach over and lay my hand on his arm, but he shrugs me off.

"But I know she's not ready for more than friendship. No matter what you think of me, I'd never break that trust."

Jesse moves like a flash. He's on Harrison before his chair hits the ground behind him.

I jump up, but Bernard grabs me, pulling me back.

"You need to leave! I don't want to look at you," Jesse screams in Harrison's face, his hands around his neck as they wrestle on the floor.

Bernard steps in front of me. "That's enough." His voice is no louder than it was at dinner, but his calm timbre blankets the room, demanding attention.

Jesse glances down at Harrison beneath him. His cheeks color as he releases his grip and stands. His gaze fixed firmly on the floor as anger pulses through his jaw.

Harrison gets up and straightens his glasses. The frame is bent slightly, and it won't lay right across his nose. He looks at Bernard. "I'm so sorry, Mr. Shelton. I didn't have any intentions of disrespecting your home like this."

With that, he walks out the door.

I grab my hoodie off the couch, and race after him. I won't let him leave without saying something first. I don't want this to be goodbye.

"You shouldn't have followed me, Brice. He needs to cool down, and this is going to make it worse."

"Did you mean what you said in there?"

He's leaning against his truck. I walk right up to him—I want to be looking in his eyes when he answers this question. I grab his glasses from his face and do my best to straighten the frame. His cheeks color when my hands touch him, and I try to imagine what it would be like if he kissed me right now.

I slide his glasses back on his face. I meant to step back, but I step closer, instead. I can feel the warmth coming off his body, and I shiver in the cold winter air.

He runs his hands down my arms. "You shouldn't be out here," he whispers, tipping my chin up so my eyes meet his.

What I see there is heartbreaking, and I know this is goodbye.

"I'm leaving this fall. I got into Central, and I finally have enough saved for housing. I'm really sorry all this happened, Rice. I *did* mean what I said in there, and one of these days I'll prove it to you. But I think it's best if I stay away for a while."

I imagine a glass heart shattering into a million little pieces, and even though I know mine is a strong muscle, today it feels just as fragile and as brave. I step closer still, and I let my lips brush against his.

He grabs me, pulling me closer, his lips parting slowly. And I lose myself in my first kiss—knowing I'll never kiss another.

18

THIS IS HOW IT SHOULD BE

THE BUTTERFLIES IN MY STOMACH ARE DIFFERENT TODAY. There are just one or two of them in there, flying lazily in circles. Not like the immeasurable amount that reside there when Harrison is around. Not that Harrison has been around. I haven't seen him for weeks, and something tells me I won't be seeing him for a long time to come. I still feel him, though. We're tethered together by soul-fiber.

I set the magazine I've been holding back on the stand beside my chair. The office is quiet; Mom and I are the only two waiting. The woman behind the desk assured us it won't be much longer.

Now that my thoughts have stilled, I hear water trickling and look around to find the source. In the corner of the room, there's a small water fountain surrounded by plants—some with big, fuchsia-colored flowers in bloom. It's lovely. The whole atmosphere of the place is so different. I hope the doctor will be, too.

It's funny when your thoughts conjure people.

A small, dark man in a white coat opens the door. "Brice?"

He stands, quietly observing me, arms crossed, and a slight smile on his face.

I push up from the chair, a deep sense of dread in my stomach. I really don't like uncertainty. Meeting someone new always makes me anxious.

Mom stands with me, grabbing my arm. "Relax," she whispers—when she's clearly anything but.

I can't let this moment own me. Whatever happens, when I leave this office, I'll still be me, and Mom will still be Mom.

Once I'm standing beside him, his smile grows. He places his hand on my shoulder. "Welcome, Brice. I'm Dr. Banting—not *the* Dr. Banting, of course—but I like to think I keep the name in good standing." He winks, turning to walk down the hallway.

His strides are long despite his small stature. I stand, paralyzed, watching him. I know I'm supposed to follow, but my mind is still trying to sort out the whole introduction.

I turn to Mom. "What?"

"Well, come on." She rushes after him.

"What?" I whisper again, the whole experience feeling a little bizarre. But, for the first time in months, I feel like I might be able to breathe again. I'm breathing *now*, but I want to be able to take those deep breaths. The kind you take when you know everything is going to be okay.

I make my way down the hall, entering the room they're standing in. "Sorry, I just…" I just don't know how to finish the sentence—apparently.

He waves his hand, clearing the air. "No need to apologize." He chuckles, shaking his head.

"What's funny?" Mom asks, a bit of an edge to her voice.

"I've never been able to figure out what it is that makes diabetics always feel the need to apologize. Trust me, young lady, you have nothing to apologize for. If anything, the world should be apologizing to you."

I don't quite know what to say to that, but I know it's true. It feels like all I do anymore is apologize—for my feelings, for my actions, for all the trouble. I feel like a burden to everyone…all the time.

"Sorry." I bury my face in my hands, mortified that my first impression is making me a cliché. I rub my hands down my face. I look up to see he's watching me. It's one of *those* looks. Like all my secrets are his to take.

"I'm really nervous. My last doctor…" I don't finish the sentence—I don't know how.

"He said she was going to die young," Mom steps in, finishing it for me. She pauses, takes a deep breath, and when she glances back at me, I can see her eyes beginning to well. She squares her shoulders and takes my hand. "He was insensitive and his pessimism made us feel terrible." The squeeze she gives my fingers is almost painful.

"Brice, I am here to help you. To *teach* you. I believe, as your doctor, my biggest priority is to keep you healthy. Not just physically but emotionally and mentally. If something concerns me, I will speak to you frankly about it. But I am an optimist, and I believe in the power of the mind over the body. So, what I am getting at, in a rather long-winded manner, I'm afraid—" he chuckles, amused by himself and I can't help but be a bit amused, too, "—I would never say something that would put your mental and emotional health at risk. I'm sorry for what the last doctor said. I've reviewed your blood sugar log and your labs, and I can assure you that there is no merit to it."

I shake my head, feeling a ridiculous amount of emotion. "What do you mean? Why would he say that terrible thing if it wasn't true?" I don't understand why he would be so carelessly hurtful for no reason.

"Well, I'm reviewing everything now, and the fact that you

have kept such a diligent log is impressive to me. Most teenagers wouldn't. Of course, it would be nice to try to stabilize your blood sugar levels, but when were you diagnosed?"

"November fourteenth," I say, wondering what he's getting at.

He laughs and I'm not quite sure what to think. I wasn't expecting *that*. I glance at Mom. Her forehead's wrinkled, and she's sitting on the edge of her chair, her purse strap in hand. Maybe we're just going to doctor hop forever and never find someone to help me with this.

"I'm sorry. That probably seemed incredibly rude, I do apologize. It's just that November fourteenth is National Diabetes day. It has been since 1991, but the reason they chose that day is because it was the late, great, Dr. Banting's birthday." He glances up from my chart, and I can tell he's waiting for me to say something.

The problem is, I'm not sure what.

I look at Mom. She gives me a little half shrug. She must not know the proper response to all of this, either.

I decide to go with the biggest question I have at the moment. "Who is Dr. Banting?"

He glances up again. This time, he looks shocked. "I didn't realize you didn't know. I probably seem a little silly going on like I have been." He closes my file. "Dr. Banting was the man who discovered insulin therapy. If it wasn't for his steadfast persistence in the name of science, they may have never figured it out."

"Wow" is all I can say. The notion that insulin wasn't always around had never occurred to me before. I hadn't even thought about someone discovering it.

"Yeah, you should look him up if you ever get a chance. He was quite an impressive man."

"I will, the next time I go to the library. So, what is it about my numbers that made *him* say that, if you don't see the same thing?" It's time to sit the history lesson aside and get to the heart of this—before it drowns me.

"You've only had this disease for a little over five months now. Your A1C, which is a blood test we do to determine blood sugar control over the last ninety days, went from being a 15.7 when you were first diagnosed...down to an 8.8 now. That is *amazing* progress. Ideally, we would like it to be 7 or below, but the progress you've made is just what we want to see. They're on the verge of releasing a new insulin that's going to be a real game changer. As soon as they do, we'll get you on it. Should be in the next few months. Until then, I would like you to stay the course and know this will get easier. Diabetes is a lot more than most people think it is. It's challenging to learn how to control it, instead of letting it control you. I believe you're on your way. Do you have any questions?"

"Is there any way to stop having the lows? They're really scary." I hate the way my voice shakes when I talk. I sound like a child afraid of monsters hiding in my closet.

"Frequent snacks are a *must*. I suggest eating at least every two hours. It doesn't have to be a big snack. This will cut down on the lows. Do you feel them?"

"Yes. I get really shaky, and my heart begins to race. Sometimes, I feel really weak, like I need to sit down. I almost always cry, and I hate it. I don't even feel sad, usually. It's like the crying is something that happens because of the low...have you heard of that before?"

"An emotional response to the lack of glucose is quite normal. I'm sorry you respond that way. I know it's probably quite frustrating, but it's a very common response. The good thing is, you're able to recognize your body's triggers. This helps to keep you safe. Do you make sure to always carry something on you?"

"Yeah, my first low I was by myself and I didn't quite know what to do, so I'm always prepared now," I tell him, thinking back to that moment with the milk and the graham crackers—the first day I truly knew what it was like to have this disease.

"Good. Being prepared and paying attention to your body—and what it's trying to tell you—are all positive steps toward managing this disease. I think you'll do just fine, Brice. Do you have any other questions? Anything else you want to talk about?"

I don't answer right away. I sit for a moment, instead, and think about all of the questions I had. Now that I've brought up the big thing—the elephant that's been taking up more than its fair share of room for quite a while now—all the little things have evaporated with it. Their absence has left me standing in the center of a stark, white, bare room with nothing to say at all.

"No. Thank you, though, Dr. Banting…for taking me as a patient." It was the only thing I could think of, and now that I've said it, I wish I could take it back. It sounds absurd—as if he chose me or something.

"You can live a full and happy life, Brice. I'm happy to be able to show you how. It's a privilege. Stop and see Judy on the way out. She'll schedule your next appointment and give you a lab order. You'll want to make sure you're fasting when you get those done. Do it about a week before your appointment." He pushes himself up from the little stool and begins walking us back out to the front.

It feels more like a visit with a friend than a trip to the doctor. I'm really grateful to Bernard for recommending him. This is doable. My steps are light for the first time in months.

The drive home is quiet. I think we're both enjoying the absence of noise. My inner voice has been so loud lately, I've been lost inside myself. This is the first time in weeks that my thoughts belong to me, and I can take them wherever I'd like.

I gaze out the window, taking in the long train of sleeping elephants that line the valley. Not real elephants, of course, but I always imagined them awake when I was sleeping, dancing through the night—only to fall back into the deep slumber of daytime. The hills don't really move, and they're much larger than a row of sleeping elephants would be.

I've spent my life in the Yakima Valley. Sometimes it's hard to imagine a world beyond it. The heat of the summer and the cold of the winter are as much a part of me as the hills that surround it. I can't imagine calling any other place home.

"I have to work in an hour. Are you going to Bernie's tonight?"

I hate nicknames. But, as much as I hate them, my mother seems to love them. She never calls anyone by their given name.

"Yeah, I wanted to thank him." I've never had a better friend. I love Jayden with every crazy hair on my head, but Bernard and I have kindred souls.

"All right, honey, just don't forget to check your sugar." She smiles at me, and even though I know she's just doing what moms do, it still stings a bit.

"Love you."

I get out and run up the steps. I hate the winter, and even though it's almost March, it's still cold and white—or what *used* to be white. Snow is only pretty the day it falls; after that it's this dirty, gray color from where our day-to-day lives have trampled and soiled it. I'm ready for the rebirth of spring.

I get to Bernard's step and blow the cold from my fingers before I ring the bell. I can't wait to tell him how much I love

Dr. Banting. I pull my hands back up to breathe on them again just as the door opens.

I drop my hands. I can't believe he's here. Today is officially the best day of 1996, and it's not even two o'clock.

"What are you doing here?" I ask, my voice a throaty whisper that mortifies me.

He smiles and those dimples show, and I forget all about my momentary despair. He loves me. Now that I know this, I can't *unknow* it, and as much as it's going to suck to wait the next two years, three months, and twenty-two days to be able to find out what that means—for now, simply knowing it is enough.

"I was hoping to get to see you today," he says, and I can hear the goodbye in his voice already. "How have you been? How's school?"

I grasp onto this line he's thrown me and scramble to think of something honest to say—something that will give him a piece of me.

"We've been studying cells in biology." I take a deep breath, feeling my cheeks color...now that I've started, I have to finish. "Something about looking at them under the microscope makes me feel alive. Seeing how much life exists inside each tiny drop has awakened a part of me I never knew existed. I don't know what it means, but I know it means something."

He's quiet for a moment, his gaze reading every minute that's gone by since we saw each other last. That's the way it always is with him—a single look, and I'm his completely. Every last bit of me.

"That's amazing, Rice. It's a great thing—knowing what it is that inspires you. I bet whatever you do with this, you'll succeed. You were born for happiness." The sadness in his voice is too much for me.

"What about you, Harrison? What are you doing?" I don't mean for the comment to sound harsh, but it does. I know he's going, and I also know he has to, but it doesn't make it hurt any less.

"I got a job up in Ellensburg. I'm moving up this weekend. That way, I'm already settled when school starts. Honestly, Rice, I can't breathe here, you know? I wish I could fill every day with you, but your brother's right, I shouldn't be thinking like this. I shouldn't be laying all of this on you. It's not fair to you, and it's not fair to him either." His honey-colored eyes are almost golden, lit by a yellow flame.

I step into the apartment. Bernard smiles, pushing himself up from the sofa. "I'm just going to go make some tea," he says, walking toward the kitchen.

I don't know what to do. My arms feel heavy, and for a moment, I imagine them as magnets—attracted to him, pulling toward him with a force so strong, I can't hold back.

I step into him, and he opens his arms, welcoming it. We stand like this, wrapped together, for what feels like a heartbeat and a lifetime combined. Our souls mixing, so when he pulls back, a part of me will be with him forever. I won't be whole until his arms are wrapped around me once again.

"I brought you something," Harrison says. Walking over to the coffee table, he picks up a book. He hands it to me. My mouth turns up as I run my fingers over the raised title of *Remember Me Two*.

"You remembered." I bump his shoulder.

"I never asked...how was the first one?"

"Oddly tied to the whole diabetes thing. I actually just finished it. It was too weird at first—just being diagnosed with this disease, then the first book I go to read is almost centered around it. I'm glad I finished, though. In true Pike fashion, the book did not disappoint."

As we stand here, making small talk, waiting for Bernard, I tell myself that I can do this—this is the kind of thing worth waiting for. *Rome wasn't built in a day.* After all of these months of hearing it, I finally understand the true meaning of the words.

PART 2

2005 - HARRISON

19

A TOAST

"To Harrison and Brice. As much as I didn't like the idea of anyone looking at my sister the way that this guy looked at her, I couldn't be happier to call him my brother." Jesse holds his champagne glass up, looks me in the eye, and winks.

I think he's had a few glasses already, and knowing him, he's just getting started.

"I know he'll take care of you, Brice," he finishes, his voice catching on her name.

She shifts forward, and I know his words have unknowingly pulled a scab off an old wound.

I pull myself up, letting my fingers graze across her bare shoulders as I do. I raise my glass. "You've got it all wrong. She'll take care of me—she'll save me from myself every day."

I was looking at him when I started the speech, but now I'm lost in her evergreen eyes. I can't help myself. I spent years holding back—eighteen to be precise. I've been in love with this girl since she was seven years old. I slowly run my fingers down her arm, goosebumps rising up behind them. I lean down and place the softest kiss on her lips. The moan that leaves her makes me wish the night were over. I can't wait for her surprise.

"Hey, hey, that's enough of that—remember? She's my baby sister." Jesse laughs. His wife, Cassie, reaches up and pulls him back down into his chair.

"I can't wait to be alone with you," I whisper to my wife when I sit back down. *Mmmm, my wife.* I can't believe this is finally real.

"Let's dance first. You only get married once, you know?" She raises her eyebrow, and her front curl breaks free from the pins holding her hair. I tuck it behind her ear and lean in, touching my mouth lightly to hers. She opens up to me, and I deepen the kiss, our tongues doing a slow dance. As much as it kills me, I have to break away…before I can't.

I pull back slowly, tracing my hand down her arm as I go. I reach her fingertips and wrap my hand around them. She stands, surrounded by a cascade of ivory silk. She didn't want white or tulle. Jayden told her she was taking all the fun out of it. I'm glad she rarely listens to Jayden.

The ivory silk pools out onto the floor, causing tiny gold beads to dance like stars in the twilight. Her hair is up in a series of knots, with daisies tucked in here and there, and curls falling out in just the right places. She's breathtaking, and I can't take my eyes off her.

I'd give up forever to touch you…

The rest of the world falls away as I hold her in my arms, and we sway to the music—our music, our song, our life. This girl was made for me.

"What are you thinking about?" she whispers, leaning her head on my shoulder.

"The only thing I ever think about."

I hear the smile in her reply. "Oh yeah? What's that?"

"You," I whisper, leaning down and trailing kisses from her bare shoulder all the way up her neck.

A low hum from the base of her throat is her only reply. I could live in this moment forever. "I love you, Rice."

She hates nicknames, all of them but that one—the silly name I gave her years ago. Her brother always called her Little Bit, and I couldn't help but add *of rice* to the end of it. I was a twelve-year-old boy, so I thought it was hilarious—a play on Brice. I expected an outrage—foot stomping or something when I called her that. I hadn't expected her cheeks to color, just barely, just enough for me to know that it warmed her. Then she turned her face up to me, and I saw the rest of my life in her eyes.

It really freaked me out. I'd never had my soul connect with someone else's like that. I knew we belonged together; our souls were made from the same ethereal mist. It wasn't so much like falling for someone else as it was a coming home to myself—becoming whole again.

"I have a surprise for you…"

Her head snaps up, her left eyebrow nearly reaching her hair line. She's adorable when she's caught off guard. I take a mental snapshot and file it, knowing this will warm me for years to come.

Jesse and I have been working on this during every free moment we've had for the last year. I couldn't have done it without him. "I can't wait to show you." My voice is so quiet, I'm not sure she heard me.

You're the closest to heaven that I'll ever be…

"Are we almost there?" Brice questions, fiddling with the silk blindfold I put on her when we left the reception at Jesse's.

He and Cassie live on a ranch out in West Valley. They

have a beautiful home and insisted we get married there in their back garden. He knew every spare penny I had was going into this surprise, and there was really no way I could turn him down.

I reach over and take her hand, slowly rubbing circles on her palm with my thumb. I feel her relax into the moment. We've only been in the car for five minutes, and we'll be driving for about another thirty—opposite sides of the Yakima Valley.

Sometimes I wish I found something suitable closer to Jesse's house. But, when this house popped up, I knew it would be perfect. I got it dirt-cheap and started applying for building permits right away. Jesse had a few guys from his construction crew help out when they could, and together we built the guest house in the back. The property came with ten acres, but I decided to keep the new addition pretty close. Bernard is almost eighty, and his diabetes has become very frail. I don't know how long it will be before we will need to move him inside. But I also know he needs his solitude. *'When you speak to the dead, sometimes it's easier when no one is listening.'* He told me that once, a long time ago when I asked him why he never tried to find someone to spend his time with. I never replied; the weight of his words had been too much to respond to. He has that affect on me often.

"You never answered my question." Her voice is a soft breath.

I feel a ripple of worry, but try to push it aside. I know it doesn't work that way. Pushing aside worry is the same as admitting defeat, and I'd never let this disease defeat us.

"We have about twenty minutes—time for a snack. I know we didn't get a chance to eat much dinner tonight and I'm starving." I really am, but I know with all the dancing, she's probably starting to dip. I let go of her hand and pull a container from the bag that's sitting between us. "Can you open this blindfolded?"

"What's in here?" She reaches out, blindly grabbing for the container. As soon as she pops the lid, the sweet smell of strawberries fills the car, and I hear a tiny moan escape her parted lips.

"I love you." I could say it a million times every day and still feel like I can't convey the depth of the words.

The dark chocolate hits her tongue, and I imagine she's lost in the succulent flavors filling her mouth. Everything tastes better dipped in chocolate.

"Thank you for knowing I would need these. I should have eaten more, but every moment was so perfect, I didn't want to miss a thing. Thank you, for all of it, but mostly these strawberries. I could've just had you and them and I would have called it the perfect day." Her laughter fills the car, warming me all the way through.

"There's some orange juice in the thermos, too—if you need it."

I watch as she pulls it out, the blindness not slowing her down as she brings it to her mouth. Her arms are trembling slightly, but I think we caught it in time. The blindfold was a bad idea. I'm sure if she wasn't wearing it, she'd be checking her sugar.

"You can take it off, Rice. It was a silly idea. Just don't peek out the window." I try to tease her. I know what this is going to do to her; hopefully I can stop it. "You can put it back on after."

She recaps the orange juice, her hands shaking more now —I'm sure it's from the emotions, as much as the low blood sugar. She pulls her monitor out of her purse. It only takes about ten seconds before she glances up at me, panic dancing through her eyes.

"27." Her voice is barely a whisper. I see the first tear fall.

I pull over into the Thriftway parking lot. We're still about fifteen minutes from the house—it's too far.

"Let's drink some more juice," I tell her, grabbing the thermos. Opening it back up, I pass it to her. My heart's racing. I imagine it matches hers, beat for beat. She's told me it feels like her heart is trying to break free from her chest when she's really low, and 27 is really fucking *low*.

She takes the container, but instead of raising it to her lips, it slowly sinks down to her lap. I reach over and re-cap it. I don't want it to spill. I've only seen her like this a few times. Usually she stays with me, and I rarely have to coach her. I release my seat belt and get out of the car. Walking around, I open her door, needing to be closer to her than the center console will allow.

"I'm so sorry I ruined the surprise." Her voice comes out in a sob, the words barely audible.

I can't deal with the emotions right now. I know they will subside once we get her sugar back up. At least she already had a chocolate strawberry, but I need her to have more juice.

"You could never ruin anything," I tell her as I open the juice back up and pour a tiny cupful into the lid.

Her shoulders are heaving with her sobs.

"Brice!" My voice comes out sharper than intended, but I need her to stay with me. "Come on, baby, you need to drink this." I wrap my arm around her shoulders, pulling her into me, as I try to brace myself halfway in and out of the car. I raise the tiny cup to her mouth, finally breathing again as she swallows the life-saving liquid.

20

SURPRISE!

I PULL INTO THE ROCKY DRIVEWAY, MY HEART RACING AGAIN. I've worked so hard on this, spent so much time here. Every swipe of a paintbrush, every hammered nail done with uncertainty. Some days, I can't see past the haze of trepidation that lingers like the last stubborn wisps of fog once the sun has fully risen—its heat enough to eradicate it from the air, yet it remains. Most of the time, I can tamp it down, but sometimes it sneaks up on me, turning my mood sour for days. I've never been unsure of her love. I feel it body and soul, the reality of it so concrete there's never been room for doubt.

No, my uncertainty doesn't belong to the love we share—it lies solely with time. I try to put it out of my head, but it's there, always—the fear that she could be snatched from me without a moment's notice. Last week, her mom called. She never calls me. So, when I saw her name on the screen, my heart lodged so firmly in my throat, I couldn't speak. I hit talk, and I turned to ash and drifted away as I waited for her to break the silence. It had been nothing—Julie confirming the time for the family dinner. I know the way I'm feeling isn't healthy, and I know I need to get over it. But living with her every day is frightening. Seeing how it wears on her. Feeling her get up in the middle of the night—her side of the bed ablaze with heat. I always give her a couple minutes before I go to the kitchen. Sometimes, I think my presence throws things off, and it's actually easier for her if I don't interfere. But, what if I didn't get up, and she didn't make it to the kitchen?

"What are we waiting for?" Her question pulls me from my relentless thoughts.

"Dramatic buildup," I joke. "Are you ready for this?"

"Yes," she replies, putting her hand on her door to open it.

"Wait." I open my door and rush to her side. I'm trying to decide whether I should take off the blindfold now or wait until we're inside. But, I want her to see this. All of it. I pull the door wide, the cool night air connecting with her skin, causing a ripple of goosebumps on her exposed shoulders. I slip off my suit jacket and drape it over her as I help her to her feet.

"Are you sure you're ready?" I whisper, my words causing a second ripple of goosebumps. I let my hand slide up to the wrap, untying the loose knot holding it over her eyes.

I revel in the sudden intake of breath as our new home fills her vision. The simple white farmhouse is everything she has always wanted in a home. All the touches I've added over the last few months are what make it something *more*—the solid wood rockers sitting under the covered porch, the large welcome sign that sits in the corner by the front door, the gerbera daisy's I know are her favorite, filling the old wash bins flanking either side of the stairs. Her movements are slow, deliberate, and I feel a low hum of satisfaction as she rubs her hand across the rail. I know there is no chance for a splinter. I feel the ever-present ache of hard work between my shoulder blades, but it was all worth it—all the sanding, scraping, and resurfacing. I'd do it all a thousand times over just to be able to give her this.

"Would you like to see the inside?"

Her eyes are a mixture of fear and wonder. I want to alleviate her fear, but I also want to save the best part for last. As much as I know that she will fall in love with every last detail of this house, I also fully expect her to tell me no. She'll change her mind, of course, but I see the list of reasons why she wants to tell me no forming behind her as she traces the W on the welcome sign I painted on leftover barn wood.

There was a barely standing old barn in the back when I bought the property. Jesse and I planned a man's camping trip one weekend, but really came over here and pulled the whole thing down. I repurposed most of it back into the restoration of the house. There are parts of it everywhere. It became a sort of game for us—who could find the best use for old wood.

"Did you?" she pauses, her eyes brimming with tears. "How? How did you do this?"

I shrug as I turn the knob and give the door a little push. I paid the neighbor kid to come light all the candles I had placed along the floor, and the effect is magical. Tiny gold flames light the way through the house and fresh roses fragrant the air —a confetti of petals decorating the trail of candlelight.

She stands on the threshold of our home, the flickering light dancing in her clear, green eyes. She wants this so badly, but because of her love for another, she is preparing herself to walk away from it. I scoop her into my arms, causing a burst of laughter to escape her.

"Harrison, I don't even know what to say. How did you do this? How could you afford this? How did you keep this big of a secret? You know he won't come, and I can't leave him, I'd never leave him…" Her words break away, tears rimming her eyes for the second time tonight.

I set her on her feet. Cupping her face in my hands, I let

myself get lost in her eyes for a moment, my never-ending desire for her taking over as I lean down and taste her red lips. I hate that she's sad on our wedding night. I can't stand to let her linger in despair any longer.

"There's more." I scoop her off her feet, walking quickly through the house. I should have started at the back and saved her this senseless heartache. "I'll answer your questions after you see it," I whisper, as she lays her head on my chest.

I reach the back door, the trail of candles forgotten as the excitement for what lies ahead takes over. The large, wood deck that connects the back to the front is lit by little white lights that are strung from the lowest branches of the big maple tree sitting in the center of our yard. I sail down the stairs, the anticipation adding a quickness to my step.

"Is that…" she pauses, her eyebrows scrunching together, uncertainty and hope at war for a place in her expression. "A house? Is there another house?" Her voice is ringed with excitement, now that hope has placed its victory flag.

"That one's not ours." I linger as I memorize her face in this moment. "That one belongs to Bernard."

She's radiant, and this time I know the tears are ones of joy.

"You want to see?"

Her only response is a giggle that erupts from her as she begins kicking her feet until I put her down on the brick trail that leads from our home to his. As soon as her boots hit the ground, she's off at a sprint to reach the lit porch of the little house. I made sure the square footage was the same as his apartment. I didn't want to take anything away from him, and I know with the shelves I installed in the front room, he'll have more room than he's had in a long time.

Out of all of the things I've done since I bought this property, this is what I'm most proud of. I brought Bernard out here last week. At first, he tried to tell me no. They're so much alike—he and Brice. He kept saying that the last thing two newlyweds need around is an old man. But once I got him to see the inside, the reality of my seriousness became apparent to him, and he knew... It was meant to be. The place was *literally* made for him.

"Come on!" She claps her hands, and the smile she's wearing shines more brightly than the full moon hanging above her in the sky. She's always been a small person, but what she lacks in mass, she makes up for in spirit. Right now, I feel her everywhere.

I leave my place on the brick path and climb the steps to my love. "He'll be happy here, Rice," I whisper, before sliding the key in the lock.

The squeal that erupts from her is better suited to the seven-year-old girl I met all those years ago. But I suppose that's the magic of joy—it has the ability to transport us through time, back to the days of carefree youth. She rarely lets go of the seriousness that has always consumed her. Seeing her so lost in the moment fills my soul in a way I've never felt before. I'm responsible for her happiness, and this is just the beginning. I want to see this kind of smile *every day*.

21

I'M NOT THE ONLY ONE WITH A SURPRISE...

I'M SPENT—LYING NAKED ON THE BLANKET I LAID ON THE floor in front of the fireplace. She's draped across my chest, her cheek resting in her palm, and she's gazing down at me. The firelight that's dancing through her eyes is making me hunger for her again, but I still haven't shown her the bedroom.

"This is going to make everything so much easier."

She has a habit of doing this—saying half a thought, expecting that I'll know the other half. Most of the time I follow pretty well, but I don't have any idea what she's referring to now. "What's going to make everything easier?"

"This house—our home. It's going to make it so much easier to raise this baby."

The satisfied smirk on her face is almost too much as I let her words take hold.

"What are you saying, Rice?" I need to hear her say it again. My mind is racing with everything this means. "Is it okay? Are you going to be okay?"

"As long as I'm careful, it'll all be fine. Dr. Banting says that although I will have to be watched more closely, I can absolutely do this. I can have our first baby." There is so much excitement in her eyes, it helps to alleviate the doubt I'm feeling.

"When did you find out?"

"A few weeks ago. I went to see Dr. Banting because of all the nighttime lows I've been having. Turns out, it's because of this little bean," she says, resting her free hand over her stomach.

She's known for a few weeks and was able to keep it from me? I can't even process that. Every time I look in her eyes, I feel like I know everything—she's the other half of me. How did I not know? *This house.* I've spent every last free moment finishing the house.

She clears her throat, her eyes cast down, and I realize I've been quiet for too long.

I pull myself up, gathering her in my lap. "This is going to be great for our sex life," I whisper, causing the smile that lights my life to bloom on her face.

"You're such a pig." She slaps me playfully before our mouths collide, and I lose myself in her silent chaos.

Her quiet breathing is the only noise in the still house. I finally got to show her the bedroom. My thoughts are racing, and I know sleep won't happen for me tonight. She's already twelve weeks along. Normal gestation is forty weeks, but they will induce her at thirty-eight…something about diabetics having big babies. Which means, in just twenty-six weeks, we'll be parents. I can't sleep with news like that on my mind.

I pull the covers back, pausing to make sure I don't wake her. Her mouth is still fluttering lightly, with the easy breath of night. *Good.* Grabbing a pair of sweats out of my bag, I slip them on and make my way to the door. If I stay in here staring at the ceiling all night, I'll go mad.

The nightlight in the hall is just bright enough to guide me toward the bathroom. I cringe as my footfall causes the floor to creak loudly. I stand motionless outside our bedroom door for what feels like an eternity before I chance moving again.

Reaching the bathroom, I flip on the light. My reflection makes me pause, ashamed of what I see. I should be elated, ecstatic, *overjoyed* by Brice's news. But I can't shake the fear from my heart, and I'm wearing it all over my face. My mom has always said that the eyes are the windows to the soul. The dark brown orbs staring back at me are heavy, weighted…on what started as the happiest day of my life.

I reach down, opening the cupboard beneath the sink, and grab a washcloth. I need to let go of this feeling, shake it off, wash it away—before my beautiful wife sees it written all over me.

As the water slowly begins to warm, I let myself imagine our child. Brice can do this. I've never known anyone stronger, and the last thing she needs is my doubt making it harder for her. I've wanted a family with this girl for as long as I can remember.

The mirror begins to steam, pulling me from my thoughts. I hold the washcloth under, then turn off the stream. I wring it out, and as I feel the warmth hit my face, I tell myself that my doubts will be washed away with any grime leftover from the day. I take one last look in the mirror, trying to see what Brice sees when she looks at me. My hair is too long, but she likes it that way. She loves to run her hands through it. I feel myself harden just thinking about the way her fingers feel across my scalp. I laugh at my inability to think of her without my body reacting this way. Will that ever change? *I hope not.*

I make my way down the hall, past our room, and into the empty one beside it. Flipping on the light, I try to imagine it as it will be. It's the perfect size for a nursery. I had planned on putting an office here, but there will be plenty of room for my desk downstairs. I wonder what color the walls will be—pink or blue? I shake my head, getting rid of that mindset. A light green will be the perfect shade, either way.

We leave for our honeymoon tomorrow. As soon as we get home, this is going to be my biggest priority. I would give her the moon if I could, and even though I haven't met the little bean growing in her belly, my love for him or her has already started to take root in my heart. We can do this. We *will* do this.

I turn off the light and make my way back to her. I could find her in the darkest night just by following the thread that connects us so completely. As I slip back in beside her, she molds herself to me, and I let the feeling of us calm the terror in my soul. We. Will. Do. This.

22

TIME TO MOVE

"Ahh, baby, why are you crying?" I ask Brice. She's standing in the middle of our old living room, a cleaning rag in hand, bawling her eyes out. She's always been an emotional being, and this pregnancy has magnified it. At least I'll know how to deal with tears when the baby gets here. I smile at the thought, receiving a death stare for it. *Oops.*

"I was just thinking about the baby." This sentence, these seven words, have saved me countless times, and I've only known about the baby for three weeks. Three beautiful weeks. I let go of the fear I was feeling when I first found out, and I couldn't be happier with our current condition. Except for the tears. *I could do without the tears.* They're exhausting.

I walk to her and wrap her tightly in my arms, hoping the gesture is enough to fix whatever has her so upset. I feel her relax into me.

"I just…I'm just going to miss it. I grew up here. I know, I know, it's just a ratty old apartment, but…" The sobs take her over again, the rest of her words lost to them.

When her mom remarried, Brice took over the lease of the apartment. I think in some ways she fully intended to stay here forever. I'm sure the move would be emotional under perfect conditions. But with the storm of hormones flooding her system daily, she's losing herself to the sadness.

"The things that matter the most are coming with us. Bernard will just be a few steps away; that's not going to change. We have something better now." I realize my mistake as soon as the words leave my mouth, and she starts to sob harder. "Not better because there was something wrong with the apartment, just better because there will be more room for our growing family," I scramble, hoping the words will be enough.

"Woohoo." Bernard laughs as he walks through the door. His step is lighter than I've seen it in years.

This move is exactly what he needed to rejuvenate his soul—his words, not mine. Although, this man has taught me so many of life's lessons; I'm not sure if any of the words I speak didn't originally come from him.

"What's going on in here?" The glee in his tone is quickly replaced with concern as he comes further into the room.

"What's the matter, little one?" Bernard pauses in front of us, his cane shaking slightly. For months I've been trying to convince him that he would be safer with a walker—something that would offer more support—but he just keeps telling me that's nonsense. His cane does just fine. I think it's become an accessory, like the hats. He told me once that a cane looks cool, but a walker makes you look old. I think it's funny that someone rounding on eighty is worried about looking old.

"Is this guy giving you trouble," he asks, nodding in my direction, causing a smile to break through her tears. I don't know what I'd do without this man sometimes.

"It's nothing to worry about, Bernard." She sniffles, which should be disgusting, but somehow, she makes it adorable. "I'm just being sentimental."

"There's always a touch of pain that comes from new

growth, but it doesn't last." Bernard pauses to catch his breath. "It'll die down, get to the point where you rarely even think about it at all. This has been your home for a really long time; it's all right to feel bad about leaving it. But there will soon come a day when the memories will just be happy," he finishes, and I'm not surprised when she steps out of my arms into his.

"Thank you," she whispers to him, and I turn away, feeling like this moment isn't mine.

Jesse walks in, his dark hair sticking through the cap he's wearing backwards, his face smudged with grime and sweat, but he's still sporting an easy smile. "I see how it is, me and my girl are doing the heavy work while you chill in here." He catches my eye with a wink.

I don't know how, but he always seems to know when he needs to show up and lighten the mood. He's been my brother for damn near twenty years—it just wasn't official until three weeks ago. The three years we didn't speak was the hardest time in my life, ever. I would have walked away from any notion of being with her just to get my friend back, but that didn't seem to matter. Not until Cassie came along and straightened him out. She walks into the room behind him, her long, dark hair in a messy bun on top of her head. She has a bandana folded and tied around her forehead, keeping the sweat out of her eyes. August in the Yakima Valley is an insane time to be moving.

Brice rushes into the kitchen and comes back with two glasses of water. "You better drink this. I don't want anyone getting heatstroke today. We need you healthy, so we can work you to the bone," she jokes, passing them the water, all traces of the tears from moments ago gone. She catches my eye and mouths the word *sorry*. I hate that she thinks she needs to apologize to me all the time, but it creates a warmth deep inside me just the same.

"Gee, thanks," Cassie says, bumping hips with Brice. "You know I'd work my butt off for you anytime. I'm always here for you, babe."

"Thank you," Brice replies, and the tears I hear in her voice are enough to make me want to get to work.

"Cassie, why don't you take a break and hang in the air conditioning for a while? We'll take a big load over." They've been working on filling the truck full of boxes from Bernard's place. All of his boxes are heavy. All of them. When I asked him what was so heavy, his reply was, *words are heavy, no matter how you look at it.* It was one of those comments that I wanted to write down and keep forever. *Bernardism's*...maybe one day I'll write a book.

23

LAY IT OUT THERE

"Two days, huh?" Jesse says, turning into the driveway.

"Yeah."

"Just, *yeah*? Are you excited? I bet it's a girl. Cassie said she had a feeling, and she's almost always right."

I don't know what to say to this. The fear is always present. I can't imagine being a parent will be different. I think the fear will just get bigger. "I'm scared shitless." I'm not sure why I say it, I don't speak my feelings out loud very often, especially where fear is concerned. I always think it gains power if you put it out there.

A wicked chuckle escapes him as he slaps me on the back. It throws me off; laughter was the last thing I expected.

"Welcome to parenthood, my friend. Trust me, it just gets worse. Wait till you hold her." He pumps his fist into his chest. "I can guarantee, you've never felt anything like it."

Crunching gravel is the only sound in the truck as his words swirl in my thoughts. I can't believe I'm going to be a dad. This has all been so surreal, but this morning when I walked into the bathroom after Brice's shower, and saw the roundness in her belly that hadn't been visible a week ago, it suddenly felt real. There's life growing inside her—life I helped create. A life that will forever change mine in the best possible way.

A slow, easy smile takes over my face, in spite of the fear in the pit of my stomach. Monday, we find out if we're having a boy or a girl. I always pictured my oldest as a boy, I'm not sure why. A month ago, we weren't even married…now we're having a family.

"Nah, we're having a boy for sure."

"What's your wager?"

"Seriously?" We used to do this as kids, but that was a long time ago. If I didn't know better, I'd say Jesse's feeling nostalgic. "Free reign? Anything goes?"

He slowly nods his head. I think the true implications of what he's done are just beginning to register.

"Lay it on me. Doesn't matter, because I'm going to win." He opens his door and the wave of heat envelops the truck cab instantly. Air conditioning fades quickly when it's pushing a hundred degrees.

"Loser hosts the barbecues for the rest of the summer." I'm not entirely sure that I'll win, so I don't want to pick something too bad. My freshman year of high school was spent with only one eyebrow. It was a lesson-learning experience for me, so now I never pick a punishment that will have a lasting effect. Especially when the winner is left for fate to decide.

I close the door to the truck, wishing I had thought about central air when I was updating the house. We have a swamp cooler in the laundry room window, but it does little to combat the ever-present heat.

Heat waves hover above the gravel, and it's not even noon. It's going to be a long day. Jesse's already at the back of the truck. The sound of the big door rolling up snaps me back to the moment and I round the truck, tucking my bandana into my shorts pocket for easy access. It's time to get sweaty.

"You're not starting without me, are you?"

"Wouldn't dream of it, brother." He glances over at me, wiggling his eyebrows as if we're in for loads of fun. This guy. I shake my head as he starts dancing to music playing just for him, grabbing the first box as his feet dance to the beat of the unheard song. "Try not to think too much about every box. I'd like to get home before midnight." He laughs as he heads toward Bernard's little porch.

Sometimes my thoughts overtake me, and I don't even realize I've stopped all movement. My mom says I've been that way forever. She always used to tell me that I'm not someone who tries something a dozen ways before I get it right. I'm someone who thinks and analyzes something until I fully understand it. Then I do it once, correctly. The truth is, most of the time I'm not even thinking about the task at hand. My thoughts are millions of miles away in a place all their own.

"There's only one way to pick up a box, Ford," Jesse says, as he grabs his second, heading back to the porch. "Get over here and open this door. That way I don't have to pick them all up twice." He sets his box down, grabs his bandana, and wipes the sweat that's already forming on his forehead. His eyes meet mine, and I see that he's set all joking aside. "I'm worried about her, too, Ford. I would rip the world in half if something were to happen to my baby sister. But she's so fucking strong. That's what you have to remember. This might be hard, but she's up for it. She always goes headfirst after the things she wants in life, and *that* girl was made to be a mother. Don't doubt her or this. Get out of that fucking head of yours and open this door before I smack your ass." He smirks, trying to contain a full smile.

I close the distance to the porch and open the door. "Think we can get it unloaded in thirty?" I ask, sliding the key in the lock.

"Shit, I would've been done already if it wasn't for your slow ass!"

I know it won't be long now before we're heading back to reload. I can't wait to move all of our things into our home. *Our home.* This is where we will spend our life together, and today and every day after is just the beginning. Because as long as we're taking air into our lungs, we can dream of tomorrow—and tomorrow is always a beautiful day.

24

TIME TO FIRE UP THE GRILL...

"Why are you so nervous?" I ask.

Brice is adorable, with her little round belly bump barely showing in the enormous gown she's wearing. She's lying on the table, knees bent, bouncing her toes. The hand that isn't resting on her stomach is covering most of her face.

She slowly lowers her hand, and I immediately wish she would put it back. Apparently, questions are *out of the question.*

"I don't know! How would you like to be poked and prodded? They will be looking at my insides! How would you like it if they were looking at your insides?"

She's been like this for the last two days. The house is a disaster of half-full boxes, and I think it's adding to her mood. She hates disorder, says it makes her mind feel boxed in. Couple that with the excitement of today, and the fear that maybe we won't find out—maybe the baby won't let us see—and what we wind up with is a very messy emotional cocktail being poured. Time for an intervention before things get crazy.

"Everything will be fine. You have nothing to worry

about." I walk over to her and place my hand over the one she has resting over our child. I lean down close enough to whisper, "Just as long as you don't fart." I smile, and I'm sure she sees it. Damn. The effect would have been better if I could have held it in. I'm not surprised when her little hand connects with my shoulder. I'm surprised that it stings a bit, though.

"Are you serious right now?" She huffs, but I see my comment had the intended effect. Now she's just irritated at me and doesn't look so nervous. "This is all very serious, Harrison."

I'm relieved for the knock at the door. I'm sure that by the end of the visit she will have forgotten all about her irritation. Her sharp intake of breath turns my attention to her. She's pulled herself up on the table, her feet now dangling in front of her.

Our eyes meet and I rush to her side, wrapping my arm around her. "It's fine, it's going to be just fine," I whisper to her, my lips connecting with her hair.

"Come in," she calls, after taking a second quick breath.

A woman walks in, eyes on the chart she's holding in front of her. She looks up with a kind smile that transforms her whole face. "Good afternoon, I'm Crystal. I'll be doing your ultrasound today. This is the big one, right?" She glances back at the chart, double-checking the information there. "So, I guess the big question is, do you want to know? Or are you wanting to be surprised?"

"We want to know," we both say simultaneously.

I haven't been this nervous since my job interview at the high school five years ago. Luckily, that went my way. Now I get to spend every day teaching in the same class I was inspired in all those years ago. Sometimes I wonder how things would have turned out for me if I had been placed in Ms. Jenkins' class instead of Bernard's. The impact he's had on my life has been tremendous. I don't know who I would have been without him always looking out for me.

"All right, let's take a look then." Crystal smiles again as she gently opens Brice's gown. "Is this your first?" she asks, squirting some kind of blue jelly on her stomach.

"Yeah," Brice answers, reaching her hand up for mine. Our fingers connect, and I feel the electrical hum that comes only from her. It warms my body, calming my nerves. "But, definitely not our last," she continues. "We have a big house and need a big family. I've got a lot of love to give." She smiles up at me, and I have to stop myself from leaning down and tasting her perfect lips.

I glance back at Crystal. She has some sort of wand thing that must transfer the image to the screen, because as soon as she places it on Brice's stomach, I see movement. It's hard to make out anything else at first. The picture is black and white and grainy, but after I look at it for a moment, it begins to take shape. I can clearly see the head and the little arms moving around.

"Oh, she's not shy at all," Crystal says, her bright smile like pure sunshine.

Her words ping around inside my head for a moment, their meaning lost to me. *She*. She said *she*. Brice squeezes my hand tightly, beginning to squeal like the little girl she was that first day I met her, all of those years ago.

"Did you say she? Did she say she? Oh my God! A girl, we're having a baby *girl*."

Her last words reverse the paralyzation that has momentarily overtaken me. I'm surprised when I feel moisture on my face. I don't cry.

"Sure did. Do you see that?" Crystal asks, pointing toward the grainy image. "Right there? Where it looks like an equal sign? That equal sign is her vagina. You are having a girl! Congrats, Mom."

She continues her work, the mouse in her hand making the arrow move across the image. She's dragging lines from one spot to another, taking measurements of her. Measurements of our baby. I grew up an only child. I have no idea how to care for a baby. The idea of that is just as terrifying as it is exciting.

Brice squeezes my fingers. I glance from the screen, to her, and see a steady stream of tears sliding down the side of her face into the mass of curls that lie beneath her. When our eyes meet, the smile she gives me could brighten the darkest night, and I know that it's liquid joy pouring from her.

Our baby girl puts her little hand up and waves her tiny fingers and a laugh escapes me. "Did you see that? She just waved."

Crystal gives me a knowing smile. I'm sure she witnesses these kinds of things all day long, but the moment feels magical to me. I want nothing more than to get down on my knees and kiss all over Brice's belly. Our daughter—my daughter—is in there. Moving and growing in a world all her own. It has never felt more real than it does in this moment.

"I have all the measurements we need. Say goodbye, Dad. Next time you see her, you'll be holding her in your arms," Crystal says, removing the wand from Brice's belly, causing the screen to go black. When she flips the light on, I feel a moment of sadness, the visual connection with my daughter lost.

"Let's go shopping," Brice says the moment the door closes behind Crystal. The smile that's living on her face looks like it could stay there forever. "Target. They have the best little girl things. I've been browsing for weeks. I'm so excited to finally be able to put things in the cart!"

She hops off the table, and when she pulls the tent of a gown off, I reach out for her, pulling her into my arms. My fingers graze across her naked skin, causing it to pebble. As I start to trail kisses down her shoulder, she melts into me, and I feel myself harden. *I didn't think this through.* I place one chaste kiss on her belly and straighten.

"Shopping, then dinner, then you. The rest of the world can wait until tomorrow. Tonight is for us," I tell her, as I step back to let her dress.

25

ONE ON ONE

"Knock, knock." I say the words as I rap my knuckles against the wood. I never wait for him to open the door. I haven't in years.

"Is that you, Harry?"

It sounds like he's in the kitchen. I pull the door closed and head toward his voice.

"I'm glad you're here. I need a hand hanging this one." Bernard is standing on a chair against the windowless wall behind his table. A large canvas is propped beneath him. My muscles tense at the sight. He shouldn't be up there.

I rush to his chair and reach a hand up to him. "Old man, what're you doing up there? Trying to get yourself killed?" He glances around like he has no idea what the big deal is.

"Who are you calling *old man*?" He laughs, effortlessly stepping off the chair. "These legs have been carrying me around for nearly eighty years now. I'm familiar with these legs. I know how to use them." He turns and winks at me, his smile full of amusement. "Now, if you're through insulting me, lend me a hand so we can get this beauty on the wall." He reaches down and turns the canvas.

"Wow." It's the only response I can give as I take in the painting I've never seen before. I know it's an early piece. The brush strokes are lighter, freer—creating a softening of the image. "When did she do this one?" I ask, feeling a familiar pang of regret for the years we were forced to spend apart. I can't figure out what I'm looking at. "What is it?"

"Boy, you are just full of questions today." He laughs, shaking his head as he admires the piece with me. "This is her first—what started her creative journey. It's a cross-cut section of a blade of grass. Those little smiling faces spoke to her... woke her up, so to speak."

I lift the canvas, surprised at the weight. It's much bigger than she normally does, and I wonder why I've never seen it before. Brice has made a living out of passion. It's the unseen that speaks to her—the things that are there under the surface. When she talks about a piece she's working on, her whole body glows. She's her true self when she's immersed in her art. I love to watch her paint. I could stand in the doorway for an hour and not even know it.

I remember the day she told me about how she felt looking in the microscope. I never could have imagined how *this* could come from that. How it'd ignited this passion and talent she had buried inside.

I step back once the painting is secure on the wall, taking it all in. The blade of grass fills most of the picture. Its shape is curved, the backside flat and smooth as if it's the wall containing the world inside. The inside edge is uneven with large knobs coming off of it and little, soft green hairs covering the surface. Inside, it looks like a series of small, smiling faces, their mouths a glowing blue color. I can't help but reach out and touch the surface of the painting there. Her work always has that effect on me—the textures calling to be touched.

"Those smiling faces are the channels that move the water

through the blade of grass. It's quite extraordinary, the things that exist unseen to the rest of us." Bernard pats my shoulder as I stand frozen before the painting. I reach up to touch it again, thrown back by the rapid slap to my arm. "Don't touch!" His voice is sharp and hollow at the same time, the tone raising goosebumps across my arms.

"What are you doing here anyway? Always just come when you please." He's pacing now, wringing his hands. "You should go. Go on, get out of here!"

His eyes find mine, and I don't know the man standing before me. I've only seen him like this once before, and that was a time I try to forget. I hope it's not too late to get through to him.

"Let's check your sugar. I think you're low." I see his monitor sitting on the counter by the fridge and go to grab it.

"I don't need you here. Get out!" He stumbles with the force of his voice and falls into the table.

My heart is racing as I try to figure out how to get him to drink some juice. I need Brice. She could break through the deepest haze. But she's in Seattle for the weekend visiting Jayden.

"See what you did? I told you I don't need you here!" He slumps into the chair, his words dripping disdain.

I ignore his harshness. Grabbing the fridge door, I hold my breath, hoping to find what I need inside. I let it go at the sight of the orange carton sitting on the top shelf. Pulling it out, I carry it to the counter. There's an empty water glass sitting beside the sink. *That'll do.* I fill it halfway. *How am I going to get this juice in him?*

"Fine, I'll go. But only if you drink this." *Please.* I set the juice in front of him of and step back.

"Fuck you and your juice!"

He swipes his arm out, knocking the glass from the table. I

flinch as it connects with the lower cabinets and shatters. *That's not going to work.*

I'm losing ground fast. The lower he goes, the more unpredictable he's going to become. I have to get something in him. I wrack my brain, trying to think of something—*anything* to get us through this.

I feel the blow from his balled fist seconds after I register his movement. *Fuck.* Eighty or not, that fucking hurt. *This is not Bernard, this is not Bernard*—my mantra as I fight to calm my anger.

I turn the rage into action. I grab another glass from the cabinet, this time, a plastic one, trying to avoid an even bigger mess. If he doesn't drink it now, I'll have to call 911. I can't let him lose consciousness. The last time he did, he began seizing immediately.

I need to catch him off guard. Do something unexpected.

Armed with new juice, I take a deep breath and call on the anger I feel every day at this disease. Fuck diabetes. Fuck everything about it. But most of all, fuck low blood sugar and its unpredictability.

"You're going to drink this fucking juice." I let the rage carry through my voice. "Quit fucking with me, old man! You'll do it for her, dammit!"

I'm shaking now, inches from his face. My anger is a palpable thing, as real as the orange juice sloshing in the cup—begging for action.

He grabs the cup from my hand, juice sloshing over the side. I've lost. *He's going to pitch it in my face.* I hold my breath as ever so slowly, it heads toward his mouth. I'm afraid to move. Anything could set him off and change his hand's course. I don't breathe again until I see his Adam's apple carrying the precious liquid down his throat. I take a much needed breath.

He finishes the whole cup, his aged body slumping into the

chair, diminishing the force and vitality from moments before. A weak, tired, old man is left in their place.

I don't say anything for what feels like an eternity. When he looks up at me, his eyes are full of regret and sorrow. I stand to retrieve his monitor. This isn't over.

"Let's take a look, see where you're at." I ready everything and reach my hand out for his. I'm relieved when I feel his shaky hand in mine. There'll be no more fighting. I prick his finger and wait. 32.

We glance at the machine's readout, both of us held captive by the number...before I snap into action. Pulling a loaf of bread from the bread box and a jar of peanut butter from the cupboard, I set out to complete the simple task—my mind calming as I do. Within moments, I set a peanut butter sandwich in front of him. I don't say anything. I don't need to now. Even if his mind is shaky, his body knows what it needs to do. It doesn't take long for him to finish the sandwich.

This is the time I hate the most. With Brice, I always fear something will happen, and her mind will never fully return to her. It usually only lasts a handful of minutes, but those moments can stretch into an eternity, waiting for her to break the silence. As I sit quietly, waiting for Bernard, the feeling is no different.

I need to move.

While Bernard recovers, I clean the mess this disease has made of his home. I glance at him after I wipe the rinsed rag across the hard wood for the last time. He's sitting taller now, his hands folded in front of him, thumbs bouncing against one another. His eyes lift to meet mine, and I'm surprised to see them shimmering with unshed tears.

"I'm so sorry, Harry. So sorry. I could never repay you the debt I owe you." The sadness on his face quickly morphs into something else as I turn to face him directly. He reaches his hand out to touch me from his place at the table before he breaks down completely. Silent sobs wrack him—the force of them causing his whole body to shake.

"Hey, hey. That's enough of that. Do you know how cool this shiner's gonna be?" I reach up and touch the tender skin, holding in the wince that wants to escape me. "All the high school kids will be talking about it. Especially after they hear the story I'm going to make up to go along with it." I laugh, hoping to break him from his sadness, hoping to free his mind from the effects of this terrible fucking disease.

He's quiet for a moment—his thoughts unknown to me. But his tears have stopped, and his breathing is beginning to even out. "Let me come—talk to them. We can at least turn this into a learning experience." His eyes meet mine, and I see that he's put his sadness to rest. *Always the optimist.* I grab his hand, wishing I could do more, *say more*, but no words come.

I'm surprised when he pushes his chair back, the legs making a scraping sound as they slide across the floor. He stands in front of me, holding his hand out. I stand, and he wraps his feeble arms around me. I relax into them, patting him on the back. The sharp knobs of his spine feel so prominent through his sweater.

"Tomorrow and I—we don't have quite the agreement we used to have. Lately, I'm not sure if it's going to show or not, so I have to make the most of today."

His words hit me like ice water to the face, and I start to feel like I can't breathe in the small space. I give a final squeeze before I step back, ashamed at my reaction.

"Don't look so surprised." He laughs, the sound like gravel pinging off glass. "It's not like I can live forever."

We both stand quietly. I feel like I've been robbed of my voice, and I pray that he gets to meet my daughter, that she will feel his scratchy beard as he lays gentle kisses on her forehead. If all his tomorrows are lost, I pray he will get that one.

He deserves to feel that kind of happiness before he leaves us forever.

"I love you, son. Just know that."

"I'm going to make up a bed on the couch. I'll stay over tonight." I leave the room without glancing back, needing to distance myself from the waves of emotion in the kitchen.

26

QUESTIONS AND ANSWERS

I step out of the shower, grabbing my towel from the counter. The throbbing in the center of my shoulder blades feels like it has its own heartbeat separate from mine. This pain doesn't belong to me. I take a deep breath in and slowly roll my shoulders, trying to will it away. Bernard's couch is tiny, and I think it was made sometime in the seventies. It's not a couch for a full-grown man to sleep on.

Brice bursts into the room, car keys in one hand, her purse in the other. "I gotta pee." She flings everything down on the counter in her haste to the toilet. "That was the longest drive ever. Ahhh… I didn't think I was going to make it."

The look of relief that overcomes her face causes my body to harden in longing for her. She's so fucking gorgeous. Her gaze is directly on me, and when she licks her lip, I let out a groan. Her eyes slowly roam up my naked body, and I want nothing more than to take her right here on the bathroom floor.

Her eyebrows furrow, and she quickly stands up, the lust she had just been wearing set aside for something else. *What just happened?*

"What happened?" she asks, reaching for my eye, and it all comes back to me. "What did you do? Did you get in a fight?"

A strangled laugh rises up, and I cover my mouth to try to block its escape. "It was Bernard." I smile and try to pull off amused, but I know it won't work. *It never does.* My thoughts are hers before I even have them.

Fear flashes across her face. She turns, dashing from the bathroom. *Shit.* I didn't realize I wouldn't have time to speak, or I would have said something differently. I slip back into my shorts, leaving my work clothes on the counter, and head after her.

The back door is wide open, and when I reach its mouth, I can see Bernard's door is wide open, too. I hope he's finished with his shower already.

"Are you okay?" Brice is looking Bernard over as if she were his mother.

I feel lighter than I have in days. I'm so glad she's home. They care for each other better than anyone else can.

"I'm fine. It's Harrison you should be worried about."

I try to be offended when he lets out a chuckle, but I can't. He hears me laugh and looks my way with a wink.

Swinging his arm back, he acts out a punch. "I sucker-punched him right in the eye, and he had the good grace to not hit me back. Then he slept on that rickety, old couch for two nights. God knows why." He looks at me and shakes his head. "You're pouring your attention in the wrong place, little one. Now, if you don't mind, I'm going to get ready for my day." He heads back toward the bathroom.

Brice stands staring after him, her hands resting on her swollen belly, absently rubbing circles across it. Her hands are always there, cradling our baby. She finally looks back at me, a small smile on her face. "I guess he's all right… How about you?" She makes her way down the porch steps until she's standing in front of me, her bare feet joining mine in the damp grass.

I reach out for her, drawn by the magnetic pull she has over me. My hands slip into her messy curls, and I pull her to me, longing for the connection of mouth and tongue. Her lips part and she takes me in—the world brightening in the best possible way. I slip my hand down her body and rest it on her stomach. I feel something brush against it from the inside, and I pull my mouth from hers. "Did she? Did she just move?"

"You felt it?"

She's been trying to get me to feel it for weeks, but I never could. Every time I placed my hand on her belly, the movement stopped, and it's been driving her crazy.

She lets out a squeal and her hand covers mine. "Yay! I thought you would never feel her. I feel her all the time. I'm so glad you can feel it. Isn't she lovely? My little lovely." The love in her voice causes a ripple of goosebumps to cover my arms despite the warm morning sun on my back.

"It's amazing." There's nothing else to say. The movement inside of her—*our* daughter's movement—is the most amazing thing I've ever felt.

Her eyes hold mine for a lifetime, the wrinkle in her brow getting deeper with every moment. "Are you sure you're okay?" she asks, biting on her lower lip.

I bring my thumb up, rubbing it across her lip, extricating it from the grasp of her teeth.

"I'm sure. I missed you like crazy, though. How's Jayden?"

"I don't know. It's always so hard to tell with her. When we were kids, I could never get her to stop talking. Now it's like she hardly has anything to say. I've been trying to figure out what happened for ten years, but I still don't know. I don't even know what's happening to her now." Her lip is trapped by her teeth once again, her hand twisting the beads at her wrist. I wish she could let this go, but I know she never will. Jayden ran away from home when they were just sixteen. She took off to Seattle, and Brice didn't know where she was for two years. She still doesn't know why Jayden left and it drives her crazy. "Sometimes I think I should just let her go. She doesn't belong to me anymore. Maybe she never did."

"Why'd you leave so early? I wasn't expecting you home until later." I grab her hand, walking back toward our house.

"I went to the science center yesterday. It was really inspiring." She pauses as we reach the steps, tears in her eyes. "I don't know where she was. She left early, saying something about a work emergency. You know, she's so vague about her work; I don't even know what she does." Anger mingles with her words, warring for a place amongst the hurt. "When I woke at three this morning, restless for a paintbrush, I just left. I'm sure Jayden will understand. It's totally her style," she says with a sad little laugh.

"I'm sorry." I pull her hand up, grazing her knuckles with kisses. "Jayden's Jayden. I don't know if you'll ever know her secrets. It might be time to just let it go. Accept that you'll never know."

"I don't know if I can do that," she replies softly. "I missed you." Her eyes tell me the subject is closed.

27

THE TEACHER RETURNS

"Mr. Shelton, what a pleasure. When Mr. Wade asked if you could come in for an impromptu lesson, I agreed immediately. It'll be a real treat to have you lecturing in our halls again," Ms. Brand says as she walks us down to my classroom.

Her silver curls bounce with each step. The way she's fawning all over Bernard causes a smirk to take over my face, and no matter how much I try to contain it, I can't. He hasn't seemed this happy in years.

"Ms. Brand, I didn't realize you were still with the school. Do you think you'll ever retire?" Bernard asks her, surprising me with his bluntness.

"Oh, heavens, no. I married the job, Mr. Shelton. You wouldn't leave a spouse late in life, would you? This is my life, the journey I chose, and I plan to see it through all the way till the end."

I'm a little surprised and saddened by her reply. I keep hearing rumors from above that the school board has been considering a forced retirement. She just turned eighty-two.

"I respect that," Bernard replies, as we cross the threshold into my classroom. Ms. Brand stays on the other side of the door frame. She rarely steps foot into a class. It's as if there's an invisible barrier keeping her out. But she owns the halls.

"Would you like to sit in today?" The slight smile on Bernard's face tells me that he knows she won't accept.

"No, no. I have plenty to do to keep this place running. I leave the teaching to the teachers." She reaches her hand out to shake Bernard's and giggles like a schoolgirl when he brings her hand up, grazing her knuckles with a kiss.

"It's lovely to see you again, Betsy." He raises his hat briefly before turning in toward the room.

"Harry, you dog. You didn't tell me you were teaching in my old room."

Bernard walks in lazy circles around the classroom, hand on his chest, slowly shaking his head. He glances over at me, the smile on his face not matching the tears in his eyes. "I had a lot of good days in here." His voice is low, full of memories. "I know what she means—being married to the job. I mourned the loss of this place almost the same way I mourned for my broken marriage. If it hadn't been for Brice showing up. Needing me..." His thoughts trail off as he sits, shaking his head. "Well, I owe a lot to you. To both of you."

"Friendship isn't measured that way, Bernard. You owe us nothing. You've given so much already." I know he knows this already. He has to.

"Boy, what did I ever give you...besides a bruised head?" His laughter fills the room, just as the first students start to arrive.

He'll have six classes to talk to today. Six opportunities to spread knowledge and understanding about a disease that's grossly misportrayed in society today. I expect to hear a lot of things that will have me grinding my teeth. I hope his smooth words will break through the stigma that's been placed.

"Good afternoon."

Bernard stands at the front of the room, his hands clasped in front of his chest, a small smile on his face as he waits for them to give him their attention—and they will. I'm not sure how he does it, but I've never seen him start a lecture without everyone's eyes on him. He doesn't ask for it—not with words.

"Before I retired, everyone referred to me as Mr. Shelton. Today, you can just call me Bernard. Mr. Wade was generous enough to let me come talk with each of you today. I'm not here to talk to you about the greats in literature, nor will I be sharing my favorite poems. Today's lesson will be much different than the ones I previously taught in this room."

He walks to the desk, leaning his small frame against it, arms crossed in front of his chest. He wouldn't let me put a chair in the front of the room. He said you can't captivate an audience sitting down. Our eyes meet, and I hold back a chuckle when he winks at me.

He turns his attention back to the class and asks, "Do any of you know what diabetes is? Have you ever heard of it?"

He's started every lesson like this today, but no two have ended up the same.

"You there," he nods toward Erica in the front row.

Good choice. I know she'll lead the lesson in a positive direction.

"I believe it's something that happens when a person's body quits making insulin," she answers, sounding a bit unsure of herself.

"True, that's exactly what happens to cause it. Very good…" he pauses, waiting for her to supply her name.

"Erica." She smiles, a touch of color gracing her cheeks.

"Surprise, surprise. Erica knew the answer," Matt says, from behind her.

It's the weirdest thing. He's always such a good kid, but

lately he's been trying to razz her. I'm not really sure, but I think it might be love.

"And you are?" Bernard asks, failing miserably at his attempt to hide the grin from his face.

"Matt, sir," he answers, in the most respectful tone.

"Nice to meet you, son," he says, the tiniest hint of amusement in his voice. "You weren't trying to make this young lady feel bad, were you?" He pauses for a moment, and Matt shakes his strawberry blonde head, color creeping up his neck and across his cheeks. *Poor kid, he's about to get schooled.* "I didn't think so. I think maybe you're just strutting your tail feathers. Let me tell you, women don't like fancy feathers. They like things like kindness and respect. You show her both of those things, and you won't go wrong."

Bernard and Matt are both quiet, their eyes locked on one another for a long moment before the spell is broken, and he begins to speak again.

"Sorry, I'm old and my mind wanders." He lets out a little laugh, shaking his head before he regains his composure. "Let's get back on topic. Matt, do you know what causes the pancreas to quit making insulin?"

"I've heard it happens if you don't take care of yourself. You know, people who don't eat right and exercise get it. Right?"

There have only been two people that have known the correct answer to this question today. Both of the kids who knew had someone closely related to them who had the disease.

"You're only partially right. While poor diet and lack of exercise can cause a person to develop type 2 diabetes, even that's a hereditary disease—meaning the people who develop type 2 diabetes have a gene that makes them more likely to develop it at some point in their life. With *type 2* diabetes, in most cases, the pancreas still creates insulin, but with *type 1* it does not. Type 1 is an autoimmune disease. Which means the body's immune system turns on its own cells, seeing them as a threat. In the case of type 1 diabetes, the immune system attacks the beta cells in the pancreas that create the insulin."

Scott Williams surprises me, popping out of his chair in the back row. "My little brother just got diagnosed with juvenile diabetes—which one is that? It's so weird. He's such a tiny little dude. I don't know how he ended up with a fat-person disease."

"How long ago was he diagnosed?" Bernard asks, no judgement in his voice at all for the tactless words of the teenager.

"About a month or so ago, I guess." Scott slumps back in his chair. "Now my mom's all worried all the time. It's like it's the only thing happening at our house and it's happening twenty-four seven. I'm over it." His shoulders fall, his face slowly heating, and I feel sorry for the kid. Moments ago, I wanted to tear into him. I know firsthand how much the rest of life can feel like it takes a backseat to this disease.

"I understand that." Bernard hops up onto my desk, the only indication that the day is wearing on him.

I glance at the clock, glad to see only twenty minutes remain before the final bell rings. It's been a long, emotional day. But a good one. If even half these kids take what they learned home with them today, then today was a good day. Eyes were opened and important information was shared.

"I bet your brother does, too. The truth is, diabetes doesn't take a day off. There's no way to pick and choose when you pay attention to it. It's there constantly. Take a look at Mr. Wade for a moment." He pauses as the class collectively turns their attention to me for the first time today. Bernard stands quietly waiting for the whispers and gasps to die down before he continues.

"A few days ago, Mr. Wade came to my house to check on

me like he always does. He wasn't expecting what he got, though…"

My thoughts drift off as Bernard tells the story he has told so many times today, sprinkling in information throughout that will hopefully help save lives. I hope when Scott walks out of this classroom, he'll have a better understanding of everything his little brother goes through each day. That alone will make today worth it.

28

SOLID WORK

"Hand me that screwdriver, would you?"

Bernard's sitting in the rocker across from the big window, today's sun shining across his lap, making little particles of dust dance in front of his face. He seems tired today, his movements slow and heavy.

He glances down at the tool he's been holding in his hand since he sat down. "I *thought* you'd be needing this." He chuckles softly, a sad smile on his face. "I remember…I remember the day we put together sweet Leila's crib. She was already with us. We didn't worry about the crib before she was born. She slept in a little basket by the bed in the beginning. But it wasn't long before she was too big for it. They grow fast. You be sure to cherish every moment. Try to live in the moment. If I could tell my younger self anything, it would be this: to quit living in the past and the future all the damn time. You have to live in the moment. Yesterday will always be a day behind you, and tomorrow will always be a day ahead. Live for today. Live for right now."

His eyes meet mine, and I feel a chill run through my soul.

I don't think his words are meant for me, but I'd be a fool not to listen. His eyes are telling me that much.

He reaches forward, extending the tool out in front of him—the dust particles flipping and floating away. Laughter floats up the stairs from the party below, only aiding in the eeriness of the moment.

I take the tool from his hand, surprised when he grabs my wrist, holding it for a moment. "Thank you for always taking such good care of my girl. She's everything to me. Of course, I love all you kids, but that one…her home is right here," he says, patting his chest. "I don't worry about her anymore, though. I know she's loved and cared for." He lets out a big sigh, squeezing my wrist before he lets go. "I don't know what's gotten into me." He shakes his head. "Sentimental old fool," he finishes with a light laugh, sinking back into the shadows, the particles reappearing to continue their slow dance.

I turn back to the crib, only needing the tool to tighten the work I've started with my hands. The dark mahogany wood of the crib looks beautiful against the buttercream color of the walls. Brice didn't want pink; instead she's chosen a neutral shade, and she's accenting it with a beautiful ocean blue. She painted a picture of fish scales under a microscope, but instead of using the natural colors, she infused it with a hue of blues and purples—mermaid colors.

"That's solid work right there." The words are soft and end with a loud exhale of breath.

The chills from moments before return.

I set the driver down, slowly turning, my heart beginning to accelerate in my chest. Bernard i's slumped in the chair, his arm hanging slack over the side. Rushing over, I gather his limp body in my arms, laying him on the floor beside the crib.

"Mom! Brice!" I yell, hoping my voice carries through the celebration below. "Help!"

I feel for a pulse, but I can't find one. I don't know what happened. He was fine just moments ago. I feel for his sternum, carrying my fingers up. I place my hands above his heart and start compressions.

"What is it, baby? What's going on?"

My mom is the first one through the door frame, the rest of the women in my life appearing one by one behind her. Julie flips open her cell phone and begins speaking rapidly.

"He just... He's gone. He was just talking to me. Now... Now he's gone..."

I continue the compressions, vomit rising up my throat as I feel his bones crack violently beneath my hands.

"Stop!" Brice pushes her way through everyone, stumbling back when she comes into view. "You have to stop... He wouldn't want that... Stop!"

She falls to her knees, cradling his face in her hands. She takes a shaky breath, tears sliding freely from her eyes. Brice grabs my wrist, pulling my hands away.

"Please...stop," she whispers, and her words finally sink in.

She's right. I shouldn't have tried—but I *had* to try.

"I'm sorry." A foreign voice comes out of me. "I'm so sorry, he... I couldn't just let him go... How? How... How do we let him go?" I can't hold back the flood, and I wish more than anything that it was just the three of us in this room. I'm falling apart in front of all of them.

Julie snaps her phone closed. Her eyes hold mine for a moment before she turns to address all the baby-shower attendees. "The medics will be here shortly. Let's clear the room, so they can get in here." She turns back to Brice. "I'm right downstairs if you need me, baby," she whispers, before shooing the small crowd out of the room.

The door closes softly behind them.

"This isn't goodbye. I'll carry you with me always. I'll

never say goodbye." Brice leans down, her lips meeting his forehead. She sits back up, her eyes finding mine. "He's still here; he'll always be here."

She falls into me, and we hold each other, crying on the floor until the gurney pushes through the door.

She pulls in a shaky breath, addressing the first man to walk in. "He has a DNR. Harrison didn't know. He just signed it last week." Her voice is detached, floating in a sea of sadness.

I stand on legs that aren't my own, in a place I've never been before. I reach out my hand to Brice—she's the only thing keeping me in the room right now. Her presence, the only thing that feels solid…*real* to me.

She grabs my hand, and the effort to stand is almost too much for her. Her belly is so rounded, it's hard for her to get her balance. It takes me a moment to register this and reach out my other hand.

We stand together, silently watching as our best friend is loaded onto the gurney. His dark skin looks ashen, sunken in without life to animate it. I feel rooted to the spot, and yet as if I have floated a million miles away.

"We were just talking…" I'm surprised when the words slip out. I know that they have no meaning now.

Brice squeezes my hand tightly as the medics disappear with Bernard. She lets go when the last voice travels beyond us and we're truly alone once more.

"I don't know how to do this. I don't know how to let go of someone I only ever wanted to hold onto…" Her words dissolve into an ocean of sadness. It knocks us from the shore to float in its desolate waves of sorrow, begging us to dive down into the deep, dark trenches of grief.

29

HOW TO SAY GOODBYE

I CAN'T SEEM TO GET MY MOUTH AROUND THE WORDS. TODAY is the day we gather with friends to say goodbye. Brice wants me to speak—says I'm good at it. A bitter laugh wells up from deep inside, and it actually feels good to let it out.

"Harrison, is that you?"

I've been standing in front of my closet for too long now. I'm sure she's starting to get impatient.

I feel her walk into the room, her grief palpable. It mingles and swirls with mine until the air becomes a toxic thing that poisons my lungs. I take a deep breath of it, wanting to feel the putrid burn of sadness as it flows through my veins.

"Hey." She slides her hand down my arm, giving a gentle tug as she reaches my fingertips. "Come on, I'll find you something. Just…just let me take care of you." The last of her words come out in a rush, and I know it's all she can do to hold back the tears that have been a near constant for her for the last two days.

I feel her belly brush against my back as her hands smooth over my shoulders. "You always look stunning in that gray button-down, and I found the perfect tie. It'll match mine." Her voice sounds lighter, somehow, and I wonder what she's talking about. She certainly doesn't own any ties.

"What—" I turn to ask, pausing to take her in. She's wearing a simple, black, sleeveless dress, and around her neck she has a gray silk tie with tiny pink flamingos all over it. On her head rests a black fedora with one pink feather tucked into the gray silk band. "—are you wearing?" I finish, a sudden rush of laughter welling up and out of me. The sadness is still there, like a shadow standing behind us, but seeing her in his hat releases me from it for a moment.

She looks down at the floor before she answers. "I couldn't sleep last night. I didn't want today to be an ordinary funeral. He wasn't an ordinary man. Then, when I got up this morning, it came to me, and I knew… I knew what we had to do. So, I went out to his house—" her voice cracks, and I know how hard it must have been for her to go there and be in his presence without him, "—and, I picked out some hats for all of us. He wouldn't want them to be left sitting, gathering dust. It might sound silly, but I feel him more closely with this on my head." She lifts the hat, tipping it toward me for a moment before she rests it back in place.

"And the tie?" I don't remember ever seeing Bernard in a tie, even when he worked at the school.

"Turns out, he had just as many ties as hats. For some reason, I couldn't leave the flamingos behind. They went so well with the pink feather." She shrugs her shoulders, rubbing the tie between her fingers. "He was so full of life, you know? It didn't matter that he was eighty. I fully expected to have another ten years with him. Even when he tried telling me, I didn't want to listen. I couldn't… I couldn't… I just…." She shakes her head, curls falling from the confines of the hat and tumbling across her shoulders.

"I know, baby. I know." I wrap my arms around her, the hat falling from her head, as I bend down to kiss her. Our sadness mingles, coloring our kiss with dark hues of burnt ember and crimson. My hand travels down, resting on her belly where I find the only happiness in our world that has been tinged by sorrow. My daughter runs her tiny foot across my hand, reminding me that through everything, life must prevail.

"We'll do this together."

"It was a beautiful service."

I nod my head in agreement, a tight smile on my face. I've heard this same thing, or something like it, countless times already. It feels never-ending, and I want nothing more than to scoop my wife in my arms and carry her to the car.

"I'm so sorry for your loss," Ms. Shrimp says, solidifying the notion in my mind that I should do exactly that.

"Sorry, but we've gotta get out of here."

Brice turns at my words, abandoning the conversation she's having with Cassie. Before I can talk myself out of it, I slip an arm behind her knees, and the other across her back, sweeping her into my arms. "Let's go."

She rests her head against my chest, whispering for only me to hear. "Thank you. Cassie was keeping the line moving, but thank you for putting a stop to the endless torture. You're my knight in shining armor."

I press my key fob and place her on her feet beside the car. Her eyes are saucers, and the wrinkles between them a deep valley. "Was that rude? Do you think they'll think we're rude? Running off like two newlyweds instead of grieving family members? We're terrible." Her words are coming rapid fire, and I'm starting to wonder if the relief of leaving early is going to be shattered by her guilt.

"Hey." I run my thumb across her bottom lip, causing the valley to flatten and her words to still. "Let them think what they want, but I don't think they'll want to think bad of us. And if they do—fuck them. Every person in there is feeling pain from losing him, but not one of them as deeply or profoundly as *you*. Not even me. You want to know what the last thing we talked about was?"

I feel the back of my throat begin to close, and it's all I can do to swallow past it. I glance down at the black tie I'm wearing, this one with a single flamingo wearing a pair of black sunglasses. The absurdity of it makes me smile, and I feel him standing there with me in the moment.

"What did he say?" She traces my flamingo with her finger before she lays her head on my shoulder, her swollen abdomen resting against me.

"He thanked me for taking care of *you*—which is exactly what I'm doing." I tilt her face up to mine and kiss her gently. "He also told me that you live in his heart, but I already knew that."

Her tears fall silently, sliding into my hand, which is 'caressing her cheek. She pulls my face back to hers, surprising me with the intensity of her kiss.

"Thank you…for being there with him. And thank you… for loving me."

Her tears become silent sobs, and I quickly turn to open the door. I guide her into the seat and fasten the belt around her.

"I didn't have a choice." The words fall quietly from my soul as I close the door. The image of him slumped over in the chair is playing over and over again in my mind, as I walk around to my side. I knew—I felt it in the chills that covered my skin, heard it in the weakness of his words. I just wish I had listened. Paid better attention. I wish I had dropped the screwdriver and stood at his side. Instead of being a coward—turning my back to him.

30

AMELIA

She pauses from the book she's reading and glances up at me. "I've been thinking..."

This is how ninety-nine percent of her sentences start. She's a thinker. Her thoughts are often deep underground rivers—courses unknown—invisible to the naked eye. A tiny smile plays on her face, and the ropes that have bound my heart for the past two weeks loosen. Smiles are a rare thing these days. I still my hands, her foot warm between them, waiting expectantly to hear where her thoughts are taking her.

"I want to name her Amelia. Amelia Grace."

Unexpected. She's been set on the name Estella for months. I take the word and tumble it around in my mind for a moment before I try passing it through my lips. "Amelia... I like it. What made you change your mind?" My hands start their slow rub across the sole of her foot again as I wait for her response.

"Mmmm... Can I keep you forever?" Brice teases, her head leaning back against the sofa, causing *the* curl to spring from its holding place and flop into her line of sight. She grabs it, shoving it forcefully behind her ear.

It won't stay—never does. She hates it, absolutely *hates* that curl. She's declared all-out war on it more times than I can count...even threatening to cut it off every now and again.

"Well?" She gives me a pointed look, and I can't help but laugh as the curl slips free again, bouncing across her nose.

I love that curl.

"Shut up!" She laughs. "I know you love them, but they drive me crazy! Seriously, I should just go get the scissors." She huffs, making it bounce again. She pulls it out straight in front of her and turns her fingers into a pair of scissors, giving it an imaginary snip.

My laughter breaks free, and I feel life awaken within me once more. I can't stop; I glance at Brice, and her eyebrow has disappeared—lost beneath the mass of curls.

"Whew," I release before the chuckles consume me again. "Sorry—I. I don't know... I don't know what happened." I take a deep breath, my lungs sucking it in with greed. When I let it go, I feel some of the sadness that has been holding me let go, too.

"I love you," she says simply, relaxing back into the couch. "Now seriously, what do you think of Amelia? I've been reading a book about Amelia Earhart. She didn't think twice about the expectations of others. She knew what she wanted in life, and she worked hard to make it her reality. She was a champion amongst women, living in a man's world. She was inspired, brave, and confident. I want all of those things for our daughter. I want her to chase her dreams on feet that know the way. I don't know, it probably sounds silly... I just... I don't know... Say something!" She laughs, shaking the foot that's in my hand.

"I love it, and now that you've told me where it came from, I love it even more. Our Amelia Grace. I can't wait to hold her in my arms."

I place her foot in my lap and run my hand up her leg, stopping when I reach her belly. It's so swollen now. So full of life. Every little movement is visible from the outside. Two more weeks, and she'll be here with us. The thought fills me with a fear unlike any other. Two weeks until I'll be responsible for the care of another.

"I have an NST tomorrow. Doc says I need them three times a week now through the end. It's kind of nice, though, just sitting, listening to the sound of her heartbeat. And when I get the room at the end of the hall, I get to enjoy the magnificent afternoon light." She lets out a sigh, her hand tracing infinity symbols across her belly—something I've noticed she does when she's relaxed and lost in thought.

"I'll take the day off, go with you. We'll have lunch, maybe hit the baby section at Target before we go."

She's had so many appointments through the whole pregnancy and never complains about any of it. I should have gone to more, taken off more days—lived in the moment like Bernard said. This is my baby, too. I want to sit in the room and listen to her heartbeat. "I'll call Ms. Brand now."

"Really? Are you sure?" she asks, sliding her feet out of my lap so I can grab the phone.

"I'm sure. I want to be there. I want to do this."

31

NON-STRESS TEST

"Let's get it for her." The little pink flamingo is soft in my hands, and I can't explain my insane desire to purchase it. I want it so badly for her.

"We don't need it. We should be saving for things like diapers—ouch—" she pauses, hand at the top of her belly, "—that one hurt."

She sets the onesie she's holding in the cart and places her other hand beneath her belly. "Good thing that appointment's soon. This feels different." Her eyebrows scrunch, in worry, and pain.

She's been having Braxton Hicks for months now. She says for the most part, 'they're painless—like a muscle flexing and releasing. The doctor says they're harmless.

"Let's go. We can show up early." I toss the flamingo in the cart, heading toward the checkout. I slow down when I notice it's hard for her to keep up.

"Do you think she's coming?" she asks as she catches up. "I think she might be coming." An excited smile lights through her pain. She's never looked more beautiful.

I push the cart to the side of the aisle and go to her. "What can I do? Do you want me to carry you?"

She shakes her head, no, placing both hands at the top of her belly. "It shouldn't—"

Her eyes connect with mine, and the fear I see there makes my heart stop. She closes them, crouches down, and lets out a scream that turns my heart to stone. Her body goes slack, and I just catch her weight before she falls to the floor.

"It shouldn't hurt on top. It's never hurt on top before," she whispers, her voice full of pain.

"I'm calling for help." I flip open my phone, punching in the three numbers.

"911, what's your emergency?"

"It's my wife, Brice Wade. She's thirty-six weeks pregnant, a type 1 diabetic, and I think she's in labor. Oh, and we're at Target in the middle of the baby section—" I look for an aisle number, "—aisle 16, and I think something's wrong. She says it hurts on top."

"I'm dispatching an ambulance now, Mr. Wade. Help will be there soon. Try to remain calm."

I laugh at the notion—calm—*yeah right.*

Brice's grip tightens on my hand as she lets out another scream that causes my flesh to pebble. Cold sweat moistens my shirt, my heart racing beneath it. I hope the medics are fast.

"Oh dear! Looks like someone's decided today is the day!"

I look up, and there's a petite little woman with hair that can only be described as purple watching us. Maybe that's what happens when you try to do a deep-red over gray, I'm not sure, but I like her immediately. The fear coursing through me needs a distraction.

"What can I do to help?" she asks, clapping her hands.

I don't have a reply, and the seconds feel endless before she begins again. "Is that your cart?"

A direct question—*I've got this.*

"Yeah, but it's the least of my concerns at the moment." I chuckle, but it sounds more like a strangled cry. I take a deep breath, willing the fear away. Hope is what I need right now.

"I'll be right back," the little woman says. With a determined look of glee, she ditches her cart for ours and disappears from the aisle.

"What just happened?" I mumble, turning my attention back to Brice.

She's continually rubbing the top of her stomach. Her eyes are an emerald forest fire—fear alive and free in the depths of them.

"She'll be all right. They're coming. It won't be much longer." I throw a string of hollow promises her way, just to say something.

"Feel it… Something happened…"

She grabs my hand and rubs it across the top of her abdomen. I feel a large bump, as if her stomach has a goose egg.

"I don't know what happened." She's crying silently now, and all I can do is hold her hand. I know nothing, have no words, and it's taking every bit of me to hold onto the flame of hope inside. *Please, God.*

"Mr. and Mrs. Wade?" a man asks from behind me, causing the flame of hope to spark back to life.

"That's us," I say, leaving Brice's side so they can reach her. "There's something wrong," I state, lamely backing into the shelves.

I watch as they do a quick check of her vitals and load her onto the gurney.

"Just in time. Here you go, Dad," the woman with the purple hair says, having reappeared beside me. She thrusts a bag into my hand, just as they start to push Brice out of the aisle. "You'll do great. You've got this." She chuckles as I rush to catch up.

32

LIFE HAS ITS OWN PLAN

"Abruption."

I say it out loud, wondering if it sounds as powerful and terrifying on the outside as it does on the inside. The couple waiting across from me gives one another a terrified look. He places his hand protectively over her belly; hers meets his there, rubbing lovingly across it. I can't look away from their hands.

Brice is in surgery. What she was experiencing was an abruption, meaning her placenta tore away from her uterine wall.

Meaning Amelia was floating in a pool of water—without any air.

They said there's still hope, but it didn't live on their faces. I didn't hear it in their words.

"Mr. Wade, let's get you to Brice's room. She'll be out of surgery soon," the nurse says as she walks in. Her shoulders are slumped, and every time our eyes meet, she looks away. "The doctor will be in to speak to you soon," she finishes, turning to lead me down the hall. I feel my heart ripping, and I imagine the blood spraying from the torn ventricles as I pull myself from the chair.

I can't... I don't want to do this...

The walk down the hall seems to last forever—the eerie silence broken only by the sound of our footfalls as we make our way to the end. She finally stops. I notice a little picture above the room number. A small leaf floating on the surface of water with a single tear running across its dark green surface. It opens a cavern inside of me. I'm helpless to stop the tears as they begin their journey down my face.

"Is Brice going...is she...is she going to be okay?" I manage. I'm falling apart in front of this woman. I can't even bring myself to care. I can't lose Brice, too.

"She's all right, Mr. Wade. She's going to be fine." The false smile on her face as she squeezes my upper arm makes me want to shove her out of the room and slam the door.

"Harry!"

Julie bursts into the room. She's gripping her purse straps so hard her knuckles are white and her hands are shaking.

"What happened—" Her words are halted, her worst fears confirmed at the sight of me. She rushes to me, and I fall into her, the silent tears giving way to sobs as we share the heartache together.

She only lets me sob for a moment before she pulls away from me, takes a deep breath, and straightens her shoulders. "Okay, that's enough of that. They told me Brice would be out of surgery soon. We have to be strong... We have to be strong for our girl," she says, squeezing my hand.

I feel her shaking begin to subside, and I try to draw strength from her, to do the same. *She's right. I can't be a puddle when what Brice needs is a mountain.*

The nurse is standing, motionless, in front of us. "I-I-I'll go get—I'll go get the doctor," she stutters, before she takes off for the door.

"She must be new," Julie says, sending motion through my hand. "She didn't handle herself very well."

The simplicity of her statement causes me to forget, for a moment, the reason for my heartache.

Two hours ago, I was feeling my baby tickle my hand with her foot.

Two hours ago, I was going to be a dad.

"What did they say? What happened?"

I don't know how to answer her question.

Still connected, I lead her to the chairs against the wall, and we sit. I've been holding her hand for an eternity, and I don't know how to let it go. We sit like this for five minutes, or a hundred, until the silence is broken as two new nurses push a bed through the door.

Their heads are covered with surgical caps, and I wonder if the patterns lend to their personalities or if they were purchased on a whim. One has roses, the other flames. I glance down at the bed. As soon as my eyes lock onto Brice, I'm out of the chair, my connection with Julie broken as I step forward.

Her curls are a tangled halo around her head. Her eyes—closed. I run my fingers lightly down her arm, and they flutter open.

"Hey," she says so softly, I'm not sure it really made a sound at all.

"Hey," I croak back, the sound of my voice causing two deep crevasses to form between her brows.

I watch helplessly as her confusion shifts to panic. She pulls back the covers and begins grasping wildly at her stomach.

"Be careful, darlin', you're going to rip open your stitches if you keep that up," the nurse with the flames says, gently taking Brice's hands, moving them away from her stomach. "There, that's better," she finishes, as Brice's hands begin to still.

When she steps away, I grab Brice's hand, needing to feel the weight of it in my own.

"Where is she? Where's my baby?" Her words slice through the air, sharp and jagged.

Her eyes search the room, frantically, landing on Julie. "Mama, where's my baby?" she cries, her whole body beginning to shake from the force of her sobs.

Julie rushes to her, squeezing into the space at the head of the bed. She wraps her arms around Brice's upper body and begins rocking quietly back and forth. "Shh sh sh sh sh…"

The nurse with the tiny roses on her cap appears beside me. "The doctor will be right in." Her eyes are deep, sapphire pools—the sadness of the day living in their inky depths.

I can't make any words, so I nod my head in acknowledgment.

"I'm so sorry," she adds, breaking the dam inside of me.

They leave the room as Brice's obstetrician, Dr. Rowles, walks in. "Harrison," he says, nodding in acknowledgement, as he pulls a chair beside Brice's bed.

Julie sits up, but her arm is still protectively surrounding Brice.

"Where is she? Where's my baby?" Brice's voice is barely a whisper.

It's a question with an answer too horrible to hear, but it has to be asked, anyway. I'm thankful for her bravery. I couldn't form the words myself.

I sit on the edge of the bed and reach for her trembling hand.

"There's never an easy way to say this, but she didn't make it. We tried everything in our power. But she was without oxygen for too long. We couldn't revive her. I'm so sorry," he replies, rubbing his hands over his aged face. "I know this isn't something you want to even think about now, but there was no damage to your uterus. You should be able to carry a child again."

"I want to see her," Brice says, her shoulders shaking with quiet tears as she holds her head high—determination on her broken face.

"I'm not sure..." he trails off, looking to the door.

"Bring her in. Let us see her," I demand, the words coming out harsher than intended.

Dr. Rowles stands, his gaze connecting with mine for a long moment before he leaves the room.

Julie slips off the bed as the door closes. She wraps Brice's face in her hands, laying a tender kiss on her forehead. "I'll be right outside," she says, dropping her hands. She stands quietly for a moment before she follows the doctor out.

I can't form words.

I'm sorry seems like the worst possible thing to say. I let go of her hand and slide further up the bed so that I can hold her, but she motions me to stop.

"Please..." She shakes her head. "I can't... I can't feel you right now," she finishes, putting her face in her hands as her shoulders are wracked with silent sobs.

I sit, statue-still, as the emotions swell like a turbulent sea inside of me. I want nothing more than to wrap my arms around her, letting my tears mingle with hers. But Julie's right. She doesn't need the weight of my heartache smothering her own.

A light tap on the door releases me from my stillness, and I stand as Dr. Rowles walks in, a tiny pink bundle in his arms. His eyes are red-rimmed glassy balls. "I'll leave her with you for a few moments." He places the bundle in my arms.

My chest aches as I pull the blanket from her. Her petite face is blurred as I take in her delicate features. Her tiny heart mouth is parted slightly, as if breath could move through it at any moment, but her skin is colorless, and her chest is still.

I feel the edge of the bed behind me, sitting before I fall. I memorize her beauty—the rise of her button nose, the swell of her cheeks. And when I run my fingers over her silky fine curls, I lose my composure—a strangled sob breaking free. I pull her to me, allowing myself a moment of grief before I lay her in her mother's arms.

Today, the color has left my world.

I pace to the window, unable to watch as Brice has her moment with our daughter. I watch as drivers pull in and out of the busy hospital parking lot, each with their own set of worries and fears.

"I saw him." Her words are soft, riddled with heartache. "When I first got out of surgery. He was wearing his favorite hat, you know, the gray corduroy newsboy one?"

I nod my head in understanding, afraid that if I open my mouth she'll quit speaking.

"He was holding her, a huge grin on his face, her tiny hand clasping his dark finger tightly. He *took her*—" her voice shifts, and when her eyes finally meet mine, they're a wildfire of anger and sadness, "—*He took her*. She wasn't his—she was *mine*... She was supposed to be *mine*." The sobs overtake her as she pulls Amelia to her chest, rocking frantically back and forth. "She was mine...they *both* were supposed to be *mine*."

I don't care what she wants.

I'm on the bed in an instant, my arms wrapped tightly around them, my body rocking with the motion as our hearts bleed out across the floor. I imagine the pain seeping under the door and tainting the happiness of this place. There is no life here, only death and heartache.

33

HOW TO SURVIVE

"Are you all right?" I ask, walking into the living room where I've come to feel like a trespasser.

She's drawn an invisible line, and I'm not allowed to cross it. I'm not allowed to touch her—even with my eyes. If I do, she dissolves into fluid sadness. She's faded—gone. I'm worried. The house is too still, too quiet, and it's been this way for too fucking long.

I round the couch, standing silently, waiting for a reply.

She's bundled in the throw her mom knitted for her when she was first diagnosed. It's hideous. The bright shade of green is an assault to the eyes. She loves it, though. It brings her comfort, which means I love it, too. Sort of.

Her gaze turns toward me, but it doesn't connect—it's slightly to the right. The way she's staring so intently at nothing, I know—she's low. I see a bowl of oatmeal in her hand. *Has it been there since this morning?*

"Brice!"

The anger in my voice surprises us both, and her eyes connect with mine, the imminent tears beginning to swell.

"You need to eat!"

She shakes her head, causing the tears to spill over, leaving red streaks in their wake.

We've been home for weeks—six weeks to be exact. The amount of time it takes for an exterior wound from a c-section to heal.

But she isn't healing.

She isn't eating, and I'm getting really fucking tired of it. I feel rage building inside of me. *I can't take it anymore.*

"You know you need to eat, right? You know you will *FUCKING DIE* if you don't eat, right? What the fuck are we doing, Brice?"

I leave the room, not waiting for a reply. I know I won't get one. I never fucking get one.

I pull open the fridge and grab the jug of orange juice. I fill a glass, then pull a straw from the drawer. This is the routine. She's living on orange juice and I can't fucking deal with it anymore. I can't. I slam the drawer and pull the phone from its cradle.

"Jesse," I say as he comes on the line. "I need you to get over here. I have to leave before I explode." I slam the phone down, not waiting for a reply, and take the juice to the living room.

I grab the monitor from the coffee table. She reluctantly produces a finger. She's as familiar with the routine as I am. *Is she just as tired of it? Is she even in there at all?*

24.

Jesus, fuck, that's low.

The tremble from my hand makes it difficult to put the dark purple straw between her lips, the liquid threatening to spill in the process. She lets go of the oatmeal bowl, its contents so coagulated they hold firm to the sides as it spins to a stop on the floor. She jumps slightly at the sound before taking the straw between her fingers and guiding it to her mouth.

Her cheeks are sunken, her skin sallow—except for the dark circles that rim her eyes. Even her green irises have lost their sheen. As the cup slowly empties, I struggle to maintain my composure. *I need to get out of here.*

"Your brother's coming," I say casually, even though I'm feeling anything but.

I'm hoping for a reaction.

I *need* a reaction.

She hasn't let them come, not for weeks. In the beginning, when all she could do was cry, she'd let them come, hold her—cry with her. Now she doesn't want them here. Just like she doesn't want me here. I'm so fucking scared for the day I wake and she's gone. She's going to die. *I need a fucking reaction.*

"Here?"

"Yeah, Rice, here."

I rub my hands down my face, the exhaustion of the last few weeks settling in like an ache in a bone—constant, throbbing—to match the ache in my chest. Exhaling a sharp breath, I stand, hearing a quick rap on the door. It swings open before I reach it. Jesse steps in, slipping his work boots off beside it.

His gaze lands on Brice before I have a chance to say anything.

"What the fuck, Ford? You're supposed to be taking care of her." He brushes past me, his cheeks flushed a livid red.

I look at her, really look at her.

Her beautiful, chestnut curls are dingy and dark, slipping from the knot that began on top of her head. Now it's hanging loosely at the side, a solid, matted clump.

How many days has it been since she combed it?

She's lost so much weight; her bones are jutted out at sharp, angry angles. I'm failing her as much as she's failing me.

I have to get out of here.

I hang my head, trying to form a response. The life raft of

anger that slipped in to propel me out of the sea of sadness burns away and I'm left flailing in the turbulent waves.

With my last breath before I'm pulled under I say, "I called you here for help. Not a fucking guilt trip. I can manage that on my own. She needs to eat."

I grab my keys from the coffee table, scattering garbage in the process. *I don't care.* I walk out the door without another word. I have no idea where I'm going, but I have to get out if I'm ever going to breathe again.

34

MOM

"Knock, knock."

I open the door to the tiny apartment. I've been driving around aimlessly for an hour, finally giving in to the pull to see her. "Mom? You home?"

"Am I ever not home?" She laughs from her spot on the tattered, blue sofa. "Question is, how did I get lucky enough for a visit?" The edge of hurt in her voice makes my skin bristle.

Why did I even come?

Closing the door behind me, I step into the room. The dim glow from the table lamp is the only thing warming the bare walls. Haphazard stacks of books and magazines cover every flat surface.

She stands, trying to clear a seat on the sofa beside her. The voices from the television do nothing to fill the vast silence between us.

I step to her as she places the last stack of magazines on the floor. I feel an old ache in my chest as I wrap my arms around her. "Missed you, Mom." It's true. As hard as it is to be here—to see her as she is now—I've really missed her.

She pulls back from the hug, running her hand down the back of her head, trying to smooth her disheveled hair. "If I'd known you were coming, I would have pulled myself together."

"You know you're the most beautiful woman in the world, always," I tell her, happy to see the light ignite in her honey brown eyes. She's exquisite in her tattered sweatpants and wrinkled tee. You can't dress down a beauty like hers.

I never understood my father leaving. I used to imagine confronting him as a child. Tracking him down, knocking on his door—demanding answers. It played out differently every time. Often, with him crying and begging for forgiveness.

Occasionally, there were lightsabers and a great battle involved. But I never had the opportunity to ask in real life. I haven't seen him since I was four.

We sit down, and she grabs the remote, muting the TV. A young Anakin and Padme continue their conversation in silence.

She turns her attention to me, and I see the swell of emotion that's been in everyone's eyes since *that* day. She reaches over, grabbing my hand. "How are you, baby?"

I feel the tears well up, spilling over.

"I'm cracking up, Mom. I don't know if I can put the pieces together again. I feel like I can't breathe in that house."

I shake my head, angry at the voice inside me, whispering that I need to run away. It wakes me in the middle of the night, chanting, like the slow beat of a drum behind every thought. "She won't…she won't look at me. She won't talk to me. I can't fix that."

Mom takes a shaky breath, pulling her legs up beneath her. Her gaze is fixed on the couch beside my leg for a million years. When she finally looks back at me, her eyes are full—tears threatening to spill at any moment. "I really did you wrong, son."

I pounce to interrupt her, but she puts her hand up, shaking her head.

"This is something I should have shared with you long ago. I think you really need it now. It's taking everything in me to tell you this, so please—just let me get it out." She squeezes my wrist, and I nod my head, vowing to hold my tongue if it means the mystery that is my mother will be revealed.

"I never told you about your brother."

"Brother?" My vow is broken instantly as I try to sort the tangle of thoughts that bombard me at the sentence she whispered so softly. "I don't understand…"

I'm helpless for anything else to say. I do the only thing I can. I sit back into the sofa, wrap my fingers through hers, and wait for her to save me from this sea of questions.

"Irish twins." The soft, sad smile she gives breaks open my heart. "Do you know what those are? Have you heard that term before?" she questions, waiting for a response.

I sift through my muddied mind, trying to supply her with one. "Close pregnancies? Back to back?"

"That's right. You always were so smart," she says in the way only a mother can, patting my hand with her free one. "It was only a few months after you were born that I found out I was pregnant again. I was a soggy mess for almost a week. In that week, I mourned what I thought I would be missing out on in your childhood because of it." She shakes her head, growling at herself. "I felt so much guilt over that week—after—"

She buries her face in her hands and begins to sob.

"Mom, you don't have to—"

"Yes, I do. I need to do this, Harrison. I do. We both need this. When you were little, after your father left, I could stuff it down inside. Ignore it. Because I had you. But that hasn't worked in a long time." Her voice comes out strong despite her breakdown.

We sit quietly for a moment, and I feel her energy flow through me where our hands are clasped. I think about Amelia—how hard it's been to lose her. How hard it is to talk about it with anyone. I look at my mom, wondering how I ever could have missed the veil of sadness she wears like a second skin.

"He would have been named Mark. Original, I know," she chuckles. "I was so hung up on *Star Wars*." Her eyes land on the screen in front of us, her cheeks coloring. "I guess *was* isn't the correct term. Oh, how it must look to you…" She gives my hand a squeeze. "I honestly do other things. I read…" She drops my hand, waving hers about the cluttered room.

I try to process everything she's telling me. Try to fit this other boy into the memories of my childhood.

"I know, Ma," I answer absently, my focus lost in the tidal wave of thoughts all around me. *Phantom people—empty spaces.*

"I shut down completely after—holding him in my arms, looking at that little face that would never be. I saw it every time I closed my eyes, every time I looked at your father. You've always resembled me more than him, but Mark would have been the opposite. So, I began building walls…until I had walled him out completely. There was no room for him. And the pain—I chose the pain. It may have been different, if he had pushed me more. If he'd taken a sledgehammer to those walls, fought his way in."

She pauses, and I think about what she's saying and the life I'm living. *She's right.* Brice and I are both doing our part in sabotaging our love for one another by making the pain bigger—by feeding it daily, letting it grow.

"So, what do I do?"

"You fight your way in. Break her open. Show her your pain. Don't hide it from her. Rescue her from the pit of despair she's trapped in."

35

SLEDGEHAMMER

I PULL INTO THE ROCKY DRIVEWAY AND LET MY TRUCK IDLE. I don't know what I'm going to find when I go in, or how I'm going to break through it. But I know I owe it to us to try.

I close my eyes and see her as she was—lying naked in front of the fire the night of our wedding—so much life in her eyes.

I want that girl.

She's mine, and it's time to break her free.

I turn off the engine and slide out of the truck. Wearing my resolve like armor, I make my way to the house. I *will* break through. Because if I don't, she's going to die.

I slide my key in the lock, walking in the front door. The house is quiet and clean. I stand, motionless, as my eyes make their journey through it, landing on Cassie where she sits in the armchair by the fire, a book laid open on her lap.

"Cassie?" I'm surprised to find her instead of Jesse.

She gives me a knowing smile, and I feel as if she's processing my thoughts like they're her own.

"He couldn't hack it either, had to call in the big guns." She pauses in her speech, flexing her arm. "What the fuck,

Harrison? If you can't do it, let us in. We're all just chomping at the bit to help, to share the heartache, you know? We see her crumbling. Truth is, you don't look much better, my friend."

I sit in the chair across from her. "Where is she? Did you get her to eat?"

"Jesse managed a piece of peanut butter toast before I got here. When he left, I gave her a shower...scrubbed her nasty ass hair." She shoots me a look. "You vowed to be here for her, Harry. She looked like she should be living on the streets, and this house was a fucking disaster." She holds my stare for a long moment before she stands, closing the book together.

I watch in silence as she makes her way to the door, sliding her feet into her crocs. She opens it, turning back before she steps out. "You have to remind her that she's important, too."

A nod is all I manage, and it earns me a sad smile before the door closes behind her.

I rake my hands through my hair. It's amazing how much lighter the house feels without the clutter and mess weighing it down. We brought sadness home from the hospital. There was no space left for trivial things like responsibility. It spread like a virus until it owned everything. It's time to take something back. It's time to swing the hammer. I just hope the walls aren't made of rubber.

Her back is to me when I walk in the bedroom door, but I know she's awake. I see it in the stiffening of her shoulders.

The moonlight shining through the thin curtains is the only light in the room. It's enough so I don't flip the switch as I walk in. I undress in silence, sliding into the clean sheets beside her. She takes a sharp breath as I wrap my body around hers. She tries to pull away; I fold myself closer.

"I'm not letting you go, Rice. I can't. Part of me wishes I

could." I'm surprised by the words as they leave my mouth. I don't want to hurt her more, but I owe her the truth.

Her silence ushers me forward.

"She would have been the center of our world. She would have been the sun, and we would have rotated around her, basking in the glow of her light. But she's not—she can't be. If she stays the center, our world will crumble around her, and we'll be sucked into the black hole she's become." I hold my breath, icy fear pricking my skin as her silent sobs wrack my body.

"I close my eyes and I see her. I want her with an ache that's larger than life," she whispers, her words so quiet, the night sounds threaten to steal them before I can make them out.

"I can't lose you, Rice. You have to let me in. You aren't alone. I want her too." I feel my words vibrate against her back. *I hope I'm not doing more damage.* "Yesterday, when I went to the store, I saw a little girl with her dad. She couldn't have been more than two or three. Her giggle rang out across the parking lot, piercing through me, shattering me. I sat in my truck and cried for her. I wanted so badly to be that man. To hear the delight in her giggle and not feel it slay me." Sharing the words returns me to the spot. I'm helpless to stop the flood of emotion that lives right behind my every thought.

I hold her, imagining my silent tears falling across her body, mingling with hers. I take in the scent of her, run my fingers up her bare arm, and lose myself in her. I pepper kisses across her shoulder up to her ear.

"We lost her, but we can find each other."

She shifts beneath me, lying flat on the bed. She pulls my mouth to hers, our lips coming together for the first time in weeks. The tears continue as the sadness flows through us, mingling in the places where we touch.

We abandon words, our souls communicating in the most primitive way.

The bed is empty when I wake. The house is silent, except for the occasional call of the songbirds outside. I grab a pair of sweats from the drawer and go in search of her. Opening the door, I hear soft music coming from her small studio at the end of the hall. Kelly Clarkson's voice rings out from the speakers as I cross the entry.

Brice is lost to everything, except the painting before her. Her microscope remains covered. *What's her inspiration?*

The hues of deep purple and indigo swirl on the canvas with a trace of light coming from some unknown source. I'm not sure how she makes the colors appear like something you could be standing in, but she does. Every painting—every time.

"What is it?"

My question startles her—the brush freezing before the canvas. She stares, lost in thought for a moment before she answers.

"Sadness, I guess, or what it feels like to *me*. I imagine those traces of white scattered about—that's you. You always shine like a beacon for me, lighting my way through the darkest night. Thank you for finding me in the darkness..." Her words trail off as her brush connects with the canvas again.

I back out of the room. Hope blooms inside me as I make my way down the stairs to start a pot of coffee. I know this is just the beginning. We have a long road to walk. I just put on a fresh pair of boots, and I'm ready for the journey. Wherever it takes us.

PART 3

2015 - BRICE

36

PAST TIME

"Mama, when can we go in the tiny house?"

Charlie waits patiently for an answer. Even though he's just four years old, I know he knows the answer already. But he's just stubborn enough to ask anyway. We go through this every time we're playing in the yard.

I look over at the little home—dark and dreary. Unused. Unloved.

Harrison takes care of it. It isn't in shambles by any means. It just has a big, gray thundercloud hanging in the cloudless sky above it. The smooth layer I've laid over the old wound shifts, feeling brand new again.

"Why do you ask? Always? You already know the answer." I look into the most precious eyes I've ever seen and smile as he weighs my question.

The dimple on his cheek is leaping from side to side as he moves his mouth this way and that. I reach for my phone, wanting to capture the moment.

It's over before I get it turned on. *Figures*. I rarely catch them in time.

"One day it'll be different. One day you'll be ready. Then

we'll get to go in. I bet it's so cool. Daddy says it has everything a big house has!"

"You'd go with me? Hold my hand?"

I feel my heart begin to accelerate. *I'm losing to a dimple.* If it hadn't been doing such an irresistible little dance, I wouldn't even be contemplating it. This boy has evil powers of persuasion. *I hope he never finds out.*

"Yes!!" He runs around me in fast circles. "Oh yeah! Oh yeah!"

Coming to the spot in front of me, he holds his hand out to help me up. His dark chocolate curls are as wild as mine, and his eyes—the same golden honey color as his dad's. He's a perfect blend. Parts borrowed from each to make a unique new whole.

I try to get my feet beneath me and push with just one hand, the weight of my front making it hard to balance. Laughter bubbles out of me as I tumble back to my bottom. Charlie's giggles dance with my own, his hands in front of his mouth, body bent at the waist, dissolving into pure delight.

"I think we may have to try a different way, Captain." Standing on my knees, I brace my weight on my hands in front of me. Planting my feet on the ground, I push off. I laugh again as I find my balance. "Whew, that was hard work."

"You did it! Can we really go in now?" His eyes are pleading, the delight from moments before nowhere to be seen as he holds his breath, waiting for my reply.

I think about the house, how long it's been since I spent time there. Ten years. Ten long years of ignoring the elephant that's sitting in my backyard. So much wasted space.

I've been hiding from ghosts that have haunted me for way too long.

"If I have the brave Captain to lead the way, I think I might just be able to do it. *If* we can find the key. Do you know where Daddy keeps it?"

I know exactly where the key is hanging. It's been taunting me from its spot on the hook for too long now. *I can do this.*

"It's in the kitchen." His left eyebrow reaches maximum height, the Garrison genes fully present in my little boy. I'm overwhelmed with the urge to bend down and wrap him in my arms. The effort it took to stand up is the only thing holding me back.

I lace my fingers through his. "You know what?"

"You love me," he replies with a dramatic sigh, and I chide myself for saying it so often. "Now come on! Let's do this."

The frantic beat of my heart is reverberating back to me like a drum in an empty room. My palms are sweaty as I slide the key into the lock. On the outside, I'm calm and collected... that's what I tell myself. A quick glance at Charlie puts that lie to rest. I stumble, momentarily, to find another one. He only looks worried because the world on the other side of the door is unknown to him. Sure, that's it. *It has nothing to do with me.*

I straighten my shoulders, take a deep breath, and turn the key.

You can do this.

Plastering on my brightest smile, I give the door a little push. It takes my eyes a moment to adjust to the dark room. I step in from the sunny porch, my hand grasping wildly for the switch beside the door.

"Wow!" The honey in his eyes sparkles as the light from above rains down on us.

It's different.

Everything is different here.

The classic cream walls have been replaced with a fresh, spring green. The long bookshelf that lined the back wall has been halved, its pieces used to build a work table. In the center of the room is a large black rubber mat, with an easel sitting on top.

Charlie erupts into delightful giggles as he comes to a stop in front of the large painting on the wall above the work table. "Look Mama, they're so happy."

He points up into the center of my very first painting from all those years ago. I had forgotten all about it and the happy little water ducts living inside each blade of grass.

"They are, aren't they?"

Peace washes over me as I stand, enjoying the wonder of nature, the beauty in the little things. Somewhere along the way, I'd forgotten that. The world inside of me had become so large, it was the only thing I could see.

I pull the chair out from the desk, slowly lowering my tired body into it. The lazy circles I trace across my belly are met with a flutter of movement from inside.

She's mine. I'll have her.

"They are! They really are!" He runs circles around the easel with the kind of joy known only to children.

He stops in front of me, his mind a combustible engine. "What is this place? Is this *your* place? For painting? Why don't you paint in here? Can we? Can we paint in here?"

I had begun setting up a small paint station for him with watercolors when I was working. It usually lasts roughly seven minutes before he's ready for the next adventure.

I don't know which question to answer first; they're fired in such rapid succession.

When did he do all this? Was it the first year? The second?

The emotions begin to drag me down as my thoughts swirl around how I continued to let him down, day after day, year after year. His love and hard work sat here, unseen. *Unused.*

Charlie's eyes never leave mine as I continue to weigh his questions. "Hey, don't forget to breathe," I tell him as his cheeks begin to color.

He pulls in a sharp breath followed by a stream of words. "Please, Mom, please? Can we—can we please?"

I reach my hand out, and he helps pull me from the chair. The heavy drapes that are covering the windows will have to go—I need natural light.

I reach the first one, pulling the cord to open it. The May sky greets me with its pristine beauty. My heart catches in my throat as I see Harrison open his truck door. He slides out, reaching back in to grab his bounty.

"Daddy's home! Do you think he'll see us?" Charlie asks, waving frantically from beside me.

"If you use your Jedi powers, he will."

I smile as he stills instantly, a look of pure concentration taking over his face.

Come on, Harrison, look over here.

My pent-up breath leaves me as Harrison turns toward us. Confusion flashes on his face, but he's quick to recover with an easy smile. The echoed drumbeat of my heart begins its staccato rhythm, deafening me to the rest of the world.

"Hi, guys. Is there anyone in here who likes tacos?" Harrison questions, pushing open the door.

The delectable aroma of authentic pork tacos tantalizes my senses, and every other thought leaves me. *I need those tacos.*

"I love tacos!" Charlie yells, jumping up and down.

Does his love for them stem from the fact that I ate them nearly every day of my pregnancy with him? There could never be enough tacos.

Harrison's golden eyes land on mine, and he holds me captive for a moment. My cheeks flush as a satisfied grin causes the deep dimples to grace his face with their presence. *The dimples get me every time.* I hope *she* doesn't have dimples. I shut down the thought as soon as I have it. She's not mine yet. Nothing in life is guaranteed. Reassuring me from the inside, I feel her move—*I'm here. I'm yours. I exist.*

I make my way across the room. The scent of fresh cut wood—his smell—finds its way through the succulent taco haze. I never understood how he could smell like that, day after day, whether he's been working with his favorite medium or not. Tree sap lives in his veins. I run my nose up his neck, drinking him in. My lips find his, and I lose myself to home for a moment.

"Eeeew gross!" Charlie makes gagging sounds behind me, and I pull away from his dad.

We share a knowing smile before I make my move. I feel the weight of the plastic handle, pulling it from him, my insulin the only thing stopping me from eating right here on the floor of this little house, but I know I have to wait. There are steps—a routine. Compliance at all costs, a must.

The screen door slams behind me. Moments later, the damp grass tickles my feet. Their laughter dances in my ears as I near the back porch of our home.

37

WHISPERS IN THE DARK

"I'm proud of you."

Faint butterfly kisses tickle my shoulder, and I feel the same winged creatures take flight in my belly. Twenty years of loving this man and he still affects me with every touch.

"Oh yeah, why's that?" I let out on a sigh.

His hand slips over my side, rubbing slowly across my lower abdomen. Settling there, his fingers lightly caress her movements, the weight of her coming to rest against him. He always calms her. Him behind me like this feels just as necessary as the enormous body pillow, cradling me from the front.

A stillness fills the air. For a moment, I think he's fallen asleep.

"For turning the key, for stepping inside."

I snuggle in closer, filling every space, so I'm completely cocooned. I let his statement linger.

"Me, too," I whisper. "I'm sorry it took so long. When did you set it up for me?" I hold my breath, afraid for the answer.

"When you were pregnant with Charlie." He lets out a strange laugh. "For some reason, I thought having him would just sort of erase all of that pain—move us through it. Like holding him would put us on the other side."

I can't respond, thinking about how awful I was after Charlie. Postpartum depression is what they called it. *I knew better.* It was grief. Holding him, breathing him in—it made the loss of her feel even more cavernous.

"Hey, I'm not trying to talk about the things that didn't happen. I was talking about what did." I hear an ancient fatigue in his voice, warning me not to slip down the rabbit hole that is our past. "Today, you were a badass, and I'm proud of you. That was all I was trying to say."

My mind is a sticky web of self-torment—one wrong step and I could be lost for days. I take a shaky breath. He deserves this. So do I. "I want to move my studio out there." The words come out in a rush, an invisible monster close on their heels, threatening to gobble them up before they can escape.

The bed dips as he sits up. "Really? Do you think you should wait until after?"

His words are left hanging. *After*—a place of dark waters both of us are afraid to enter.

"I think I've waited long enough. It's time to tell my old friend goodbye. It's time to honor him and all the words he left behind. You didn't get rid of any of that, did you?"

"Of course not. Everything's stored in the bedroom. I'll take the day off tomorrow and help you go through it." He settles back in.

The idea of freedom from the ghosts of my past lulls me to sleep.

The weight of the small, pink bundle is simultaneously as heavy as the earth and as light as the sky. The world around me

—white. I'm not sure if I've been here for a year, or twenty. I don't know how I know to keep walking, I just do.

My feet still as I bear witness to a spinning leaf fall from above. I laugh, and it echoes back to me, causing a flurry of leaves to follow the first.

I don't know how I know my laugh is the catalyst for the cascade of green filling this white space, but it is. The appearance of color lightens my step, and I start walking once again.

The soft sound of water over rocks fills my ears, and I start to hum. *I don't hum. When do I ever hum?* As confused as I am by it, I can't seem to stop, so I relax into it, finding that the melody twists beautifully through the sound of the water. The temperature cools, and I know I'm almost there.

I reach the water's edge. It's clear like that in a bathtub, uncontaminated by the white ground below, with smooth, glass rocks visible beneath—but just barely. I close my eyes, wondering for the first time about the absence of the sun. Thinking of it—I feel its presence on my back, warming me from above. Opening my eyes, I smile at the shadow that now cuts across the water before me. *Some things should just be.*

The weight of the bundle in my arms becomes too much for me, and I know she belongs in the clear water—it's why my journey brought me here. I bring my arms down, pulling the blanket from her face. Her little rosebud mouth, suspended in animation before me, causes a cascade of emotion to fill this pristine place. Such a perfect, little mouth. I take great care placing her into the water, pleased to feel that it's warm to the touch.

The movement of the water slows. I gasp in wonder as color begins to bleed from the blanket below her. The clear water shimmers with shades of lavender and blue, silver lacing its way between them. My eyes are drawn to the silver ribbon as it coils and moves, creating the most beautiful pattern. I glance back to the blanket just as she sinks below the surface.

Everything stills. *It must be finished.*

I stand, preparing to leave this place, but movement on the water catches my eye. I lean forward just as the surface breaks and hundreds of colorful butterflies paint the sky.

She's home now.

I open my eyes to darkness and the sound of Harrison's even breaths beside me. Squinting, I can just make out the numbers on the clock—1:37. The middle of the night.

I need to paint.

It's been weeks since I took a brush to canvas, all desire missing. I slide Harrison's arm off of me, pushing my pillow to the floor. With a grace that can only be obtained by a woman in her third trimester, I push myself out of the bed, holding my breath as I watch him roll to the other side, snuggling in. *That was close.*

Making my way down the hall, I stop at the first door beside ours. The night light casts a soft glow from inside. My sweet baby boy is fast asleep, his little, blue elephant held tight to his chest—the soft satin of its blanket grasped between chubby fingers. I feel an ache that only love can bring, and I thank God for letting courage find me when I thought sorrow was my only friend. I back out of the room and continue to my studio.

I flip on the light, happy to see a blank canvas already on the easel. Slipping in my earbuds, I scroll through my playlist, seeking "Disturbed." It's just what I need. I've been obsessed with this song for weeks. As "The Sound of Silence" fills me, I load my palette with purple, blue, and silver. Then I dip my brush into the paint.

Placing the first stroke on the canvas, I let the emotion and vision of what I just went through slip from the brush's tip, and, like magic, the water from the dream reappears before me. Once the blues and purples are in place, I take my finest brush and dip it into the metallic paint. The ribbons of silver dance from the bristles, taking on the appearance of lace over water. I feel a single tear slip from my eye.

Goodbye.

38

TRIP TO THE PAST

THE OIL SIZZLES AND POPS AS I PLACE THE NEXT BATCH INTO the hot pan. How long will it be before the tantalizing scent reaches them in their own private dreams?

Thirty-six weeks pregnant, and I feel as light as a feather. I grab a piece from the plate, unable to resist any longer. The taste explosion pushes me over the edge. I moan. As the sound leaves me, I feel his breath across my bare neck. His lips taste the skin there, and I moan again.

"You're so fucking sexy when you eat bacon," he whispers. Reaching around, he steals a piece from the plate. "How did I get lucky enough for this kind of treat?" Harrison asks, grabbing the coffee pot to fill the cup I set out for him.

"I had the weirdest dream," I say, laughing at myself. I say this about as often as most people say "good morning."

"And?"

"And it was good. I feel really good." I let the words settle for a moment. Their simple truth washes over me as I scoop the last of the bacon from the skillet. *I. Feel. Good.*

I drain most of the grease from the pan, then grab the colorful array of veggies waiting on the cutting board. The sweet peppers' fragrance freshens the air as they begin to warm with the mushrooms.

"I called and talked to Jim." He pauses to sip from his cup, letting out a soft sigh as he swallows. "I'm yours for the day."

Jim Reynolds took over when Ms. Brand passed a few years ago. She'd been dodging retirement for years, somehow charming her way out of just one more year each time the board met to discuss it. Harrison had been happy that she passed before they managed to get her out. He said it was how she wanted it.

"Perfect, because I called your mom, and she said she'd love to spend the day with Charlie."

"Grandma Steph?" Charlie walks in, rubbing the sleep from his eyes. His hair's a nest of wild curls. "Do I really get to spend the day with Grandma Steph?" His excitement is tangible as he pulls his chair out at the table. "Did you make us breakfast, too? Is it a holiday?"

Questions are never-ending when you're four.

"It's not a holiday, Captain, but the rest is true."

His obsession with all things nautical earned him the nickname when he was just two. I've always sort of loathed nicknames. Until him. I used several when he was a baby, but Captain is the one that stuck. He loves it.

"Where do you want to start?"

Harrison flips on the light to the small bedroom, and I take a step back. I wasn't anticipating so much. I knew Bernard wrote regularly, but I wasn't expecting *this*.

"I organized it a few years ago, so the journals are boxed by decade. The stories have their own boxes, there." He points to the far corner where there are two boxes separated from the rest.

"How did you…" I trail off as I walk into the room, dumbfounded by the amount of work my husband poured into this.

"Bernard was one of the building blocks of my foundation. I looked up to him. I loved him. I chose my career because I wanted to be like him. This is what I needed to do to deal with his loss. Honestly, I felt like I understood him better, *knew* him better, *after* he died than I ever did in life. His journals and philosophies on life helped me through those rough years. I'm not sure we would be where we are now without him."

"I'll start with the 90's," I say, running my hand over the box marked 2000's. I'm not ready for that yet.

"Not every box is full, and honestly, I haven't read them all. I boxed the 60's, 70's, and 80's together. I tried to read those a few years back, but it's all very dark and personal. It didn't feel right to read them."

Our eyes meet and the history we share is exchanged in this moment. He breaks the contact, grabbing the box labeled *90's*. He walks it to the small sofa that's taking up the back wall, setting it in front of the familiar relic.

The rough material scratches the back of my legs, sending my mind to earlier days, to conversations that long ago became whispers in the wind—faint words trickling through the haze of time. It brings back the hurt of losing Bernard that I had buried beneath the loss of Amelia.

Last night's dream felt like a release from all of that pain, and I know I need to do that here, as well. It's time to reconnect with my old friend.

Harrison crouches down in front of where I'm sitting, taking my face in between his hands. The years pass between us in silence, and I sense that he's about to leave me here, alone, in this room full of memories.

"Stay with me," I whisper, the words barely audible.

He's quiet, and I catch the quick glance he takes to my

belly, having the same thought I'm wrestling with. *Will she be okay?* Will the penalty for my emotion be more crushing pain?

"Maybe we shouldn't do this," I toss into the room, much louder than anticipated.

His fingers slide through mine and I *feel* his calm. I close my eyes, trying to let it wash over me.

"You need this, Brice, and if you want me by your side, then that's the only place I'm going to be. She'll be okay. You both will." His last words come out in a whisper—a promise he doesn't hold the power to make, but I snatch it up anyway, needing to believe in his words.

The cushion sinks with the weight of him as he takes the seat beside me. I'm envious of the length of his shorts, wishing I had chosen something other than the summer dress I'm wearing. Lately, dresses are the only things that're really comfortable. I laugh, surprising us both.

"Care to share your joke with the class, Mrs. Wade?" Harrison says, in his steel-wool voice, making me laugh again as the rumble of his timbre washes over me.

"I was just thinking about this dress, and how it's the only thing comfortable to wear now. I wish it was a little longer, so this rough, old couch wasn't scratching the backs of my legs. Then the irony of thinking that anything at all is comfortable, when I could be my own continent… But my skin is still mini sized and…. Well, you get the picture." I let out a sigh, trying to find a comfortable spot in a body that's anything but.

"You just have to embrace it." He stands up, his hands moving to the button on his shorts. I laugh again as he releases it, his shorts falling to the floor. "Really *feel* the texture and put yourself back there. It's all part of the experience. The first time I read his journals, I was totally naked. Fully immersed," he deadpans, scooting back and forth on the cushion, burrowing in.

"I wondered where that rash came from," I reply, my tone

matching his in seriousness. I love us and our ability to be totally ridiculous together.

"All right, 1990s, here we come," he says, rubbing his hands together in front of him before he pulls the lid off the box.

I've been reading for hours, but I've finally reached it. *Me.* I knew I'd find myself here, in these pages, but I wasn't exactly sure *when*. Would it be that first time I met him when my brother was carrying me to the car? Or that dinner party when our lives first became entwined?

Turns out, it was neither.

Jesse came over today to borrow some books and talk about life. His little sister was just diagnosed. It's breaking his heart. He's such a caring kid. He was surprised to hear that I have it too.

I think it's funny when people react that way. I don't know how many times I've heard, "I thought only kids get that." Like the result of being a kid isn't growing into an adult. Like all kids with diabetes have Peter Pan syndrome. It's funny how our minds work. He did better than most, though—knew more. I'll give him that.

I glance over at Harrison who's lost in the past with me.

"I found myself." The words sound funny in the room that's been quiet for so long.

"You're the main topic of discussion for the next ten years, babe. The main character of his ever-changing story," he replies, not looking up from the words on his page. He chose the 50's. Apparently, Bernard was pretty wild in his twenties.

I turn my attention back to the spiral notebook that's resting on the shelf that is my belly and lose myself in the memories of those first years. Some of the words leap from the page to be stored in my heart forever.

She showed up like a salve for a wound that had been seeping for years. All other treatments haven't touched it, but she's miraculously doing the trick. Thoughts of Leila don't hurt anymore. I didn't think that was possible after feeling the pain for so long. Who knew what this old man needed was the friendship of an odd little sprite?

She was angry today. Injustice is the gasoline that always seems to make her fire burn bright. But like anything fueled to burn, it quickly faded to ashes. I can always see the mark it leaves behind, though. It sits in the drop of her shoulders that are already so burdened by the weight of this life.

She made me a painting. It's the most impressive thing I've ever seen. I didn't know what it was at first, but when she told me that they had looked at grass under the microscope in her bio class, and those happy little faces are actually the water ducts that live inside each single blade...

I feel like cupid for two little lovebirds.
    Harrison came by today. He's almost done with his first semester at Central. I'm so proud of him. He was always my favorite student. He gave me a letter for Brice. She's going to be over the moon. My days were so gray before these two colored it with their love for one another.

Jayden ran away. Brice's heartbroken, and I can't seem to find a way to make it better. Truth is, my heart's in pieces too. Something must have been really terrible to cause her to go—without a word to her best friend. I pray night and day that she's all right.

She's lost all color. Every now and then I see a glimpse of it behind the shadows in her eyes, but I fear that I'll never see it fully return.

Gloria passed last night. A low in her sleep. It's what I fear every morning. I'm glad Brice always stops by on her way to school. Sometimes, I think she knows I need it. We've talked about it a few times—the nighttime lows. She says she always wakes up, heart thumping, in a cold sweat—how could anyone sleep through that? She laughed like my worry was ridiculous, but I saw the flash of fear in her eyes.

Brice's bracelet broke yesterday; green beads flew across the floor. We tried to find them all. I could tell by the way her eyes continued searching after we had given up, that some were lost. When she came over this afternoon, it was back on her wrist, only different. The lost beads had been replaced with black ones.

Medicare denied my insulin today. I've been on the phone all day trying to get it straightened out. I'm glad I always fill before I'm out. At least it will give me a few days. I hope those assholes don't make me jump through a thousand hoops to get it. I'm so tired of always having to fight to live.

I'm so tired today. If it weren't for Brice and her ever-present friendship, I might never leave this bed.

My stomach rumbles, causing the words on the page to swim out of focus. Hearing the noise, Harrison closes the notebook on his lap and smiles over at me. "Sounds like my girls need to eat. What are you hungry for?"

The truth is, I haven't been hungry for much the last few days. I think it's because I'm out of room. "Some fruit would be nice," I say, the idea of it making me salivate.

39

GOODBYE FROM THE GRAVE

It's been a week since I first started reading Bernard's journals, and I wonder for the thousandth time why I waited so long. I feel emotionally lighter than I have in years, and delving into his thoughts makes me feel as if he's standing right beside me again.

I fluff the pillows on my side of the bed, even though I know the action is pointless—no amount of air is going to keep my body from squishing that sucker flat the moment I lie back onto it. Giving up the futile task, I toss a swollen leg up onto the bed. With a Herculean effort, I pull my massive form up with it just as Harrison breezes out of the bathroom and joins me. The minimal amount of effort it takes earns him a glare. He laughs.

"Do you want to die? Because I'll kill you in your sleep and make it look like an accident," I bark, hating myself as the nasty words slip out. I know it's not his fault he has it so easy. I really hate this uncomfortable body I'm living in.

"One more week, babe. That's all."

"You say it like it's nothing. You do realize that each day is equivalent to a year at this point, right?" I huff, causing the curl to spring free from my top knot.

One of these days, I'm going to cut the sucker off. No matter how tightly I secure my hair, it always manages to break loose—as if its sole purpose is to drive me insane.

Harrison snuggles close and rests his hand on my belly, causing our girl to graze the surface like she always does at his touch. "Any thoughts on names?"

I stiffen as the question settles against me, lying like a wedge between the two of us.

"We can name her when we're holding her, you know that."

I wish he'd quit asking. I can't do it. I cannot name her until she's here. I couldn't with Charlie, and I can't with her. It's just too much.

"See who she is before we go choosing names."

He's quiet as I lean over and grab the spiral notebook off my nightstand and begin to read.

Brice,

I've been writing to you for a while. I just didn't bother to put your name at the top of the page until now. Words are easier to leave behind when you know that someone will care enough to read them. I know it will be you sitting in the center of the vast sea of them that I've left behind. No one else has that kind of patience, except maybe Harrison. You two are two peas in a pod. They always say opposites attract, but I've never witnessed a love like yours before.

I hope all of these ramblings bring you some sort of comfort, because I know how you'll grieve for me. I'm sure it will resemble the way you love me—with your whole self, without apology. That's such a rare gift—the gift of unconditional love. I hope that you cherish it and give it away again when your heart's ready. I don't know how I was lucky enough to be the one to receive it the first time, but I'll be eternally grateful that I did.

As I feel the number of days ahead of me dwindling down, I want to be sure that you understand how much your friendship has meant to me. You were the light in the dark for me, and you gave me purpose when I had none. Thank you for so many things: your beauty, your grace, and most of all—your kindness.

Your friend,
Bernard

I close the book, its pages trembling in my fingers.

"Did you know there was a letter to me in there?"

Harrison eyes me warily, weighing his words before he speaks. "I did. I also knew that you'd find it when you were ready. It wasn't for me to decide when that was."

"I left it for so long. I feel like I should have thought about him and you. Instead I couldn't see past me—or *her*." The words have been trapped inside me for so long, it feels freeing to let them escape into the room. "I'm sorry. For the way I treated you. I wasn't strong like you were. I'm sorry for that, too…for how weak I am."

He reaches up, tucking *the* hair behind my ear, and kisses me gently. "You're the strongest person I know," he whispers, deepening the kiss at the end of his words.

40

ROLLER COASTER

Glancing at the clock, I stifle a yawn. 1:35. I have twenty-five minutes before Stephanie should be back with Charlie. My eyes are so heavy. The dishes in the sink can wait.

My body feels like it's sinking through the sofa as I lie down. The world around me quickly fades to black as all light and sound are snatched by the darkness of my subconscious.

"Mom!"

I hear Charlie. He's scared. Where is he?

"Charlie?" The word tumbles out of my mouth—a sour dessert. Where am I? "Charlie?"

"Brice, oh honey, thank God you're all right. I was so scared for you. Are you okay? Do you feel all right? We should check your sugar, make sure it's come up enough," Stephanie says.

She's sitting beside me on the sofa, and I'm sitting up. How am I sitting up? My heart begins to race as the coffee table comes into focus, and I see all the wrappers.

"What happened?" I ask. My mouth is so sticky and dry; I run my tongue across the roof a few times trying to create some bit of moisture. "Did I eat all that?" *Please say no.* It looks like Halloween night—haphazard wrappers strewn about, some with half-eaten bits of goodness still inside.

Stephanie glances over at the table, seeing what I'm seeing, as if for the first time. "Shit! Brice, I'm so sorry honey, you were just so low. You weren't making any sense, and Charlie said you needed candy, lots of candy. I just—I was scared." She wrings her hands together, each clutching the other so tightly the knuckles are white—bloodless.

"It's okay. Thank you for saving me." As soon as the words leave my mouth, the emotion springs free. Silent tears stream down my face. I can't. My body feels so heavy, my thoughts incomplete.

I shift, the weight in front of me confusing my senses even more. My hands grope my belly—my belly. *Oh God.* "Where's my monitor?"

"Momma, you were funny! You didn't know anything!" Charlie is jumping around, trying to disperse his nervous energy.

"Finger's out of your mouth, Captain. Mom's all right." I try to ease his mind, but the words sound false to my ears.

"Are you sure?" His eyes are full of sadness, laced with fear.

The sound of the door opening prevents me from responding to the question I don't know the answer to.

Moments later, Harrison walks around the sofa, dropping his briefcase on the floor. "Are you all right?"

His hands are everywhere all at once—on my face, across my shoulders...before they finally rest with mine, on top of my *still* abdomen. I can't process any of this. I need a moment to think.

"I need my monitor—"

Before I finish the sentence, Stephanie's handing it to me.

I unzip the case and push the button, bringing it to life. 22

—my last reading—flashes across the screen and my heart rate increases.

I slide the strip into the slot, my fingers making quick work of the familiar task. Cocking the gun, I place it to my finger and discharge the needle. A tiny squeeze produces what I need. I place the drop at the end of the strip and hold my breath as the five seconds flash by.

527.

Oh fuck.

The sound of the tub filling drowns out all other noise, giving me its own kind of silence for my thoughts. My hands cradle my abdomen, and I shake them every few moments. I need to feel her move. I won't be able to breathe until I feel her move.

Turning off the water, I lean back into the tub, trying to relax. Maybe I'm just too tense. Taking deep, calming breaths, I try to clear my mind of everything except the feel of the water lapping against me.

She's okay. She has to be okay. Please—please let her be okay.

Harrison's voice finds me through the walls. "You just... It was too much, Mom. I get it, though. I get it."

I imagine them standing in the kitchen beyond. Hopefully he has his arms around her. I hate that she's feeling this way because of me. None of this is her fault.

"The insulin will kick in, bring it down."

My hand makes lazy circles across my belly, silently willing her to respond. *Come on, little one. Show me you're okay.*

An elbow, or another body part just as sharp, scrapes across the inside, and I cry out, overcome with relief.

The quick rap of knuckles against wood, followed by a sudden burst of air and energy, leaves me feeling exposed.

"What happened? Are you all right?" His hair is a touch too long and, mixed with the anxiety painted across his face, gives him a disheveled look. I love it when it's at this stage—right before a haircut.

"She moved."

The anxiety morphs to confusion as he processes the two simple words. "But that's a good thing, right?"

"Of course!" I laugh as a foot, visible from the outside, stretches across the taught ball at my center. "Did you see that?"

He drops to his knees on the hard, tile floor, grabbing my face in his hands, his forehead resting against mine.

"I love you." A whisper so soft fills the air around me as his mouth collides with mine, and I lose myself in the incessant night sky that is our love.

41

D DAY

THE SOFT RUMBLE OF HARRISON'S TRUCK STIRS THE STILL AIR of the kitchen as I slip my feet into the tattered blue flip-flops sitting by the door. They're the only thing I've been able to get into for weeks. It's only 4 a.m., but the sky is already beginning to fill with light.

I inhale the fresh, clean air that only early morning can bring and let it wash through me.

Today will be a good day.

If the possibility exists that my thoughts can control the outcome of the day, I will think as many positive ones as needed to get us through to the other side. In a few short hours, I'll be holding her in my arms.

I *will* be.

I feel the dark, negative thoughts vying to get in, but I push against them. I won't let them in. *I won't.*

Harrison opens the passenger door of his truck, standing by as I heft my swollen body up into it. There isn't a part of me that doesn't feel super-sized—even my hands are twice what they were before. Settling into the seat, I clench and release my swollen fingers in front of me and laugh, imagining them staying this size as the rest of my body returns to normal.

"I'm surprised Charlie isn't up yet. He's so excited about his sister." Harrison smiles.

I can see the excitement he speaks of dancing in his own eyes. *She belongs to us already.* Every one of us. I inhale deeply and smile back at him, willing my excitement to shine more brightly than my fear. Fold it up, tuck it away—there's no room for it here today.

"He'll probably end up sleeping in. He was up so late last night, silly boy."

I gaze out the window, the hop fields stealing my thoughts. The grid of ropes and posts stand straight in a line, creating beautiful vines that are just beginning to reach up toward the sky. Their bottoms are lush and green, the tops getting ready to produce the stout ingredient found in every ale. The crops have grown up around us as the years have gone by—alfalfa fields disappearing, replaced on every side by the thick vines; a more lucrative crop. By the end of August, our home will stand at the center of a heady jungle—the leaves and sprinklers providing a much-needed reprieve from the hot desert sun.

Farm trucks and occasional pieces of equipment are the only vehicles passing by. They begin their work early, lessening the hours spent under the hot sun. I wonder about them, about the families they have at home. Do they have what they need? Men who work as hard as they do are rarely paid their worth.

"Are you thinking about names? Can I get a hint? I know you've already got some picked out. You have to. I'm sure there has been a parade of names running through your mind since the day they said she was a girl." Harrison chuckles, enjoying this game yet again.

He should know by now that I'm not going to utter a word. The truth is, I haven't thought of any. I keep thinking I'll know who she is when I look at her. Until then, the conversation is off limits, and yet he insists on bringing it up *all the time.*

"I guess you'll know soon, won't you?" I raise my brow, my mouth a sarcastic smirk.

"There she is," Dr. Rowles says, bursting into the room, as if I were lost or something.

"Yep, right where they put me, Doc." I can't help the sarcastic tone in my voice. My anxiety is a live wire dancing inside me, igniting a line of snarky behavior. I take a deep breath, trying to will my nerves to calm. "Are we ready for this?" I ask, beating him to the question I know is coming.

"I think so," he replies, eyeing the cath bag hanging on the rail of my bed and the IV site on my wrist.

Luckily, Marilyn's here. I was fortunate enough to have her for my nurse with Charlie, too. She has a knack for starting IV's. I spin the beads that live on my opposite wrist, thankful no one has told me to remove them. I've worn them for so long now; they feel like a part of me. The color is now more black than green, every time the bracelet has broken, beads have been lost. Seemed fitting to replace them with ones that are the color of Jayden's soul. Everything that I went through, everything that I lost and she never came. I swallow the thought, plastering my biggest smile on my face.

Dr. Rowles turns his attention to Harrison. I let my eyes travel with his. He's sitting up inside the long windowsill that runs along the back of the room, everything about him loose, relaxed.

"What about you, Dad, are you ready for this?" Dr. Rowles smiles expectantly, enjoying himself now that he's managed a way to take his question back.

Harrison takes a moment to answer, looking at me instead

of Doc. A slow, easy smile takes over his face, and I have one of those moments where I could cry out loud for all of the emotion that hits me when his deep dimple appears. It feels like a physical thing—a heart pang.

"I'm ready, Doc. Let's do this. Let's make today great."

I love this man.

On cue, the door springs open. Marilyn and Connie walk in, pushing a gurney between them. "Are we ready?" Marilyn asks, and I smile at the irony.

I'm trapped in an eighties sitcom.

"Connie, get a glucose on her before we go. If we're good, number wise, we'll proceed," Dr. Rowles says, leaving the room to prepare.

My heart begins to race, thumping the loudest in my throat as Connie scans my hospital band, then the monitor case. She grasps my hand, swipes my finger with alcohol. I jump when the needle is discharged. It doesn't matter that I've done it thousands of times to myself through the years. It's totally different when someone else does it.

Please be a good number.

She glances at the monitor, a bright smile lighting her face. "101. Let's do this."

They help me onto the gurney, my heart competing with the rhythm of the wheels rolling down the long hallway. I feel disjointed from what's happening—a spectator in someone else's show. We stop in a small room with a sink, and both nurses begin to wash up. Harrison stands between them at the long basin. They each take care to scrub between their fingers and up their wrists.

I'm about to be cut open.

My only job is to lie, quietly, as the show proceeds around me. Harrison's eyes connect with mine, and I force a smile.

He mouths the words *I love you* to me, and I take them, holding them tight. I can do this.

They all dress in light blue paper scrubs that cover their clothes. The only part of their faces showing are their eyes, and I feel exposed, alone, as we proceed through to the next room.

A cold, sterile table lies in the center of the room, and I'm transferred once again. This time, they tell me to sit, knees up, head forward. I'm trying to contain my shaking. I know it will just make this next part harder. But my body has a mind of its own right now, and the tremble that's coursing through me won't go away.

"Try to relax, Mrs. Wade. In a few moments, you won't feel a thing," David, the anesthesiologist, says from behind me.

I feel a cold swab along my spine, then the first jab of a sharp needle. I begin counting in my head, trying to remove myself from the pain as the needle bites again and again. As I reach thirty, the biting stops.

"Go ahead and lie back on the bed," he says, his voice low and calming.

I try to imagine the contraption sticking out of my back as I lie down on it. Once my head is resting on the bed, the lower half of my body disappears as a sheet is raised in front of me, the magic potion entering my body through the portal they've inserted in my spine.

Harrison stands beside me, his hand in mine, his view—both sides of the curtain. I know when they start based on the steady increase of pressure from his hand. I take deep breaths, trying to stay calm when I'm anything but.

I feel sharp pressure in my chest and cry out. "I think there's something wrong with my heart."

David takes a quick check of the monitor then smiles down at me. "Everything looks all right up here. I believe you're just feeling the pressure from them. She'll be out soon," he whispers, giving my shoulder a kind squeeze.

I lose Harrison completely to the other side of the curtain and see for the first time that Dr. White, Charlie's pediatrician, is standing off to the left of me beside a metal scale. He smiles kindly when he sees my attention trained on him.

The soft murmur of voices is interrupted by a sharp, beautiful cry. Harrison reappears, tears in his eyes as he says, "She's gorgeous! Absolutely gorgeous! I'm so proud of you, Rice!"

The emotion tumbles from within as I watch the flurry of activity take place before me. Marilyn hands the little wailing red being to Dr. White. He sets her on the scale, wiping blood and fluids from her face. He suctions her nose, mouth, and ears, causing her cries to escalate.

"She has nice strong lungs," he jokes, as he measures her height and weight.

I laugh through my tears.

"She's a healthy seven pounds, eight ounces, and twenty and a half inches."

He picks her up, arms and legs flailing as she continues to scream. He lays her gently in my arms.

Our eyes connect, and the rest of the room disappears. She stills, her cries going silent. She wraps her little fist around my finger, and we stare, lost in the universe that exists in each other's eyes. I feel my heart expand, making room for her to live there forever.

42

THE REBIRTH OF A NAME

"If you need anything at all, just push this red button," Connie says, showing me the center button on the remote for my bed. It has a little white nurse on it—simple, easy.

I smile up at her, wishing I could still the shaking. They say it's a side effect of the medicine they use when they do the spinal block, but it feels like shock to me. My body has just been cut open, the perfect little being that had been cradled at its center plucked from her internal home. It leaves an emptiness—a shock to the senses.

"Thank you for everything," Harrison says as Connie walks toward the door.

She smiles the warm smile of a practiced nurse. "You're welcome. Thank you for letting us be a part of it. Congratulations to both of you. She's beautiful."

The door closes with a soft swish of air and I close my eyes, take a deep breath, and try to align my center light. I continue to take deep breaths, exhaling them slowly, trying to will the quake to stop.

I open my eyes when I feel the bundle in my arms begin to

stir. I don't know how long they were closed—it felt like just a moment, but the change in the light tells me that's wrong.

I hear a giggle and turn to see Charlie standing beside the bed. Harrison gives a little wave from the corner.

"Good afternoon, sunshine," he says, his voice full of gravel from the long day. "Did you rest well?"

"It just felt like a minute. How long was I asleep?"

"A couple of hours, not long," he replies, stretching his arms up above his head. I wonder if he's been in that chair the whole time. "Your mom brought Charlie up about an hour ago. He can't wait to see her." He nods toward my arms.

"Is she really mine? My baby sister?" Charlie begins bouncing, his excitement too much to contain. "I didn't get too excited before she came, Mama, just like you said. But I'm soooo excited now!"

"Reel it in, Captain. Show me your calm, and Daddy will set you up here," I tell him, glancing at Harrison for confirmation.

His brow furrows, but just for a second before his easy smiles takes over again. I adjust in the bed, thankful the medicine hasn't worn off. The pain won't really come until later tonight when the effects of the spinal block completely wear off.

"It'll be fine. We'll be extra careful."

Charlie stills, his shoulders slightly hunched, as if he paused mid-action. "I'll be calm," he whispers out the side of his mouth, and I laugh, causing an uproar of tiny wails from the bundle in my arms.

Charlie throws his hands over his mouth, his eyes taking over the rest of his face. I laugh again, my heart so full. Happy tears begin their slide. "Put him up here, Harrison."

"Yeah, put me up there!" Charlie throws his arms straight up, his feet beginning to bounce again.

"Shoes off, then you've got yourself a deal." Harrison

smiles down at him, and it only takes a moment for his shoes to be ditched in a haphazard pile beside the bed.

Charlie snuggles in beside me, his eyes full of wonder as he reaches his hand out and traces a finger down her upturned little nose. He pulls back in surprise when her little fist comes out, her fingers wrapping possessively around his. I watch the exchange quietly, holding my breath as I commit it to memory.

He leans down, so his face is just above hers, and whispers, "I love you, little sister."

Harrison bends down, placing a kiss on my cheek, breaking the stream of tears flowing from me. "What's her name, Rice?" he whispers. I know this time he needs an answer.

I don't say anything as I think about what I'm going to name her. Thoughts of the past consume me, and I dig deep for the courage to let it all go. I think about Amelia and Bernard. I held his story, and even though it didn't belong to me, I belonged to it in a sense. It stained me—changed the color of my world. I look down into the face of my beautiful, perfect baby girl, and I find the strength to let it go the only way I know how—by giving the name a new story.

"Leila Grace."

I pause, watching my words wash over him. *I don't know what he's thinking.* I hope he understands. He and I have never spoken of Bernard's daughter, Leila. But judging by the look on his face, he's the holder of secrets, too.

"I want to name her Leila for him, but for me, too."

"It's perfect," he whispers, a single tear running slowly down the outside of his face.

I let go.

Bernard warned me that I had no more control than the weatherman. Right now, I'm an unsuspected tsunami on a hot summer day. My emotions—waves with claws and teeth. I'm helpless to do anything except let go. Let go of all the loss. Bernard's. Harrison's. Mine.

"Don't cry, Mama." Charlie puts his tiny hand on my face. Pulling me toward him, he peppers my cheeks with kisses.

"They're happy tears, Captain. I just love you all so much, I'm overflowing." I smile, placing a single kiss on his nose.

"I think it's time to introduce this girl to her grandmas."

Harrison knows what I need. He takes Charlie, putting him back on the ground. "Put your shoes on," he tells him, ruffling his hair. Turning, he picks up Leila, his lips brushing my cheek as he does. He holds my eyes for a moment before the three of them leave the room.

I take a shaky breath as the door swishes behind them. I close my eyes and breathe. I open them a moment later and he's back.

Sliding his shoes off, he carefully crawls into the bed beside me. He rests one arm behind my head, and I snuggle into him the best I can with all of the tubing and monitors covering me.

"I love you," he whispers, kissing the side of my head.

We let go together. We let go of the loss. The gain. We just be together—in this amazing world full of emotion and wonder.

"I love you, too."

43

PEOPLE PARADE

"Are you ready for this?" Harrison asks, walking into the nursery.

I smile down at Leila, snapping the last two snaps on her sleeper, its light cotton fabric perfect for her first barbeque. "That question again. What is it with that question?" I laugh, letting it fill me with happiness as I bundle my little burrito. "Yes, the princess and I are both ready. Are you ready? Is the Captain ready?" I raise my eyebrow in mock seriousness and laugh when his mimics mine.

"Of course, my lady." He gives a quick bow, and I shake my head. "Can I deliver the princess to the garden for you?" His honey eyes grow serious, and I see the pleading there.

I straighten, feeling the ache in my abdomen, and smile. "That would be lovely, thank you."

He takes her from me, and lays her in the basket. It's become her favorite resting place. Seems she has a soul for adventure just like her big brother, who decided this old basket was a better place for his sister to rest than the boring, frilly cradle. I'm not really sure where the basket came from, but seeing Leila nestled in it, I'd bet money that its woven reeds have held an infant before.

"Grandma's here!" Charlie yells, racing into the room. His top lip is stained red, a telltale sign that summer has descended upon us.

"Which one?" I laugh, my question causing him to pause in his tracks.

His eyes sparkle with glee. "Both of them! They came together!" He begins to bounce, filled with the excitement a day of family and sunshine brings.

"We better get out there then," I say to both of them.

Charlie turns, bounding out of the room with as much energy as he entered with.

Harrison walks up to me and runs his thumb across my bottom lip. He leans in and places a feather-light kiss there, reaches around me, and picks the basket up off the bed. "Let's do this." He smiles his easy smile and extends his free hand for me to hold onto.

"She's gorgeous," my mom says for the third time in the last ten minutes. I've been keeping track of the various compliments and the rate in which they're coming.

"Such a *gift*."

This one is in the lead. Every person here has said it at least twice. The truth is, she's all of those things and more. I just hope everyone realizes, soon, that they don't need to continue to say it.

"Did you know Mama has a new studio?" Charlie asks, effectively gaining the attention of everyone around him.

"Really?" Jesse asks, his eyes imploring mine.

"I'm set up in Bernard's house," I tell him, self-consciousness settling like a pebble in the pit of my stomach. I avoided it for so long; I know they all thought it was odd. "Harrison made it really lovely in there."

I scan the yard searching for him, hoping he'll come save

me from the feelings that are creeping in and stealing my breath.

"Great, let's see it," Jesse says. Standing from the picnic table, he reaches his hand out to Cassie. She stands with him, effectively starting a trend around the table that quickly spreads to the chairs beyond. *Great, I guess we're doing this.*

I give an easy smile, my heart racing, eyes beginning to fill. I glance away quickly, hoping he didn't see. Taking a deep, shaky breath, I try to recapture a bit of control over my traitorous body that's crumbling like the sand at the water's edge—my emotions the stormy sea crashing on its shore.

I take each step on legs that belong to someone else. They feel like rubber, detached. *Just breathe.*

Cassie walks up, looping her arm through mine. Her head dips toward my shoulder and she whispers out the side of her mouth, "Can you believe I married this fucker? We'll get him back later." She winks, an amused smile on her face. "We've got this, sister. You and I."

I laugh, the weight of the angry sea lessened with her closeness. "Thank you. I was about to show my crazy," I whisper back, climbing the steps to my new space.

"Do you need to do a quick check before this little tour? I know a little man that would love to show off your space. I'm sure he would take over as tour guide." She dips her head toward Charlie, who's entertaining the small crowd gathered behind us.

I pause, taking a quick check of my body.

My heart is still racing, the rhythm filling my ears, and my face is tingly, my lips feeling like a foot that's been sat on for too long.

"Yes," the word slips out, a hot tear on its tail. "Will you come with me?" I ask, my voice shaky. I don't panic every time I'm low, but when I do—when the fear grips me—it's hard to do alone. I need someone to care for me, to guide me through it.

"Of course," she whispers to me, turning to address the rest of the family. "Charlie's going to lead this little tour. I expect you'll all be respectful to the Captain." She pauses, staring hard at Jesse Jr., her oldest son. "Try to keep your questions to a minimum. We'll be back in a minute." She laces her fingers through mine, and we walk quickly to the house. "What do you need me to do?" she asks, as we walk in, her dark eyes full of concern.

"My monitor is in my purse. Get it for me?" I slip into a chair at the table, hot tears continuing their trek down my face.

She glances around the room, her eyes landing on my purse on the counter. Rushing to it, she pulls out the little machine from inside.

"Have you heard of the continuous glucose monitor?" Her question distracts me from my emotions. I'm grateful for it.

"A bit," I pause, thinking about my time with a pump. "It's hard to explain, but I don't like feeling even more dependent on something else. I know I'm dependent on the monitor and the insulin pens, but—I don't know. It's different. I'm glad those things are available, and they help so many, but it's not for me."

She busies herself, opening the case to my monitor, quickly setting it up for me. "Here's your poker." She hands over the little contraption, all cocked and ready to go. "It's loaded." Her face is full of seriousness, as if a misfire could cause a catastrophe.

I chuckle, earning a wrinkled brow in response.

I grab it from her, the quake in my hand enough to reignite the panic I was feeling. I press the gun to my finger, and push the button, releasing the needle into the tip. I squeeze a small drop of blood to the surface and place it on the strip. Five seconds later, 37 is staring back at me.

"Holy Moses," Cassie says, eying the monitor screen. "Time for a drink," she recovers with an easy smile.

"Where did you girls run off to?" my mom questions, in that tone that only moms can master.

I'm still working on mine; I'm hoping to improve once Charlie and Leila are older. Right now, there is just too much cuteness for a stern mom voice, but I'm sure they will help me perfect it as they grow.

I smile, and Mom's eyebrows crease. "What are you smirking about?"

"Nothing, it was nothing, Mom. My sugar was a little low," I say, hoping Mom doesn't notice the hitch in Cassie's left brow. Maybe it's not genetic; maybe it's environmental. She's been around us all too long. *Nope.* She saw it because now hers is raised to match it. *Here we go.*

"How low? Didn't you eat? Honey, you have to eat more. You do too much." She paces around the room of my studio, absently rubbing Leila's back while she lectures me. It's only the four of us in here. Everyone else already abandoned the small space for the ease of the outdoors.

"It's fine. I'm fine now."

"She is. I took good care of her." Cassie smiles, bumping me with her hip. "Girl, this painting is gorgeous. Are you selling prints?" she questions, leaving me for the painting of my dream.

I positioned it across from the big window. The evening light catches the silver perfectly, making it appear fluid in its journey.

"Isn't it something?" Mom joins her in front of it. "She's so gifted."

"I'm not sure I'll sell prints of this one," I reply, knowing how well it would do if I did. It feels too intimate, though—a piece of me.

I started posting art on Instagram last year and was amazed by the amount of people interested in it—in me. "I think it's just for me." I run my finger down the painting's edge.

"Wow," a voice from the past says from behind us, making my palms prickle.

I haven't seen or heard from her in ten years. Not since the morning I pulled my swollen body up off her couch and left her place. I couldn't chase her anymore, looking for answers I would never get. I finally realized she held the truth like it was her only power, and I'm not the type of person who's comfortable being fed lies.

I've never been more thankful for my mother and the ease in which she travels through life. "Jayden Marie Hart! Oh my God! I can't believe you're here!"

As soon as the words are out of her mouth, I know she's the one who set this in motion. I cast my eyes in her direction. She shrugs her shoulders, giving me a sheepish smile.

"Jayden—wow. Girl, it's been a long time, sort of like seeing a ghost," Cassie says, wrapping her arms around her. She pulls back, hands on Jayden's shoulders. "Let's go get you something to eat, introduce you to the Captain." She turns her around, the two of them leaving us standing alone.

I take a moment, trying to gather my thoughts—they're igniting like fireworks on the Fourth of July, scattering across the expanse of my mind so quickly I can't grasp a single one. Luckily, I don't have to.

"You lost so many, so much. All of the people you held closest to your heart. I couldn't stand by and do nothing." Her eyes hold mine, searching for a reaction. "I had to try and give you the only one I could, back. I know she hurt you, and her lies are insufferable. But you are the only person that girl has. We all have flaws, Brice. Luckily, the people who truly matter love us in spite of them," she says. Passing Leila to me, she makes her way to the front door.

I let her words wash over me as I snuggle my sleeping beauty closer. My mind escapes to that time, the effective way that I tried to cut off everyone that meant anything to me. Jayden was the only one I hadn't let back in.

Mom is right. It's time to forgive and move on, time to grow and change.

I glance up, surprised to see her standing before me.

I take a moment and study how the years have changed her. Her once long hair is cut short now, a sharp line angling down her jaw. She holds herself differently. Instead of the scared little girl she used to be, a confident woman stands in her place. Our eyes meet, and we smile.

"I missed you, Bri," she whispers.

"Me too." I pause, trying to gather this string of words so they flow out smoothly. "You don't have to tell me what happened. I know it was bad, whatever it was. But I want to know you *now*—no more secrets, no more lies."

Panic flashes through her blue eyes as she searches for her own words. "I can't tell you the whole truth. I've made a life out of weaving lies, catching spiders in the webs I lay."

Her gaze holds mine while I try to sort what she said.

"I can't tell you much; I've sworn not to. Believe it or not, that's an oath I'll always keep."

What? I pull a deep breath. "I guess the only thing I can do is just love you anyway."

I laugh with this mysterious woman I know everything and nothing about.

"I guess so."

We loop arms, stepping out the door. I pull Leila closer and let the laughter beyond carry us to the people I love.

"I'm glad you're here, Jay."

44

NEW FRIENDS IN OLD PLACES

"Are you sure they hold meetings there still?" Harrison asks as he spoons a bite of carrots into Leila's mouth. She giggles, causing half of it to spill from her cheeks.

Six months have gone in the blink of an eye, and I doubt that time will slow at all in the next eighteen years. It will only gather speed like a locomotive, barreling down the tracks of life.

"I don't know, honestly. But if they don't, at least I tried, right?"

I know I could look online or call the library and find out, but I like it better this way—adventures unknown. I woke the other morning with the certainty that I needed to go back, reconnect.

"Can we come, Mama? Can we, can we, can we? Please?" The spark of the idea grows to a blaze as I watch his face—so full of wonder for all things unknown.

Harrison's eyes find mine, and we have a whole conversation without words. He blows air through his lips, making Leila erupt into giggles again, before turning his focus to Charlie. "Why don't we go explore the library while Mom meets with her friends?"

"The library! I love the library! Is it time to go?" Charlie bursts from his seat at the table, running from the room.

"Well, I guess dinner's over." I shake my head at Harrison.

He shrugs his shoulders, giving me his easy smile. Life is like this now—easy, even when it's not. The pain that held me for so long has finally let me take a full breath. My lungs are able to expand because the monstrous talons of grief no longer hold me in their clutches. I've broken free, allowed myself to heal.

Stepping into the library, I pull the beanie from my head, stomping the snow from my boots. Charlie joins in, his enthusiasm apparent by the force of his stomps.

"Ok, Captain, that's enough. Remember the library rules."

I reminded him at least four times on the drive over. Sometimes, his zest for life is hard to contain. Squatting down in front of him, I dust the snow from his captain's hat and unzip his jacket.

He steals my heart as he leans in, kissing the tip of my nose. "I hope you make lots of friends, Mama. I'll be good, I promise." He winks and gives me his dad's easy smile.

The well of tears I feel doesn't surprise me. I've always had an ocean of feelings inside. Sometimes they grow so much, I have to let them out. I've accepted that.

I stand up and give Harrison a quick kiss on the cheek before I turn my attention to Leila, who's snuggled happily in her daddy's arms.

"I love you, baby girl," I whisper, kissing her smooth cheek.

"You've got this, Rice." Harrison runs his free hand down my arm, giving mine a quick squeeze before letting me go.

I stand, quietly watching as they disappear into the maze of rainbow-colored shelves. I lose the last bit of Harrison and turn my attention to the door to the left of me. I smile, remembering the first time I came here.

My thoughts conjure the sound of his voice as he led me down the steps that day.

"You'll make a lot of friends here," he had said. I never really let it come to that, but I have hope I still can.

Walking into the large room with the fireplace, I see that it's mostly empty. An older man and a young boy are the only two occupants. I turn to go, just as the man lifts his face from the table sitting between them.

It's J.C. Even though it's been more than twenty years, his face is the same, age only showing at the corners of his eyes and the creases of his smile. "Are you here for the diabetes support group?" he asks.

"I am." I'm thankful my intuition was right, that they're still meeting here. "I'm Brice, we met a long time ago."

"Brice! Oh wow, it's been a long time," he says with a laugh. "I remember you—you were Bernard's friend. He talked about you all the time." I see a flash of sorrow pass through his eyes. Bernard's loss was felt here, too. "This is my man, Christopher. He's new to the club this year." He nods toward the boy across from him who turns to look at me, a shy smile on his face.

He's probably eleven or twelve. He has dark hair, and hazel eyes stare up at me from behind dark frames.

"Nice to meet you, Christopher. I'm Brice." I take a free chair at the table they share. "What are you playing?"

Blue cards are laid out across the table, each card depicting an odd little creature.

"Pokémon," Christopher answers. The smile on his face

tells me this is his game, not J.C.'s. "It doesn't matter, though, we can stop. I was beating this old man, anyway. He's got no game." He laughs, and J.C. shakes his head.

"It's a game without rules, I tell you," J.C. says, defending himself.

"So, you have diabetes, too?" Christopher asks as he quickly begins to pick up the cards.

"I do. In fact, I just had my 20th anniversary in November."

"Has it been twenty years? Crazy." J.C. shakes his head. "Do you still talk with anyone?"

"I haven't. I wonder about Lori a lot, though. Do you know what happened to her?"

"I actually hear from Lori all the time. She created a diabetes support group on Facebook. It has over five thousand members. She's doing really well. I'll write down the site for you before you leave. It's a great place to find information and connect with others. I bet she'd love to hear from you."

"That'd be great."

The room lapses into an uncomfortable silence, and I'm surprised when Christopher's the one to break it. "Should we give our suck and sweet?"

"What's that?" I ask, confused.

"Something my mom started doing after she read it in a book. She goes around the table at dinnertime, making each of us tell the best and the worst thing that happened in our day. That way we connect with one another," he replies, shrugging his shoulders.

"Why don't you start." I smile, liking this kid and his mom —the reader. Maybe I'll make a few friends today.

"My suck—my omni pod failed on me, and my sugar climbed to 347 before I figured out what happened. My sweet —it's back down now, and I got to whip J.C. in a game of Pokémon." He smiles, shuffling the cards in his hands.

"What's an omni pod?"

"This." He pulls up the sleeve of his shirt to reveal a pod stuck to the backside of his arm. "It's how I get my insulin. I don't really like it, though, so my mom is working with the doctors to get me on something that will work better for me. I have a few friends in the online support group that love them, but it's not for me."

"I get that. I was on the pump for a few years, but I went back to the insulin pens. I'm glad there are so many options for people, though," I reply.

"I've been on the pump for years now. It's definitely made my life easier. What didn't you like about it?" J.C. asks, his voice full of curiosity.

"I don't know…it made me feel more dependent on something other than myself. If that makes any sense." I join my hands in front of me, feeling a bit foolish.

"I could see that," he replies, and I feel better. I always fear judgement, especially about my medical decisions. "As long as you have good control. Whatever works for you."

"That's what my doctor says." I laugh.

"Hey, hey." A woman with dark, curly hair walks into the room, her arms full of books.

"Hey, Mom. The meeting isn't over yet," Christopher says, answering my unspoken question. "You can join us, though."

"I'm Cristy." She sets the books down, offering me her hand to shake. "I thought it would just be these two. There hasn't been anyone else for weeks."

"I'm Brice. It's nice to meet you."

"Type 1?" she asks, taking the fourth seat at the table.

"Twenty years." I smile into her kind face.

She reaches over, grabbing Christopher's hand, and I see the hope in her eyes. Hope for twenty years, forty years, a lifetime.

The conversation ebbs and flows as the minutes tick by on

the clock. By the end of the hour, I feel as if I've known them all forever, and I'm thankful for the dream that made me come.

"Same time next week." J.C.'s the first to stand from the table, grabbing his coat from the back of his chair. "I hope you come," he adds, a sad smile on his face as he turns and begins his journey up the stairs.

"I'd like that," I whisper as the room empties.

I clip the seat belt around Charlie and take my seat in the front, my heart full and thankful.

I see Cristy and Christopher get into the car in front of us and laugh, noticing the familiar sticker on her back window—a large book that covers all but a black top knot held by a red ribbon. Diabetes isn't the only thing that Cristy and I have in common.

"Look," I say to Harrison, pointing at the sticker. "She's a nutcase, too."

His eyebrows scrunch together for a moment as he tries to make sense of what I just said. "That readers' group you belong to?"

"Yeah."

He reaches over, lacing his fingers between mine. "That's great. I'm glad you made some new friends."

I bundle a sleepy Leila in my arms and sit in the rocking chair in her room. The soft glow from the night light is the only thing illuminating her tiny face. A big yawn escapes her, and our eyes lock, the gentle rocking our only movement.

A small smile graces her lips as her eyes slowly drift shut. I continue to rock slowly, my eyes never leaving the beautiful face before me as my thoughts wander over my day. If the talons of this illness ever wrap their clutches around her or Charlie, I know I'll find the strength I witnessed in Cristy today somewhere inside of me.

I get up every morning and I fight—for myself—and all the people who love me. It's not a fight I'll ever be able to walk away from, and in a strange way, I wouldn't want to.

This is my life, and every day I end it warrior strong. Because there is no other way. Not for me.

The End

ACKNOWLEDGMENTS

I want to first say thank you to my readers. This was a very personal story for me. I was diagnosed with type 1 diabetes when I was 11. It's been quite a journey. Last year I was having trouble with hypos (low blood sugar) that I could not raise (which is really scary) and began looking for answers in the diabetic community. I stumbled upon this amazing group ran by a woman named Lori. I really want to urge anyone who has a chronic illness to search out others like yourself. It is a great way to find help with things that no one other than someone living with the same condition will understand. That being said, here is the link for Lori's group. https://m.facebook.com/groups/1601260853424557 It was joining this group that inspired me to write this book. I saw a post from a young lady who said, I wish I had the power to touch someone when my sugar is low and make them feel what I feel. Just for a minute. Then they would know. Reading her words, I realized that I do have that power. Through writing I hope that I have given you all a better understanding of this disease. I may not be able to give you the feelings physically, but I hope that emotionally I have.

I want to give the biggest thank you to my family. Brian, Sebastian, and Cassidee. I can't thank you enough for all of your support and love each and every day. Writing a book is no small project and it takes months and months of continual hard work. That work takes time away from those I love, whether I'm sitting at the computer or just lost in side my own head, but these three, they don't complain. They stand beside me, encouraging me the whole time. You guys are the best, my life would not be complete without you and your love.

Next, thank you to the PLN's. Cassie, Leila, Julie, Crystal, and Stephanie. Thank you ladie's for all of your support and encouragement all the way through. Having found you guys is one of the biggest gifts I have ever stumbled upon in this life. You are all so amazing and talented and I'm so happy to be able to call myself one of you. Erica, your knowledge and talent amazes me. You are so intelligent, thoughtful, and kind. I could never thank you enough for all of your help with this project. Kirsten, you are the best beta bitch ever, thank you for all of your help and feedback. Kat, thank you for the beautiful cover, you are such a gifted designer. Cristy, you are such an amazing T1D mom, your spirit and strength are so evident in your love for your son. Jen, thank you for coming through in a pinch and making the inside of the book beautiful. Becoming a PLN changed my life, so of course I have to say thank you to Tarryn Fisher, for bringing together such a strong kickass tribe of woman.

Thank you to the diabetics who shared their stories to help me create mine. Lori, J.C., Kristina, and Christoper. I hope you like what I have done with the things that you have shared.

Those of you that work with me, either in the past or present, Dr. Buck, Eric, Wayne, Tori, Jesse, Jamie Garrison (I gave Brice your last name as a thank you for the information on DKA you shared) Marilyn, and Connie, using your names was my way of saying thank you for the amazing dedication to compassionate care that you show our patients every day. It is an honor to work with you all.

Last but never least, Mom, thank you for teaching me kindness each and every day. I love you.

SOCIAL MEDIA

If you would like to stay up to date on future projects you can follow me on Facebook and Instagram.

Manufactured by Amazon.ca
Bolton, ON

34784086R00151